Palmetto Island

Change
of Tides

ASHLEY FARLEY

Hannah navigates her kayak into the inky shadows alongside an abandoned dock. The sun rises above the horizon, its rays chasing away the night sky with beams of pink and lavender and yellow. At low tide, the stench of dead fish and decay assaults one's nose, but having grown up on the island, Hannah is used to the odor. Oysters are visible on the banks of the marsh. Shrimp flitter across the water. And egrets poke their yellow bills in the mud. The occasional squawk of a bird is the only sound in an otherwise silent landscape. Hannah cherishes these fleeting moments as the inlet comes to life around her.

Taking in a deep breath, she steadies the telephoto lens and stills her body. She passes on the opportunity to shoot a blue heron fishing for minnows. Hannah has hundreds of such images stored on her hard drive. She's holding out for the prime shot, the photograph that will get her more Instagram followers and result in paid downloads on the stock image websites. Such shots are few and far between. But today is her lucky day.

An osprey flies in from the right, his clawed feet landing

gear as he glides across the water. Hannah presses the shutter as the osprey emerges with a wiggling mullet gripped between his claws. The osprey careens to the left and swoops back around, coming straight toward her. She holds the shutter down as the camera records the magnificent creature's movement in a continuous stream of images as he flies over her head.

Lowering her camera, she calls out to the osprey, "Show off!" She tilts her head back and lets out a woo-hoo. She previews the images on her camera's viewfinder. One, in particular, steals her breath. A shot of a lifetime. What a fabulous way to start her day.

Hannah paddles the kayak back down the creek to the floating dock at the town's marina. She slides the kayak out of the water and hoists it onto the storage rack. Slinging her waterproof camera bag over her shoulder, she hurries up the ramp to the boardwalk. She increases her pace to a jog as she passes Shaggy's, her favorite Lowcountry seafood restaurant, and the Island Bakery, the coffee shop and cafe her mom owns and operates. She bypasses the front door—the bakery doesn't open until nine—and rounds the corner of the two-story brick building, cutting through the back alley to the rear entrance.

Inside the coatroom—an oversized closet with wooden lockers for cafe employees—she kicks off her wet Crocs and hangs her camera bag on her designated wall hook.

"Morning, Mom!" she calls out to Birdie in the adjacent kitchen before taking the stairs two at a time to their second-floor apartment. Waking Gus from his sweet dreams is the highlight of her day. When he blinks his pale blue eyes open and sees her, Hannah's heart melts as dimples appear in his chubby cheeks.

But today, when she enters their bedroom, his tattered stuffed alligator, Atticus, is alone in his toddler bed.

In a singsong tone, she calls, "Gus, it's time to get ready for school." She goes into the bathroom that connects their bedroom to her mom's. "Gus! Where are you? Are you hiding from me? This isn't funny, buddy. You're scaring mommy."

With a racing heart, she conducts a quick but thorough search of the tiny apartment before flying back down the stairs to the kitchen.

"Mom! Where's Gus? He's not upstairs."

Birdie looks up from the commercial-size mixer. "What do you mean? He was sleeping when I came down a half hour ago."

"Well, he's not there now." Panic gripping her chest, Hannah passes through the kitchen to the cafe. Birdie follows on her heels, and when there's still no sign of Gus, Hannah whips out her phone. "I'm calling the police."

"Let's not panic yet, sweetheart. He's probably with Max."

"I hadn't thought of that. I hope you're right," Hannah says crossing the room to the front door. "Do you have your keys?"

Removing a set of keys from her apron pocket, Birdie unlocks the front door, and they race across the wide brick sidewalk to the Palmetto Hotel.

They pass through the lobby, where guests are waiting to check out, to the lounge where more guests are enjoying a continental breakfast. Hannah stops in her tracks, her hand against her pounding heart, at the site of Max and Gus sitting together at a table by the window. She's sipping coffee, and his tiny hands are wrapped around a plastic sippy cup.

"Gus! Thank goodness."

Gus jumps down from his chair and runs over to them. "Mama! Birdie!"

"You little devil! We've been looking all over for you." Hannah scoops him up and hugs him tight. "You scared me to death."

Gus sticks out his lower lip in a pout. "But I wanted to see Maxie."

"You should've asked Birdie or me. We would've brought

you to see Max. You know you're not allowed to leave the apartment alone."

Max stands to face them. "I should've called you. He appeared in the lobby a few minutes ago. Little rascal told me his mommy knew where he was, that you watched him walk over."

"Shame on you, Gus! We're going to have a serious talk about telling lies."

He buries his face in Hannah's neck. "I'm sorry, Mommy."

Hannah presses her cheek against his blond head. "What am I gonna do with you?" she whispers into the locks of hair that curl around his ear. Her son is becoming more of a handful every day. She needs to get him out of her mother's apartment, away from the waterfront, before something really bad happens.

When Hannah leaves to get Gus ready for day care, Birdie stays behind with Max. Lowering herself to Gus's vacated seat, she says, "I need a minute to compose myself. I'm too old to have such an energetic grandson. I thank the Lord every day for blessing me with a daughter. I would never have survived a son."

Max slaps the table near Birdie's hand. "Hush up, Birdie. You sound like you're seventy, not fifty-three. I got along fine with my son. You would have, too."

A faraway look crosses Birdie's face. "Cary would've been a wonderful daddy to a little boy. Maybe he would've stayed . . ."

"Don't go there, Birdie Fuller. I've never known a man who loved his child more, daughter or son, than your husband loved Hannah. He didn't leave on account of Hannah. He left—"

Birdie's lips turn downward. "Because of me."

"Stop putting words in my mouth, damn it. Cary left because he got himself into financial trouble. *And* because he couldn't keep his pecker in his pants."

"You know, as well as I do, my drinking drove him to cheat on me." Through the window, Birdie watches a little boy and his daddy, wearing bucket hats and carrying fishing rods, walk down the boardwalk toward the marina. "My grandson is all boy. He really needs a father figure in his life. Hannah won't admit it, but I think she realizes it."

"That situation may remedy itself," Max says.

"What do you mean?"

Max runs her fingers through her cropped blonde hair. "This mess she created will one day come back to bite her in the butt. The South can be a very small place. One day someone is going to put two and two together."

"I agree," Birdie says with a solemn nod. "However, while I don't approve of what she did, I respect the choice she made regarding Gus's biological father. My relationship with Hannah is finally on solid ground. I wouldn't dare jeopardize it by expressing my opinion."

Max's deep blue eyes go wide. "Who says this father figure has to be Gus's real baby daddy? Hannah's a beautiful young woman. And smart as a whip. Why doesn't she find some nice young man to marry her?"

"Ha. She hasn't been on a single date since Gus was born."

Max flashes a playful grin. "Maybe her mama should lead by example . . ."

Birdie cuts her eyes at Max. "Lead by example how?"

"I'll show you. Do you have time for coffee?"

Birdie checks her watch. "I can stay for a few more minutes."

"I'll be right back." Birdie admires Max's trim figure in her butt-hugging jeans as she sashays over to the bar where self-serve coffee urns stand tall alongside containers of yogurt, boxes of cereal, and trays of pastries provided by Island Bakery. Max is the same tomboy Birdie knew as a child. She wears her blonde hair boyishly short, a style that accents her high cheekbones and round face. She's constantly instigating mischief, and she has the energy of ten women their age.

Max returns with two coffee mugs on a tray and her laptop tucked under her arm. She hands Birdie a mug and reclaims her chair. "Okay, so hear me out before you shut me down. I joined the MatchMade dating website, and I think you should too."

Birdie stares at her over the rim of her mug. She takes a tentative sip and lowers the cup. "What's the point? We live in a small town. How can we meet someone new when we already know everyone?"

"It's not about finding someone new," Max says. "It's about finding someone with whom you're compatible, someone who shares the same interests as you."

Birdie rolls her eyes. "What interests? Birdie Fuller likes to bake and spends free time with her child and grandchild."

"Stop making yourself out to be the most boring person ever. You're an interesting woman, Birdie, with a lot to share." Opening the laptop, Max's fingers fly across the keys. "Here's Pete, the barber, and Tim, the pharmacist. You could have a match made in heaven with one of them."

Birdie snorts. "I'm not interested in dating Pete or Tim. Or any other man for that matter."

Max taps a few more keys. "I don't believe it. I got a message from Stan, asking me to go out for a drink on Thursday night."

Birdie's brow shoots up. "Stan Morgan? The man who owns the sporting goods store?"

"Of course, Stan Morgan. What other Stan do you know on the island?"

"None." Birdie pinches her chin as she considers the match. "I can see the two of you together. You're both energetic and outdoorsy."

"Stan was one of Danny's best friends," Max says. "That would be like dating my brother."

"Seriously, Maxie? How often have you seen Stan in the six years since Danny's funeral?"

Max frowns. "Not that often, now that I think about it."

"Danny would be thrilled to know his best friend and wife are growing old together." Birdie takes another sip of coffee. "Besides, they say the strongest relationships are built on friendship. Where's the harm in having drinks with him?"

"I guess there's not any."

Birdie sits back in her chair. "But count me out. I'm not joining any match-making website. Your date for drinks with Stan is the confirmation I need. Dating means drinks. And I don't do drinks."

"You're being ridiculous. Couples do other things on dates. Like spending the day at the beach. And taking walks along the boardwalk. And kissing. And making whoopee," Max says with a gleam in her eyes.

Birdie smacks her thigh. "You're horny! That's what this is about. Well, here's a newsflash for you, Max. Men aren't worth the trouble. Save yourself the heartache. Buy a vibrator."

"I already have three, thank you very much." Max slams the laptop shut. "Come on, Birdie. Why not give the website a try? Do you want to live your sunset years alone in an apartment over a bakery?"

"I like my apartment, thank you very much. And my bakery is soon to be a cafe. Besides, I'm not alone. My daughter and grandson live with me."

Max casts her eyes at the ceiling. "Which is a subject for another day."

"Hannah will move out when she's ready. Until then, I enjoy having her around."

Max's expression softens. "I know. And it does my heart good to see the two of you getting along so well. But Cary has been gone for three years." Max holds up three fingers. "Three years, Birdie. You and Hannah need to move on with your lives. Or . . ." Max's eyes narrow as she studies her more closely. "Please tell me you're not waiting for Cary to come back and beg for your forgiveness."

Birdie dismisses the idea with a flap of her hand. "Of course not."

"Then why haven't you divorced him yet?"

She looks down at her coffee. "Because the process is more complicated with Cary missing."

"More complicated, but not impossible. Cary left you for another woman. He isn't coming back. You're still in love with him, aren't you?"

Birdie shakes her head. "I stopped loving him long before he left."

"Then prove it by joining the website. Seriously, Birdie. We're not getting any younger. Running your own business and helping raise your grandson suits you. I've never seen you happier. Why not share that happiness with someone? Be a role model for your daughter. Take the first step toward moving on with your life."

Looking away, Birdie is silent for a long minute. "I sense that change is already in the works for Hannah."

Max moves to the edge of her seat. "What do you mean?"

"She has a meeting in Charleston later today with a young man interested in buying her company."

"Is she gonna sell it?"

"I don't know. She's going to find out more about his offer today."

"Will she stay on board with the company?"

Birdie can see the wheels in her friend's brain spinning. She has as many questions as Birdie. But no one has any answers yet. "I don't know. She hasn't gotten that far yet. She claims she's not moving to Charleston."

"She should. It would be the best thing that ever happened to her."

Birdie slumps down in her chair. "Maybe. But I don't want her to go."

"I know, hon." Max takes hold of Birdie's hand. "You may not believe this, Birdie, but if it happens, you will survive without her."

Would she? Birdie's not so sure about that. For too long, Birdie and Hannah have been stuck in place, waiting for an outside force to come along and give them a push. Hannah has grown increasingly restless these past few months. She's ready for the next stage in life. This opportunity in Charleston may be the push she needs. If this young man persuades Hannah to move to Charleston, Birdie won't hold her back. If only Birdie weren't so terrified of being alone. If the threat of her past demons weren't lurking in the shadows.

TWO

Miss Daisy is a tall woman in her early sixties with thick glasses and a stern voice that keeps her five young charges in line. Every morning, she greets her students on the porch of her sunny yellow house. Today, Gus is the last to arrive. Parking the stroller at the gate of Daisy's white picket fence, Hannah unbuckles Gus and hands him his backpack. Planting a wet kiss on her cheek, he bounds up the sidewalk, past Miss Daisy and through the front door. Hannah joins Daisy in the doorway, and they watch Gus tackle his best friend to the floor.

"Gus snuck out of the apartment this morning," Hannah says, and relates the events of her son's brief disappearance. "He's becoming more and more of a handful. Is he causing trouble for you?"

Daisy's eyes are on the little boys as they roll around on the floor in a fit of giggles. "Honey, you have nothing to worry about. Gus isn't a troublemaker. Mischievous, maybe. But not mean-spirited. He and Robbie are good boys."

Daisy is the authority on kids, and Hannah is relieved to hear her son doesn't have serious character flaws.

The teacher continues, "But mischievous boys are curious. And they like to explore. Which means you can't take your eyes off them. Especially when you live on the water."

Hannah's lungs deflate. "I'm aware. Our living arrangements are a problem in more ways than one."

She retraces her steps down the brick sidewalk and retrieves the empty stroller. Daisy lives on one of Hannah's favorite streets in Palmetto Island's main residential section. The fence extends around the large backyard, providing ample room for the kids to run around and play games. Gus needs a yard almost as much as he needs his own bedroom. Hannah has saved enough money for the down payment on a house. She's been working with a Realtor for over a year, but so far, she hasn't found her dream home.

Hannah has convinced herself that moving out of her mother's apartment and into her own place will fill a deep void. She feels empty inside, as if something is missing, but she can't pinpoint what it is. She adores her child. She has a career she enjoys. And she's happy living on the inlet in her hometown, surrounded by people she's known all her life. But is it enough? Is she settling for the status quo because she lacks the courage to try something new?

As she walks down Central Drive back toward town, she contemplates her meeting in Charleston for later in the day. She's only left the island twice since Gus was born. Both trips were to Charleston. The first, two years ago, she helped her best friend, Liza, move into an apartment when she started medical school at MUSC. And the second time she took her computer to the geniuses at the Apple Store on King Street for repair.

Who is this Ethan Hayes? And why is he so interested in her company? After reaching out to her a half dozen times over the past month, he finally convinced her to meet with him in person. He, too, owns a web design company. Only Ethan's firm, Bay Digital, employs four designers and occupies office space in downtown Charleston. Hannah, on the other hand, flies solo from her desk in the bedroom she shares with her son in the apartment they share with her mother.

Hannah is ready to expand Hannah Fuller Designs. She routinely turns down business because she lacks the bandwidth to handle new clients. Ethan wants to buy her company. She's told him she's not interested, but he refuses to take no for an answer. What if he wants her to stay with the company and work for him? Would she move to Charleston? Flutters dance across her chest at the thought of a new life in a new city. When was the last time she experienced such excitement?

Her heart sinks. What is she thinking? She can't move to Charleston. The risk is too great. Charleston is closer to Columbia, where her baby daddy lives. She's worked too hard to protect Gus to throw it all away now.

As Hannah crosses over Ocean Avenue, she looks up and down the island's primary thoroughfare in both directions. She's designed websites for most of these businesses. Johnson's Pharmacy. Scoop's Ice Cream Parlor. The Sandwich Shack. Freeman's Hardware. Beulah's Boutique. The owners are not only clients, they're her friends. She couldn't possibly leave Palmetto Island. Without the salty air, her lungs would collapse and she would die. She'd miss her mornings on the water and her long walks with her mother along the waterfront. She'd miss the bakery. She enjoys creating recipes for baked goods and coffee drinks. But mostly she would miss their regular customers.

She continues down the sidewalk to the small park that separates the northern and southern branches of the waterfront. Palm trees frame the four corners of the park with a water fountain in the center. Betsy, the town's most beloved homeless person, is eating her breakfast on a park bench. The rolling cart housing all her earthly possessions is parked on the ground at her feet. On the coldest winter nights, Max provides Betsy a complimentary room at her hotel. Betsy's tanned skin is like leather and her hair a shock of tight white curls. While no one seems to know Betsy's true age, Hannah believes she's younger than she looks, that weathering the elements for decades has prematurely aged her.

Hannah sits down beside her and eyes the remaining crumbs on the wax paper sheet in her lap. "What did you have for breakfast this morning, Betsy?"

Betsy's eyes bounce around, hinting at her unstable mind. According to rumor, she lost two young children and a husband in a car accident in the early 1990s and hasn't been the same since.

"A donut. Peaches and cream. It was quite tasty." She pats her stomach. "Is that one of your recipes?"

"All the donut flavors are mine, Betsy. You know that. Two of your favorites, the lemon-glazed blueberry one and the strawberry shortcake donut, are on the menu in honor of Memorial Day this coming weekend."

Betsy claps her hands. "Something to look forward to. You and your mama are awfully good to me, Hannah."

"You're like family, Betsy. We're here for you, if you ever need anything."

Betsy sweeps her arm at the bakery building. "I been watching them over there. What're they doing to the window?"

"Today's the big day. Mom is officially changing the name from Island Bakery to Birdie's Nest Cafe."

Betsy repeats the name. "It has a nice ring to it. Much more personable than Island Bakery."

"I think so too. And she's adding a few items to the menu, including sandwiches. Try them. I think you'll like them."

Betsy licks her lips. "I'll do that."

Hannah rises from the bench and gives Betsy's shoulder a

squeeze. "You have a good day, now. Try to stay out of the sun."

Joining her mom in front of the bakery, Hannah and Birdie watch the professionals smooth out the decal bearing their new logo, which features an illustration of a bird's nest bearing different colored eggs and the new name in yellow script.

"What do you think?" Hannah asks.

"I'm positively thrilled. You did a wonderful job on the logo, sweetheart. I'm blessed to have such a creative daughter." A dreamy expression crosses her mother's face. "*Cafe*. Don't you love the sound of it. I can't believe we've finally made it official."

Hannah draws Birdie in for a half hug. "You did all this, Mom, with very little help from me. I'm proud of all you've accomplished these past three years. And I'm not just talking about the business."

Tears glisten in Birdie's eyes. "That means a lot. More than you know." She wipes her eyes with the heel of her hands. "Shouldn't you be leaving for Charleston soon?"

"I have plenty of time," Hannah says. "You won't forget to pick Gus up from Daisy's, will you?"

"Of course, not. I've already spoken to Sadie. She's going to close the cafe so I can be there right at five."

Hannah turns away from the window. "What will you and Gus do while I'm gone?"

"I thought we'd go for a walk on the docks. Then I'll feed him dinner, give him a bath, and put him to bed."

"I should be home way before bedtime," Hannah says. "Hopefully no later than six."

"Take your time, sweetheart. Don't run out of your meeting on my account. And, for heaven's sake, don't get a speeding ticket."

Hannah laughs. "I won't."

Mother and daughter walk over to the railing and look out

across the inlet. "Mom, promise me, you won't take your eyes off Gus. Especially while you're down on the docks."

Birdie places a reassuring hand on Hannah's back. "Stop worrying, Hannah. I will watch him every second."

"He's a sneaky little bugger."

"Yes, he is. He proved that this morning. He scared me to death."

A comfortable silence settles between them as Hannah's mind drifts back to the past. "Gus's disappearance reminded me of the day Dad went missing. Remember how scared we were? I can't believe we haven't heard from him in three and a half years. Why don't you ever talk about him, Mom?"

A gentle breeze blows a strand of Birdie's blonde hair in her face, and she tucks it behind her ear. "I try not to think about your father. Running off my husband is my biggest failure in life to date."

Hannah doesn't argue with her mother. They both know Birdie's alcoholism was a problem in their marriage and family life. "What if Dad didn't disappear?"

"Come on, Hannah. He cleaned out my bank accounts. That money didn't just get up and walk away."

"True. But anything could've happened to the money. Maybe he had a gambling problem we didn't know about."

"Then how do you explain his mystery woman?" Birdie asks, her eyes on a charter fishing boat fueling up at the marina dock.

"Maybe she wasn't really his woman. Maybe she was a rumor blown out of proportion. You know how this town likes to gossip." Hannah angles her body toward her mother. "I had nothing to do with the problems in your marriage. Dad and I were tight. I don't understand why, if he's still alive, he's never contacted me."

Birdie looks from the fishing boat to Hannah. "What are

you suggesting, sweetheart? Are you saying your father is dead?"

Hannah shrugs. "Maybe. His law firm was on the verge of pressing embezzlement charges against him. Avoiding jail is a valid reason to commit suicide. What if he jumped off the causeway? The bridge is tall enough, the impact would've killed him, and the current taken him out to sea."

Birdie cups Hannah's cheek. "I'm sorry, sweetheart. I never realized how much you need closure."

"Don't you want closure, Mom?"

Birdie drops her hand. "I don't need it."

"Why? Because you're holding on to the hope that he'll come back to you one day?"

"Don't be ridiculous." Birdie's gaze shifts back to the activity on the dock.

"Why is that so ridiculous? It's been three and a half years. You're an attractive woman. Why haven't you started dating again?"

"Ha. Look who's calling the kettle black."

"Gus is the only man I have time for in my life."

Birdie loops her arm through Hannah's. "We both need to try a little harder to venture out into the world. Maybe this Ethan fella will offer you the chance of a lifetime."

"Maybe." Hannah rests her head on her mom's shoulder. "I have this unsettled feeling, like things are getting ready to change, and it scares me."

"The only thing in life that's constant is change, Hannah. Like the change of tides. The water goes out, and you're at your lowest, but then it comes rushing back in, and you're riding high again."

THREE

"You inherited me when you bought this bakery," Sadie has said to Birdie many times. And it's true. Sadie worked for the previous owner for ten years. What would Birdie do without Sadie? She's reliable. The customers adore her. And she's a whiz at baking. Not to mention that many of their tried-and-true recipes are Sadie's grandmother's originals.

Sadie and Birdie have become friends during their time spent together in the kitchen. While Max has known Birdie most of her life, Sadie is better adept at reading Birdie's emotions. And she's a heck of a lot more respectful when quizzing Birdie about her feelings.

"Penny for your thoughts," Sadie says as they roll out pie crusts for the weekly quiche special.

"I'm just thinking about a conversation I had with Max earlier." Setting down her rolling pin, Birdie goes to the swinging door and peeks through the window at her employees in the showroom. Melissa, the college student she hired for the summer, is processing an order for their only customer while

Amanda, the coffee bar manager, refills sugar shakers at the tables along the banquette.

Returning to the worktable, she asks Sadie, "How long after your divorce did you start dating again?"

Sadie casts her green eyes to the ceiling. "About three years, I reckon." Sadie sprinkles flour on the stainless-steel table and attacks her ball of dough. "After my husband left me for his mistress, I made a vow to never love another man. Anyway, I was too busy being a single parent to two young sons to think about dating and romance. But then I ran into Billy in the produce section of the Piggly Wiggly, and—"

"The two of you picked right up where you left off in high school." Birdie loves this story. She's heard it a dozen times.

"Life would've been a heck of a lot easier if I'd married him instead of Marty, the deadbeat, to begin with."

"But then you wouldn't have your boys."

"That's very true. And I wouldn't trade them for anything." Sadie's face softens as it always does when she speaks of her teenage sons. She's a striking woman in her late forties with a creamy complexion and dark auburn hair which she wears in a tight bun on top of her head. "Why do you ask? Do you have some handsome fella wanting to court you?"

"Max has joined some cockamamie dating website. And she's got it in her head for me to join too. I don't think I'm ready."

"Maybe you're more ready than you think. I didn't realize how lonely I was until I started seeing Billy again."

Birdie wipes a strand of hair out of her face with the back of her hand. "But I'm still married to Cary."

"A technicality that you can easily remedy. You should've filed them papers long ago." Birdie feels Sadie's eyes on her, but she doesn't look up. "Honestly, though, I'm not sure how I feel about them dating websites. Seems kinda pointless in a town this small when you already know every available bachelor over the age of forty."

"That's what I told Max."

"You're a beautiful woman, Birdie. You'll find someone when the time is right. When you're ready to let go of the past."

Birdie doesn't respond. What past is she holding onto? She's clinging tight to her daughter and grandson. But they are her past, present, and future. Even if they move to another town, Hannah and Gus will still be a part of her life. She sometimes misses the waterfront home she was forced to sell after Cary left. Maybe one day she'd like to get out of the apartment and into a house. But she's not obsessing about it. She's a successful businesswoman. South Carolinians are raving about her baked goods all throughout the state.

She thinks back to her conversation with Max. Could she still be in love with Cary? She dismisses the possibility. She stopped loving him long before he disappeared. Didn't she? She remembers what Hannah said on the boardwalk. *Because you're holding on to the hope that he'll come back to you one day."*

That's hogwash, she thinks to herself. And she'll prove it by joining the dating website.

Leaving Sadie to finish the quiches, Birdie enters her small office off the kitchen. Seated at her computer, she creates an account at MatchMade and fills out her profile. In the space provided to tell a little about herself, she types, *Attractive middle-aged woman seeking* . . . What is she seeking? Fun? Romance? Companionship? All the above.

Deleting her words, she spends the next hour reading what other men and women have written about themselves in their profiles. Some are more personal than others. She can't imagine saying such things to strangers. Birdie keeps her message simple. She describes herself as hard working with family being the most important aspect of her life.

Birdie uploads an image of herself Hannah took with her fancy camera. She'd snuck up on Birdie one day while she was standing at the living room window, in deep thought as she gazed out at the foggy inlet. She chooses this photo to show potential suitors her serious side. Which is how she sees herself. She's no longer the party girl of her youth. That girl left a long time ago.

Once her profile is to her liking, she clicks Enter and falls back in her chair. A wave of fear washes over her. What if someone asks her to go out for drinks?

You'll say yes, Birdie. You'll order a club soda with a lemon twist.

Birdie isn't outdoorsy like Max. What will she say if a man invites her to go sailing?

You'll say yes. You're not too old to learn something new.

While Cary often took Hannah fishing and hunting and kayaking, he never asked Birdie to go on any such outings. Instead of looking for romance, perhaps she should pursue new hobbies or extracurricular activities to keep her busy when Hannah and Gus are gone. She's getting the cart before the horse, anyway. Hannah may end up buying a house nearby, and she'll get to see them every other day and on weekends.

Hannah rarely dresses up except to go to church on Sundays. Most days, depending on the weather, she wears jeans or shorts with T-shirts. But today, she feels all grown up in slim-fitting light gray pants and a starched white shirt, her mahogany hair twisted in a neat bun, as she makes her way down a cobble-stone side street off Charleston's prominent East Bay Street.

Hannah arrives at the renovated warehouse building

promptly at three o'clock. She climbs the stairs to Bay Digital's office on the second floor. The space is hip with exposed brick walls, worn hardwood floors, and desks arranged in clusters to encourage collaboration on projects. Ethan emerges from his office to greet her. With sandy hair and warm brown eyes, he is far more handsome than his photograph on the company's website. He looks the part of a successful entrepreneur, his tall frame dressed in casual business attire—blue-and-white checked shirt, tapered khaki pants, leather driving shoes, and a casual navy windowpane blazer.

Ethan introduces Hannah to his staff before showing her to his office. The room is handsome with an Oriental rug, a heavy live edge wooden table he uses for his desk, and an oversized floor-to-ceiling window offering a glimpse of the harbor.

He motions Hannah to a grouping of four cognac-colored leather chairs. "Can I offer you coffee? Tea? Water?"

"I'm fine. Thank you."

He lowers his tall frame to the chair nearest her. "So, here we are."

Hannah holds her hands out, palms up. "Here we are. I'm not sure why, though. I told you on the phone, I'm not interested in selling my company."

"I intend to change your mind." He settles back in his seat. "Tell me about yourself, Hannah."

Is this a job interview? Hannah wonders. "Well, I graduated from—"

"No, Hannah. I don't want your resume. I've done my research. I know every bit of public knowledge about you. I'm curious about what makes you tick. If you had to name one thing that motivates your work, what would it be?"

"Hmm." What drives her the most is her son. *I know every bit of public knowledge about you.* She doubts he knows about Gus, and she's not ready to tell him. "I'd have to say the inlet. I feel a special connection to the wildlife."

Ethan gives a nod of appreciation. "I've studied your photography. Your talent is outstanding. You're a unique individual with much to offer the industry. And your work speaks for itself. I'll be honest, Hannah. I'm more interested in you than I am in your clients. But I'm willing to buy your company in order to bring you on board." The amount he offers makes Hannah's eyeballs pop.

"What would be my role within your company?"

He extends his hand toward the closed door. "I have my share of capable designers. I need someone to manage the creative aspects of the business, which will free up my time to bring in more clients. Bigger clients with more complicated needs. Working with me, you'll be designing websites for major corporations, not mom and pop businesses."

Hannah's brows knit together. "I have relationships with the owners of those mom and pop businesses. What will happen to them after the acquisition?"

"Nothing. We'll continue to service their needs." For the next half hour, as Ethan talks about the complexities of his firm, Hannah grows more intrigued with his proposition. "I want to work with you, Hannah. What do you say? Are you ready to move to Charleston?"

"And hence the sticking point," she says. "As I told you on the phone, Ethan, I'm not interested in moving to Charleston."

Ethan groans. "Charleston is a great city, Hannah. Have you spent much time here?"

"Practically none." When he appears surprised, she adds, "I know that's hard to believe when Palmetto Island is only an hour away."

"I've been to your Island. And I admit the place has a certain charm. Your small town limits your potential. Our clients will love you. You're personable and attractive. What color are your eyes, anyway?"

Hannah's face warms. "My mom calls them olive."

He leans forward in his chair. "I appreciate your tenacity, Hannah. I admire a girl who knows what she wants. Will you at least consider moving here?"

"If you'll consider allowing me to work remotely from Palmetto island."

Ethan hesitates before answering. "I'm not thrilled about the idea. I want you here. Where you can manage your staff in person. Let's make a deal. I'll consider allowing you to work remotely, if you'll let me show you around Charleston."

"Deal." While he's showing her around, she'll be convincing him she doesn't have to be present to be effective at her job.

He flashes a grin. "But be warned. I can be persuasive. By the time I'm finished, you'll see there's no better place in the world to live than Charleston."

She laughs. "Fair enough. I'll keep an open mind. When do you need my decision?"

"Take all the time you need." Ethan chuckles. "Well, maybe not a year. But I'm willing to wait a couple of months."

"I shouldn't need that much time, but thank you, anyway."

"Speaking of time." He glances at his watch. "It's almost five o'clock. Can I tempt you into having a drink with me? I'll start my tour of the city by showing you my favorite raw bar. It's a short walk from here."

She'd told her mom she'd be home by Gus's bedtime, but she's too intrigued by this man and this job opportunity to leave just yet. "Sure. But can I use your restroom first?"

"Of course," he says and shows her down the hall.

While in the restroom, she thumbs off a text to her mom, explaining she'll be home later than expected. She rejoins Ethan in the lobby, and they exit the building, heading back up the cobblestone street away from the water.

As they stroll up East Bay Street, she feels herself coming alive at the sights and sounds and smells of the city. And the people. Not the tourists dressed in Hawaiian shirts and sundresses. She sees plenty of those back home. The professional-looking men and women wearing casual business attire intrigue her. Charleston appears to be a healthy mix of city and vacation hot spot.

"I'm surprised at the number of people out on a Monday evening."

"There's always something going on in Charleston."

"Do you live downtown?" The only part of downtown Hannah knows is the area near MUSC where Liza lives.

Ethan nods. "My parents still live in the house where I grew up on Legare Street. I own a waterfront condo around the block from the office. Mount Pleasant is a wonderful option. If you can stand commuting across the Ravenel Bridge every day."

When they reach the restaurant, Ethan holds the door open, and she enters ahead of him. A young crowd is drinking draft beer and eating oysters on the half shell at the wooden bar that occupies one side of the restaurant. The buzz of conversation drowns out the country music playing in the background. Hannah relaxes as tension leaves her body. She feels as though she's returning to civilization after being stranded on a deserted island for three years.

Gus begs Birdie to read him another book. Hannah, who falls for this request every night, thinks it's adorable. She brags, "He's going to be the next John Grisham." But Birdie understands her grandson's delay tactic. He's avoiding lights out as long as possible.

Despite his pleas, after saying his prayers, Birdie tucks the covers tight around his small body and kisses Gus goodnight. She fastens the baby gate at the top of the stairs and goes down to the kitchen where she throws together a simple salad of baby spinach and rotisserie chicken with balsamic vinaigrette dressing. Setting her plate on a bamboo tray, she turns toward the stairs, stopping in her tracks at the sight of Cary standing in the coatroom. She shakes her head, as though her mind is playing tricks on her. She's imagining him. He's been on her mind too much today. She's glued to the floor, her arms and legs paralyzed. Is she having a stress dream? Is he a ghost? But then the sound of the voice she remembers all too well penetrates the silence.

"Really, Birdie? A bakery?"

The tray slips from her hands and crashes to the floor. Silverware clatters across the concrete and the plate cracks into two pieces. "How did you get in here?"

He inclines his head at the open back door. "You left the door unlocked."

She must have forgotten to lock the knob when she and Gus returned from their stroll on the waterfront. There's little crime on the island. She's never felt the need to lock her doors. With an energetic toddler around, they'll have to be more careful. She should've learned her lesson when Gus slipped out this morning.

She finds her voice. "What do you want, Cary?"

He pushes the door closed and steps across the threshold into the kitchen. "Aren't you going to welcome me home?"

Her head snaps back as though he slapped her. "Welcome you *home*? Have you lost your mind? At the risk of stating the obvious, this isn't our home. I was forced to sell our home when you took our money and ran off with your girlfriend. Where is your mystery woman, anyway?"

He hangs his head. "She took my money and ran off with another guy."

Birdie holds her chin high, shoulders back. "Good! Serves you right. Now you know how it feels."

"I guess I deserve that," he says, still staring downward.

"Damn right, you do. And so much more." She gives him the once over. He's shed at least twenty pounds and gained muscles in his shoulders and arms. "Nice tan. Where have you been? Hawaii?"

"Yes, actually." He looks up as a flush spreads across his cheeks. "On Maui."

Pain grips her chest as she thinks about the heartache he caused when he abandoned them. While she was drinking herself to an early grave, he was living it up on Maui? "What are you doing here, Cary?"

He gestures at the suitcase at his feet. "I need a place to stay until I can get back on my feet."

Birdie lets out a loud gasp. "You have some nerve," she says, her voice loud and angry. "Do you seriously think you can just waltz in here and pick up where we left off?"

A little voice calls from the top of the stairs. "Birdie."

Cary's gaze shifts from Birdie to Gus and back to Birdie.

"Yes, sweetheart," she yells up the stairs. "I'm right here. Get back in bed, and I'll be up to check on you in a minute."

Cary narrows his olive eyes. Hannah's eyes. "Is that Hannah's child?"

"Whose else child would it be? In case you've forgotten, Hannah had just found out she was pregnant when you left. She worshipped you, and you abandoned her when she needed you the most. Just this morning, our daughter admitted to me she thought you might have killed yourself. I understand why you left me. But the two of you were so close. Why didn't you ever contact her, Cary? Why didn't you let Hannah know you were alive?"

He shakes his dark head, his once salt-and-pepper hair now all pepper. *Is he dying his hair now?* "I have no excuses. I made some mistakes, and I hurt a lot of people. I want to make amends."

26

"What about the money you embezzled from the firm? From Jonathan, your best friend? He gave you a second chance, and you stole from him again. Seriously? What were you thinking?"

"Jonathan and I go way back. I'm hoping he'll let me work off what I owe him."

"Ha. Good luck with that." Using the largest half of the broken plate, Birdie scrapes up the ruined dinner and dumps it into the trash can.

"Please, Birdie. I have nowhere else to go."

At the sink, she washes and dries her hands. "Sorry. I can't help you."

"You must still feel something for me," Cary says to her back. "Otherwise, you would have divorced me."

Birdie turns and crosses the room to the coatroom. Standing before him, she can finally admit that a part of her has been hoping Cary would one day return. She's been clinging to the fond memories of the good years they spent together. The early years. But seeing him standing in *her* kitchen—her cafe, the business she's poured her heart and soul into—serves as a poignant reminder of the loneliness she felt during their last years together. If she had any lingering feelings for him, they're now gone. Their marriage is over. Birdie can finally search for some form of happiness.

"Divorce is a formality, one that I never got around to addressing. But now that you're here, I'll have my attorney draw up the papers right away. Be sure to sign them before you leave town again."

She opens the door and motions for him to go. "Goodbye, Cary. I would say it's been nice seeing you again. But it hasn't."

When he starts to object, she opens the door wider. "Please, leave."

With stooped shoulders and head lowered, he crosses the

threshold. Birdie slams and locks the door and dashes up the stairs to the safety of her apartment.

After checking on Gus, who has fallen back asleep, she paces the floor in the living room. Her craving for alcohol hasn't been this bad in months. She refuses to travel back down that path. She can't let Cary derail her life again.

She brews a cup of lavender tea and settles on the sofa to watch the sunset. The tea takes the edge off her frayed nerves and, as she gathers her wits, pride replaces the fear and anger. She did something she'd never been able to do during their marriage. She stood up to Cary. And she will continue to stand up to him.

Birdie is still sitting on the sofa, empty mug in hand, when Hannah arrives home a few minutes after eight. She goes straight to her bedroom to kiss Gus goodnight. When she returns, she plops down beside Birdie. She removes the elastic from her bun and her mahogany hair spills over the sofa cushions.

"Sorry I'm late. Ethan took me out for oysters. We had a lot to talk about. We were at the restaurant for over two hours."

"That's nice, sweetheart."

"You wouldn't believe their offices, Mom." Hannah rattles on about her meeting with Ethan, but Birdie is too distracted to pay attention.

Hannah smacks her mother's arm with the back of her hand. "Mom! You're not listening. Is something wrong?"

Birdie doesn't know how to break this kind of news. Best just to come right out and say it. "Your father's back."

Hannah's face falls. "What do you mean, he's back?"

"He showed up here earlier," Birdie says, and tells Hannah about her visit from Cary.

"I can't believe this." Jumping to her feet, Hannah walks in circles as she rakes her hands through her long hair. "Dad dumps us for his other woman, and now that she's dumped him, he comes running back to us." She stops and glares down at Birdie. "Has he lost his freaking mind, Mom? Seriously, Maui?"

Birdie stands to face her daughter. "At least you have closure, sweetheart. Your father is alive. You have another chance at a relationship with him."

Hannah gawks at her. "You're as delusional as Dad. I don't want to see him. And I don't want him anywhere near my child." She storms into her bedroom and closes the door.

Cary's return has given Birdie the closure she needs to move on. But the situation is more complicated for her daughter. Hannah's suspicions have been confirmed. Never once in the three years he was living on Maui did her father try to contact her. That is a bitter pill for Hannah to swallow. Now that Cary is back, the old hurt will resurface. Not only did he break her heart, he broke her trust. And he'll have to work hard to earn that trust back.

FOUR

Too angry to sleep, Hannah tosses and turns for most of the night. For three years, her father has been sipping mai tais and soaking up the rays on a sandy white beach in Hawaii with his girlfriend. He's been enjoying the life of luxury, meanwhile Hannah didn't know if he was alive or dead. Her question still gnaws at her. Why, in three years, four months, and twenty-four days, didn't he try to contact her? Not a single phone call or text message or email. As much as she hates to admit it, mourning his death would hurt less than his betrayal.

Just before dawn, Hannah gives up on trying to sleep and rolls out of bed. Throwing a lightweight fleece on over her pajamas, she kisses Gus's sweaty forehead, grabs her camera bag, and slips quietly out of the room, closing the bedroom door behind her. Gus understands about his mommy's early morning work. If he wakes to find her gone, he knows to go to his grandmother's room.

Hannah brews a coffee in the kitchenette and hurries down the stairs. Throwing open the back door, she stumbles over a large round object the shape of a tree trunk. The coffee flies out of her hand, but she catches herself before falling. The object groans and moves into a sitting position. From beneath his hooded sweatshirt, Hannah recognizes her father's handsome face and the green eyes that are so like her own.

"What the heck, Dad? Are you homeless now?"

He scrambles to his feet. "Hannah! Sweetheart, it's so good to see you."

When he tries to embrace her, she shoves him away. "Don't come near me."

"I understand you're upset. And you have every reason to be. But wow. Look at you." He spreads his arms wide in front of him. "You're all grown up. You're a young woman now."

"I don't know why you're here, but nobody wants any of what you're offering. So, beat it, Dad." She kicks at the ground, nearly losing her balance.

Cary steps toward her. "Are you okay?"

Hannah rights herself. "I'll be better when you leave."

"Don't be this way, honey. Aren't you the tiniest bit happy to see me? I saw your son last night. He's quite the handsome young man."

Hannah jabs her finger at her father's face. "Stay away from my son. And from me. You are not welcome here. We want nothing to do with you."

Closing and locking the door, Hannah spins on the heels of her flip-flops and sprints down the back alley to the park.

Her father calls out after her, "Hannah! Wait!"

She is relieved when she hears no footfalls on the pavement behind her. Rounding the corner of the cafe, she hurries down to the marina's floating dock, slides her kayak into the water, and paddles off into the predawn light. When she's a safe distance away, she stops rowing, resting the paddles in her lap while she catches her breath.

He called her grown-up. Hannah looks down at her fleece and flannel pajama bottoms. She hasn't grown up one bit since he left. She may no longer be in college, and she's managing her own web design business. But she's still on her mother's health insurance plan, still living in Birdie's apartment and not paying rent.

Despite being surrounded by the vast inlet and ocean beyond, she feels the world closing in on her as she thinks back to yesterday's conversation with Birdie. *The only thing in life that's constant is change. Like the change of tides.*

Hannah has seen some very low tides since her dad left. The months after his disappearance when she was nursing a broken heart, not only for Cary but for the ex-boyfriend who cheated on her. The following summer when she and Birdie were at each other's throats as they awaited Gus's arrival. The first months of Gus's life when he screamed night and day from colic. For the past two years, she's been paddling against the incoming tide without making any headway. She isn't living her life. She's hiding behind Birdie's coattails, afraid to venture out into the world.

When she reaches her favorite spot, Hannah pulls alongside the abandoned dock and readies her camera. Surveying her surroundings, she spots a lone heron. The elegant curve of his long neck against the green marsh with the backdrop of the rising pink sun makes for a stunning image. She raises the camera and focuses the lens, her finger hovering over the shutter button. As she often does, she thinks back to the Christmas her father gave her the camera and telephoto lens. Seven days before he disappeared. She lowers the camera again without engaging the shutter. After his disappearance, using the camera made her feel closer to him, their one remaining bond too precious to give up. She conveniently overlooked the likelihood he purchased the equipment with embezzled funds. Doesn't that make them both guilty?

Without taking the lens off the camera body, she stuffs the entire apparatus into her bag. She navigates the kayak around the dock and heads for home. Her phone pings in her jacket pocket with a text from Ethan. *Are you out on the water? The golden flecks in your olive eyes sparkle when you talk about the wildlife.*

Her face warms. The thought of him lounging in bed, wearing only pajama bottoms with his muscular chest bare, stirs something deep inside of her that has been asleep for far too long. She's considering how to respond to his text when her phone vibrates with an incoming call.

"Morning, beautiful," Ethan says in a husky voice.

"Good morning, Ethan. You're awake awfully early."

"I woke up thinking about you. Can you come to Charleston on Saturday? We'll go out in the boat during the day, and I'll take you to dinner afterward."

Hannah's mind races. Spending a day and night in Charleston intrigues her. A lot, actually. But who will take care of Gus? "I have to check with my mom. She's counting on me to help in the cafe over the holiday weekend." This isn't a total lie. Hannah often helps when they're busy or short-staffed.

"Okay. Just let me know. My parents have a carriage house if you need a place to stay."

Parents? Does he introduce all his business associates to his parents? "Thanks, but my best friend is in med school at MUSC. I'd probably just stay with her." Hannah promises to get back to him later today before ending the call.

She paddles slowly back to the dock. She and Ethan had shared much about their lives over oysters the previous evening. He spoke of his life growing up on the Battery and his college years at the University of Alabama. And she told him about her love of photography and the wildlife in the inlet. But she never mentioned Gus. Her son is the one aspect of her life she keeps private at all times. Before she proceeds with the acceptance of his offer, she'll have to tell Ethan the truth. What if he doesn't want a single mother of a young child in a prominent role in his company?

The sound of loud knocking wakes Birdie from a deep slumber. Slipping on her worn terry cloth robe, she hurries down the stairs to the back door. Cary is standing in the alley with his hands pressed together under his chin.

"If you're praying, I suggest you be careful. Lightning may strike you dead."

"I happen to have a good relationship with the Lord."

Birdie raises an eyebrow. "Oh really? Has the Lord forgiven you for stealing from your business partner and abandoning your wife and daughter?"

"I'm not praying. I'm begging." Cary lowers his hands from his face. "Please, Birdie. I need a place to stay. Only for a few nights until I can find a job. I literally have one dollar left to my name." Tugging his wallet out of his back pocket, he opens it to reveal the dollar bill. "Melinda canceled all my credit cards."

Melinda. Birdie's archenemy in high school was named Melinda, and she can't help but think of her whenever she hears the name. "If you're looking for sympathy, you won't find any here."

He takes a step toward her. "You're a Christian woman. Can't you take pity on a poor soul like me?"

"Enough with the bull malarkey, Cary. Even if I wanted to help you, which I definitely do not, my apartment is too small. Hannah, Gus, and I are crammed in here like sardines as it is."

"You have a sofa, don't you?"

"Yes. And one small bathroom. I'm sorry, Cary. You'll have to find somewhere else to stay. Maybe one of your friends will take you in."

When she moves to shut the door, he sticks his foot out blocking her progress. "I tried them all before I came to you. I'm persona non grata on the island."

"Are you surprised?"

Staring at the ground, he shakes his head.

"You're better off starting over in a new town where no one knows you." Birdie plants a hand on her hip. "If I give you a coupla hundred bucks, will you go away and never come back?"

"I'm not looking for a handout. I can't start over somewhere new until I make things right with the people I care about on Palmetto Island."

She grips the doorknob. "If you really cared about us, you would never have betrayed us."

He moves forward, leaning against the doorjamb so she can't shut the door. "I was weak, Birdie. I let Melinda convince me I deserved a better life. Not that I was ever unhappy in our marriage. But I was bored. And I think you were too."

When he tries to finger her cheek, Birdie brushes his hand away. "Don't touch me."

"Melinda's a financial genius. She quadrupled my money in a matter of months. I was planning to pay Jonathan back and wire you enough so you wouldn't have to sell the house. But she went berserk on me. She hid my money from me in offshore accounts."

"That's illegal."

"I'm aware."

"Then why didn't you turn *Melinda* into the cops?"

"Because I was equally guilty. And I didn't want to go to jail. Although I've been living in a different kind of prison. With Melinda as my captor. With no access to my bank accounts, I was at her beck and call. Then one morning last week, I woke up to find she'd disappeared."

Cary appears so wounded, Birdie almost feels sorry for him. "Just as you did to me."

He nods. "Melinda left me three twenty-dollar bills and a one-way plane ticket to Charleston. Despite everything, I'm relieved to be away from her. She's an evil person. I hope she gets what's coming to her."

Cary's steady gaze makes Birdie uncomfortable, and she looks past him into the kitchen.

"I don't expect you to welcome me back into your lives after the terrible things I did. I just want a chance to show you how sorry I am. I want to make it up to you and Hannah if you'll let me."

"Make it up to us how? You have one dollar to your name. You have nothing to offer us."

"I can be a grandfather to Hannah's little boy."

Cary was a doting father to Hannah. He would undoubtedly be the same to Gus.

Cary goes on. "I can help around the cafe. I'll do whatever you ask of me. I just need a little time to get back on my feet."

Birdie's resolve weakens. She's not without feelings. If his story is legit, Cary is every bit the victim she and Hannah once were. "You'll have to follow my very long list of rules."

"I'd expect nothing less."

Birdie lets out a slow breath. "Hannah won't be happy about this."

"All the more reason to give me this chance."

She holds up a finger. "One sign of trouble and you're out of here."

"I'm not here to cause trouble, Birdie. I'm here to make amends."

She opens the door wider to let him in. "Something tells me I'm going to regret this."

Hannah stores the kayak on the rack, but instead of going straight home, she stops in at the hotel to see Max. She's always been close to Max, has always talked to her about the things she couldn't discuss with her parents. Her mother's best friend is a good listener and has a way of helping Hannah see situations in a different light.

She finds Max behind the counter, finishing up with a guest. "I need to tell you something. Come with me." Leaving the guest service representative to cover the front desk, Hannah drags Max outside to the boardwalk. "Guess who's back in town?"

Max's blue eyes darken. "Your daddy?"

"Yep. Just like that." Hannah snaps her fingers. "He reappears as suddenly as he disappeared." She brings Max up to speed about her father's visit with her mother last night and about stumbling over him in the alley behind the bakery.

Max falls back against the wooden railing. "Your poor mama. This must be so hard for her."

"Do you think they'll get back together?"

Max shakes her head. "I hope not. She claims she's over him. She's worked so hard to stay sober. This could be a real setback."

"Tell me about it. Dad's been shacking up with some woman in Maui all this time. Can you believe that? Hawaii? Surely, Mom has more pride than to take him back after learning that." Propping her elbows on the railing, Hannah buries her face in her hands. "How am I supposed to act around him, Max?"

"I can't answer that for you, sweet girl. This is a difficult situation. You need to take it as it comes. You might start by hearing his side of the story. Let him explain why he did the things he did."

"Then he'll say he's sorry and ask me to forgive him. But he doesn't deserve my forgiveness."

Max pulls Hannah in for a half hug. "Sometimes forgiveness does more for the person doing the forgiving than the person asking for it."

"What's that supposed to mean?"

"The anger will fester inside of you if you don't address it. Over time, you'll become bitter. You should reconcile with your dad while you have the chance. You might later regret it, if you don't."

"I'm not interested in reconciling with him." Hannah pushes away from Max, placing her back to the water. "It was easier when I thought Dad committed suicide. I felt sorry for him. Knowing he's been alive all this time and didn't contact me . . ." She throws her hands in the air. "Whatever. I hate him so much. I just want him to leave town."

"*Hate* is a powerful word, Hannah. You're angry with your father, and understandably so. But keep that beautiful heart of yours open. Give him a chance to make amends."

Hannah turns to face Max. "Seriously? Would you be able to do the same thing if you were in my shoes?"

Max laughs. "Not a chance. But I'm not compassionate and loving like you." She smacks Hannah on the butt. "Now go home to that adorable son of yours. And give him a hug from Maxie."

As she rounds the corner of the building, Hannah is relieved to see her father is no longer in the alley. But when she enters the coatroom, she hears the sounds of Cary's voice and Gus's giggles coming from the apartment upstairs.

Dropping her camera bag on the built-in bench, Hannah crawls on all fours up the stairs. Her father and son are lying belly down on the hardwood floor, playing with Gus's wooden train set. She watches grandfather and grandson interact. When Hannah plays with Gus, she rolls the train around the track and calls out, "Choo, choo." But her father makes two engines collide with loud crashing noises, and Gus topples onto his side in laughter.

Cary is not what Hannah had in mind for her son's male role model. "What do you think you're doing? I told you to stay away from my son."

She scoops Gus up off the floor and carries his wiggling body to their room, depositing him on his bed. She wags her finger at him. "Stay here until I tell you to come out."

Ignoring his sobs, she leaves the room, closing the door behind her. She marches over to where her father is now standing beside the abandoned train set. "Who let you in here? And where's Mom? Mom!" she hollers.

"I'm right here, sweetheart."

Hannah turns to see Birdie, dressed for work in jeans and her yellow logo polo, emerging from the hallway leading to her room. "Why is he here?" she asks, her arm outstretched with a finger pointed at Cary.

"Your father's going to stay with us for a few days until he gets his life together."

Hannah's brow shoots up to her hairline. "Have you lost your mind?"

"Probably," Birdie says, slipping a clean apron over her head. "But he's in trouble, and we should help him out."

"Are you kidding me? And where was he when we were in trouble? When you were struggling with alcoholism, and I was pregnant. Have you forgotten that he abandoned us?"

Her mother's expression turns to stone. "I will never forget that, Hannah. But I'm capable of being the better person. And so are you. When you hear what your father has to say, you'll feel—"

"Nothing. I will never feel anything for him again except . . ." *Hate is a powerful word, Hannah.* She turns back around to face her father. "I feel nothing for you. Nothing whatsoever."

The sound of Gus's cries grows louder from behind her

bedroom door. "Is Gus all right?" Birdie asks. "Why is he crying?"

A stab of guilt grips Hannah's chest for taking her anger at her father out on her child. "Nothing good will come from you living here. Stay away from me and my son."

Hannah storms out and goes to her bedroom. Sitting down on the bed, she takes a screaming Gus in her arms. He swings his little fists at her, and she locks her arms tight around him. "Let's both take some deep breaths so we can calm down."

When she inhales and exhales loudly, he follows her lead. The tension leaves his body, and she hugs him close. "I'm so sorry, buddy. I shouldn't have gotten angry."

He wipes his runny nose on her fleece. "Are you mad at me, Mommy?"

"Not at all." Hannah holds her son away from her body so she can see his face. "That man out there is my father. Your grandfather."

"I know! He told me. Are you mad at Pops?"

Pops? Gus didn't think up that name on his own. "I haven't seen him in a while. It's complicated grown-up stuff, sweetheart. Nothing for you to worry about. Hey, what say you and I get dressed and go to Rudy's Diner for breakfast?"

"Can I have pancakes?"

Pancakes are a special treat, reserved for Sunday mornings only. She tousles his hair. "You may have pancakes."

Gus places his soft hand on her cheek. "Can Pops come?"

Hannah forces back another wave of anger. "Not this time, sweetheart."

Her father has cast his spell on her son, just as he did to Hannah when she was a child. But this apartment is too small for both Hannah and her father. Maybe the town is too small as well. For the first time, she ponders the possibility of moving to Charleston.

FIVE

Two cups of strong coffee along with a spinach omelet allow Hannah the clarity she needs to assess her new predicament. She's taken advantage of her mother's generosity for far too long. The time has come for her to make a move. But she needs to make the right move. Not only for her but for Gus.

"Is there any chance you could keep Gus this weekend?" Hannah asks Miss Daisy when she drops him off a few minutes later. "I'm going to Charleston to see a friend."

"I would love to have him. I'm also keeping Robbie. The three of us will have a grand old time."

Hannah's gaze travels to the boys who are chasing each other around the living room. "Are you sure it's not too much trouble? I'll only be gone from Saturday morning until around noon on Sunday."

Miss Daisy's lips part in a reassuring smile. "Stay as long as you like. We'll be fine."

Feeling ten pounds lighter, Hannah takes the long way back to the waterfront, meandering through the neighboring streets. She sends a quick text to Liza, asking if she can crash at her apartment on Saturday night, followed by a message to Ethan, accepting his invitation for a day on the water and dinner afterward. She receives prompt responses. Both Liza and Ethan are looking forward to seeing her on Saturday.

When Hannah glances up from her phone, she notices a *For Sale* sign in front of a quaint house on Summer Street. The story and a half Cape Cod-style home has dormer windows, white wood siding, black shutters, and a blue front door the color of the summer sky. Pots of pink geraniums welcome visitors on the brick steps leading up to a columned front porch.

She clicks on her Realtor's number. Shannon answers on the first ring. "Hannah! Your timing is impeccable. I was just getting ready to call you. I've found the perfect house for you. Three bedrooms. Updated kitchen. Fenced-in backyard."

"Let me guess. The address is on Summer Street?"

"Yes," Shannon says in an incredulous tone. "How'd you know?"

"I'm standing in front of it now. When can I see it?"

"Showings start on Friday. Prepare yourself. This one will go quickly."

"Can you get me an appointment? I'm flexible. Morning or afternoon."

"Sure thing. I'll be back in touch when I have a time," Shannon says and ends the call.

Hannah remains in front of the house a minute longer, imagining pumpkins on the porch at Halloween and a magnolia wreath with a red velvet bow on the door at Christmas. Despite her father's sudden return, her future is looking brighter. She has choices. Charleston or Summer Street. Either way, after three years, she is determined to make changes in her life.

Cary leaves the apartment midmorning, dressed professionally in a tailored summer suit and starched white shirt. Birdie walks him to the door, and when he leans in to kiss her, she pulls away. "What're you doing?"

"Sorry. I forgot where I was for a minute. It feels so natural for you, wearing your apron, to be saying goodbye to me at the door on my way to work."

"It may feel natural for you, but it's awkward for me."

"Right." He straightens, smoothing out his lapel. "Well, wish me luck."

"Good luck," she says, meaning it. The sooner he gets a job, the sooner he can get out of her apartment.

But when he returns that afternoon, his expression is grim. It's past closing time, and they sit at a window table in the empty cafe.

Cary blows on his chai tea, takes a tentative sip, and sets the mug down. "I don't get it. Jonathan and I have known each other since we were kids. I was certain he'd give me my old job back."

Birdie tilts her head as she studies him. His bewilderment is genuine. Has Cary always been so naïve? "You stole money from his firm, Cary. Not once, but twice. He can't give you back your job, even if he wanted to. His partners and associates would think him a fool."

"I guess you're right. At least he agreed not to press charges. He's giving me three years to pay back the money."

"That's incredibly generous of him. I don't know why you are complaining. You should be grateful. Did you ask if he'd be willing to provide a recommendation?"

"I didn't ask, but I'm sure he will."

There's that naïveté again. Or is it narcissism? "You shouldn't take anything for granted. Where else are you applying?"

"I haven't thought about it," he says, his gaze still lowered.

"There are other smaller law firms on the island. But I wouldn't get your hopes up. Like I told you this morning, you're better off starting over in a new town where no one knows you."

He looks up at her. "Are you trying to get rid of me?"

"I *am* getting rid of you. I'm divorcing you. I spoke to my attorney at length earlier today. The paperwork will be ready for us to sign in a few days. Ninety days after he files in court, the divorce will be final."

His shoulders droop. "Is this what you really want?" he asks in a quiet voice.

Birdie's jaw drops. "What *I* want? *You're* the one who left me, remember?"

"I remember. But that was a mistake. Do you think there's any chance we could try again?"

"Nope. What part of *I'm divorcing you* don't you understand?" She clasps her hands in her lap to keep them from shaking. Cary's presence is triggering a craving. She needs to get to an AA meeting soon.

"I *do* understand. I just thought . . ." He flashes his most charismatic smile, the one that once made her heart do somersaults across her chest. She's relieved to find his charm no longer works on her.

"You thought what? That I've been pining away for you all these years while you were living the good life with *Melinda* on Maui." Her gaze falls to her hands in her lap. "This hasn't been easy for me, Cary. But I have finally closed that chapter of my life. I'm ready to move on. You need to respect that while you're living under my roof."

"I do respect you. More than you know," he says, his tone barely audible.

From the window, Birdie watches tourists strolling about on the boardwalk below. "You should really consider starting over in a town like Raleigh or Charlotte. In a place where no one knows about your past."

"But my family is here. My daughter and my grandson. I'm not leaving."

"Then you might have to settle for a job in a field other than the law." Pushing back from the table, she leaves him sitting alone in the semidarkness.

On Wednesday afternoon, Max barges into the kitchen through the swinging door from the showroom. With barely a glance at Sadie, she rips into Birdie. "You're asking for trouble, Birdie. Nothing good will come from having that man in your apartment. Cary is your nemesis. Your weakness. He's a black widow spider who will tangle you in his web and spit his venom under your skin. You've worked so hard to stay sober. I'd hate for him to drive you—"

Birdie's hand shoots up. "Enough already. You've made your point." She looks at Sadie for support, but the woman's brown eyes are wide as she nods her head.

"I'm sorry, Birdie. But I agree with Max this time. You're playing with fire where that man is concerned."

Birdie falls back against the counter. "Geez, you two need to chill out. I'm keeping a tight lid on the situation. And don't worry. I went to a meeting last night. I'm fine. I promise, I'm not going to start drinking again."

Max plants her hands on her hips. "Oh really? And just how do you plan to protect yourself from that no good, two-timing—"

"I've made it clear to Cary he'll have to find somewhere else to stay if he steps out of line. He's trying hard to find a new job."

"Humph! He had a perfectly fine job with a respectable law

firm before he took all their money and flew off to Hawaii," Max says, her voice escalating with each word.

"Okay. That's enough. You're disturbing my customers. Let's go outside." Taking her by the arm, Birdie marches Max out the back door.

Outside, Max jerks her arm free of Birdie's grip, and they face off in the alley. "Have you given any consideration to what this is doing to your daughter? Hannah is furious with Cary. And rightly so. She needs time to adapt to him being back in town without having to live under the same roof with him."

Birdie folds her arms over her chest. "Okay, Miss Know-it-All, what do you suggest I do?"

"Make Cary stay somewhere else. He and Hannah can sort out their problems in due time."

"But he has nowhere else to stay, Max. I encouraged him to move to another town. I even offered to give him a little money. But he's determined to clear his name and restore his reputation on the island."

Max's expression tightens. "How admirable of him. I dare say folks around here won't be too eager to forgive him."

"That's what I told him. Do you have a room you can spare?"

Max shakes her head. "I'm booked solid for the weekend. But even if I did, you know how protective I am of my guests. I wouldn't allow Cary anywhere near them."

Birdie lets out a sigh. "Look, I have no intention of allowing this situation to continue indefinitely. I'll give him a week. Two tops. When he finds a job, I'll loan him money to rent an apartment."

Max tucks her chin to her chest as she studies Birdie. "You're falling for him again, aren't you?"

Birdie glares at her. "I most certainly am not. I'm having divorce papers drawn up as we speak. For your information, I created an account on MatchMade, and I have a date for Saturday night."

"No way! You go, girl." Max offers up a high five. "Who's the lucky guy?"

Birdie's cheeks warm. "I'm not telling."

"Oh, yes, you are." Max pinches the skin on Birdie's forearm. "Tell me!"

"Ouch! That hurts, Max. It's Harold. Now let go."

Max releases her skin. "Harold Gordon, your accountant?"

"Yes," Birdie says, rubbing her arm. "And you'd better not laugh."

Max's forehead lines deepen. "Why would I laugh? What's wrong with Harold?"

"Nothing. Except he's the most boring man alive." Birdie grimaces at the thought of spending time with Harold. "I haven't been on a date in decades. I figure I'll use the opportunity to refresh my skills. He's taking me to the Lighthouse, so at least I'll get a nice dinner out of it."

"But you don't like to go out to dinner."

Birdie shrugs. "Eating out is part of dating. I'll have to get used to it."

"You'll do fine. Order a nonalcoholic beer."

"No way! That's like wearing a sign that labels me an alcoholic. Ordering a club soda is less in your face."

"Whatever works for you, girlfriend." Max loops her arm through Birdie's, and they stroll down the alley to the park.

"When are you going out with Stan?" Birdie asks, pulling Max down beside her on the wooden bench.

"Tomorrow at six. We're just going to Shaggy's. I'm not sure what to expect."

Birdie nudges her. "Sure you do, Maxie. You know Stan. He's easy to talk to. And interesting. He knows so much about so many things."

A flush creeps up Max's neck. "What if he tries to kiss me?

I was joking the other day. The thought of making whoopee with someone other than Daniel scares the heck outta me."

"Then don't think about it. You're not going to have sex on the first date." Birdie shifts toward Max. "Just be yourself and follow his lead. At least you'll have the benefit of alcohol to break the tension."

"True." Max moves in close to Birdie, their blue-jeaned thighs pressing together. "I'm sorry I was so hard on you earlier. I underestimated you. I was worried you would fall for Cary again."

"I was married to him, Max. Despite the way he treated me, I still have feelings for him. Not the feelings a wife has for her husband. But I don't wish him any ill will." Birdie chews on her bottom lip. "I had no idea Hannah would be so upset about her father staying with us. They were once so close. I want that for them again."

"You can't solve all the problems in the world, Birdie. You need to let Cary and Hannah figure their relationship out for themselves."

With Cary thrown into the mix, Birdie's apartment is like an ant bed with everyone crawling all over one another. She's forgotten what it's like having a man in the house. Toilet seats left up. Grimy beard stubble in the sink. The sight of his suits hanging next to her clothes in the tiny closet. To make matters worse, Hannah becomes openly hostile as the week wears on, snapping at everyone around her including her son. She rarely lets Gus out of her sight, but when she does, he runs straight to Cary. Gus worships his Pops. Cary is larger than life, a fun-loving man who so easily makes him laugh. Gus and Cary share the one thing Hannah and Birdie lack—testosterone.

On Friday evening, Birdie catches Hannah in her bedroom,

peeking around the doorjamb at her father and son who are watching a fishing program on television in the living room.

Birdie goes to stand beside her daughter. "Your dad is really good with him, you know," she says in a hushed tone.

Hannah's eyes remain glued to the pair on the sofa. "He's trouble, Mom. He can't find a job, because no one in this town trusts him except you. You invited him into our home, and now my son thinks he's a superhero."

"Gus needs a male figure in his life. Whether you're willing to admit it, you know it's true."

"My son needs a male figure he can rely on. Not one who's likely to disappear on a whim." Hannah turns away from the door. "I looked at a house today on Summer Street."

Birdie's throat swells. Hannah is pulling away from her. While Birdie knows the time is overdue, it doesn't make it any less hurtful. She forces a smile. "That's exciting. Tell me about it."

"It's just what I'm looking for. Small with three bedrooms and one bath on the first floor with an attic I can easily convert into a bedroom with a play area for Gus when he gets a little older. This might be the one, if I don't accept Ethan's offer."

"What offer? This week has been a little nutty. You haven't told me about your meeting with Ethan."

"Because Dad's always around and I've had no time alone with you. Ethan wants to buy my company, and he offered me a managing position as creative director in his firm." Hannah opens her closet door and flips through a row of dresses. "I'm going to Charleston tomorrow. And I'm spending the night."

"But it's Memorial Day weekend. I need all hands on deck." Birdie doesn't mention her dinner plans with Harold for Saturday night.

Hannah tugs a small suitcase out from beneath her bed. "I can be back early on Sunday to help in the cafe."

"I'm not worried about the cafe. I'll put your father to work if necessary. But I don't see how I can keep Gus."

"You don't need to. He's staying with Daisy. She's keeping Robbie too. Gus is thrilled about his first sleepover." Hannah folds two dresses into the suitcase, tosses in her bikini, a pair of wedge heels, and an assortment of shorts and T-shirts.

"Is this a date with Ethan?"

Hannah barks out a laugh. "Not hardly. He wants me to move to Charleston, and he thinks showing me around the city will help me decide."

"Oh. I didn't realize moving was part of the deal." Given the choice, Birdie would rather have Hannah and Gus down the road on Summer Street than an hour away in Charleston. But she doesn't want to say anything that might sway her daughter's opinion. This is Hannah's future, her decision to make alone.

"I'm just doing it to appease him. I'm hoping he'll agree to let me work remotely from here. I can't leave the island."

"Why not?" Birdie asks, even though she knows the answer.

"You know why." Hannah goes to the bathroom for her cosmetics bag and zips up her suitcase.

"Ryan could just as easily find you here as in Charleston."

"It's been over three years, and he hasn't found me yet." Hannah places the suitcase beside the door and faces Birdie. "Besides, Palmetto Island is out of the way. Only vacationers come here. And Ryan's family goes to Pawley's Island every summer."

"What's the worst that can happen if he finds you?"

"He'll take Gus away from me."

Birdie points at the doorway. "You're a good mama to that little boy. No judge in his right mind will take him away from you. Gus might benefit from spending time with his father. And you can stop hiding in fear."

"Does a mother ever stop being afraid for her child?" Hannah asks as she packs Gus's clothes in a duffel bag.

"No. But this is different. Your fear of Ryan finding you is controlling your life."

Hannah zips up the duffel and drops it on the floor next to her suitcase. "You know how much I love the island, Mom. This is not an easy decision for me."

"I know, sweetheart. And I'll support you whichever way you decide."

Hannah surprises Birdie by throwing herself in Birdie's arms. "I'm sorry I've been such a bitch this week. I just have so much on my mind and having Dad around doesn't make it any easier."

Birdie smooths her daughter's hair. "I know, honey. And that's all my fault. I should've asked you before I agreed to let him live here."

"You don't need my permission, Mom. This is your apartment. We've gotten so close these past few years. I consider you my best friend. Let's make a promise that neither of us will let Dad or anyone else come between us."

Holding Hannah at arm's length, with tears in her eyes, Birdie says, "I promise, sweet girl. I value our relationship too much to let anyone ruin it."

SIX

Hannah arrives in Charleston in time to have coffee with Liza before she's due at the hospital for rounds. Liza shares a large house on Ashley Avenue with several other medical students. As they walk two blocks from the house to the MUSC campus, Liza says, "I can't believe you're seriously considering moving to Charleston. Tell me everything."

"I wouldn't say I'm seriously considering moving. I'm thinking about it." She describes Ethan's offer. "Do you think I'd like it here?"

"You would *love* Charleston. If I have my way, I'm never leaving."

Hannah stops walking. "Wait. What happened to meeting your guy in medical school and moving back to Palmetto Island after you finish your residency?"

A smirk appears on Liza's lips. "I don't remember saying that."

"You know darn well you did. I even remember when and where. It was three years ago. About a month before Gus was born. We were having coffee at the cafe."

"Whatever. Part of my prediction came true."

Liza starts walking again, and Hannah falls in line beside her. "You mean the guy part?"

"Yes! I can't wait for you to meet him, Hannah. Stuart's the best. He's originally from Charleston. He doesn't want to leave and I love it here, so we're planning to stay. Besides, MUSC has a lot to offer young doctors."

"Should I be hurt? This is the first I'm hearing about this guy, and you're already talking to him about your future."

"I didn't tell you, because we haven't been together long. And it all happened so fast."

When they arrive at Halo, they order coffee and muffins and take their food to the second-story porch. Seated at a table on the balcony, Liza pulls out her phone. "What's Ethan's last name? I'm texting Stuart to see if he knows him. Although I'm sure he does. Everyone knows everyone in Charleston."

"His name is Ethan Hayes."

Liza's thumbs fly across the screen, and seconds later, her phone pings with the incoming text. "Yep. They're good friends. They graduated high school together. Hey! Maybe we can meet y'all for drinks after your dinner. We should be done at the hospital around nine."

"Maybe." Hannah sips her coffee. "I hope I didn't give you the wrong impression. Ethan and I aren't dating. Our relationship is strictly professional."

"Yeah, right." Liza pinches off a bite of muffin and pops it into her mouth. "If that's true, why does your face look all love-struck when you talk about him?"

"Love-struck? I don't think so. I'm intrigued about the possibility of working with him. A failed romance would ruin our professional relationship."

Liza cocks a manicured eyebrow. "Who says it will fail?"

Hannah can't help but laugh. "Enough about Ethan." She

settles back in her chair. "Tell me about Charleston. Why do you like it here so much?"

"Hmm. Let's see. There are so many reasons." A gentle breeze ruffles Liza's thick auburn hair as she stares over the balcony toward the hospital. "Charleston is like Palmetto Island on steroids. There's no shortage of outdoor activities and the food is amazing, the best in the South. Mostly, I like the people. Everyone is so chill. I promise, Hannah. You'd fit right in."

"Even with a baby?" Hannah asks, picking at her muffin.

"Gus is a toddler now. But, yes. People will welcome you, even though you're a single mom. At least my friends will."

Hannah hopes Ethan will be as accepting of her when she tells him about Gus.

Silence falls over the table. Hannah wonders if Liza's parents have told her about Cary's return. She's trying to figure out how to broach the subject when Liza stands abruptly.

"I've gotta go. Stuart's waiting for me." She slaps a silver key on the table. "Here's the spare key to my house. Don't lose it. Text me when you figure out your plans for tonight."

Liza blows Hannah a kiss, tosses her black leather tote over her shoulder, and disappears inside. Seconds later, she emerges from the building and crosses Ashley Avenue, where a guy in a white physician's coat is waiting for her on the sidewalk. Stuart is tall with chestnut hair, and he smiles down at Liza as she approaches. Removing her white coat from her tote bag, Liza slips it on, and they walk off arm in arm in the opposite direction.

Finishing her muffin, Hannah takes her coffee with her for the walk back to Liza's house. The air is already stifling and trickles of sweat soon roll down her back. But she's in no hurry. She has an hour to spare before Ethan picks her up. She admires the old homes—some in better shape than others—with slanted porches and secret gardens that have housed fascinating characters for more than a century. She walks past Liza's house to Colonial Lake, where parents with small children and dogs amble along the sidewalks surrounding the tidal pond. She imagines fishing and picnicking at the lake with Gus on Saturday mornings. She admits she feels comfortable here. Charleston is like her favorite pair of denim cutoffs.

Ethan arrives in a silver Porsche Cayenne. Is he making *that* much money designing websites? Hannah wants in on this gig.

"I thought we'd take a quick tour of the city before hitting the water," he says as they speed off down the street.

Ethan fidgets with the radio and then opens the sunroof. Is he nervous? He points out various landmarks as they cruise through the downtown streets. There's more foot traffic on the sidewalks than cars on the road, which is not surprising for a holiday weekend. They drive through the College of Charleston to Upper King and back down to the City Market.

"What do you think of Charleston so far?" he asks as he whips his Porsche into the parking lot at the Yacht Club.

"The jury is still out. Although, if I move here, I may sell my car and walk everywhere."

He laughs. "Many people do. But I'd suggest getting a bicycle."

Ethan removes two coolers from the back, handing the lighter one to Hannah. They walk down the dock to a center console boat about thirty feet long, with a navy hull and teak trim that distinguish it as a Hinckley. Hannah, having grown up on the water, knows a thing or two about boats.

"Beautiful boat," she says.

"Thanks. It belongs to my dad, but I use it more than he does."

Ethan takes the cooler from her and helps her on board.

They untie from the dock, and once they're underway, he opens a cooler and hands her a beer. She follows his lead when he strips off his shirt and spreads sunscreen on his toned limbs. Feeling his eyes on her breasts, she wishes she'd worn the less revealing of her two bikinis.

He increases speed, and above the sound of the engine, Hannah yells, "Where are we going?"

"To join some friends on a secluded beach."

"Cool," she says, sliding onto the pedestal seat beside him.

Twenty minutes later, a flotilla of anchored boats comes into view. Kids their age crowd the beach. Some wade at the edge of the water, beer cans in hand, while others throw Frisbees and dance to music blasting from speakers on one of the larger boats.

Ethan and Hannah anchor the boat and join the party. He introduces her to so many people she can't remember their names. Everyone is friendly, and some of the girls she meets, she'd like to know better. When was the last time she made new friends? College. When was the last time she had so much fun? Before Gus was born. She wouldn't want to party like this every weekend, but where's the harm in blowing off a little steam every now and then?

Ethan spreads a blanket out on the beach, and they dig into their picnic.

"Did you make all this?" she asks, sweeping an arm at the containers of fried chicken, deviled eggs, and pimento cheese sandwiches.

He gives her a sheepish grin. "I may have had a little help."

"Your mama?" she says as she gnaws on a chicken leg.

"My mama's housekeeper, Gloria. She has a soft spot for me."

"Ha. I'm sure she does."

"Ready for another?" Ethan asks, offering her a beer.

She shakes her head. "No thanks. I've had enough."

They finish eating and clean up their trash. When Hannah goes into the water to pee, she swims out to the boat and stretches out on the front bench seat to sleep off her buzz.

She dozes off, and sometime later, Ethan collapses onto the opposite seat, waking her. She cracks an eyelid to find him curled up on his side with hands pressed together under one cheek, watching her.

"You're incredibly beautiful." His arm shoots out, and he runs his finger across her bikini-clad breast.

She smacks his hand away. "Our relationship is professional, Ethan."

He walks his fingers across the upholstered cushion toward her. "Who says we can't mix business with pleasure? We might hit it off, become one of Charleston's power couples."

Pushing his hand away again, Hannah props herself up on her elbows. "And if it doesn't work out?"

He hunches his free shoulder. "It doesn't work out. Not the end of the world."

"Unless we end up despising each other."

"If that happens, we'll go our separate ways," Ethan says.

She swings her legs over the bench. "Meanwhile, you have all my clients, and I'm stuck living in Charleston."

He sits bolt upright. "Hey? Why so serious?"

Because I'm a single mom. I can't afford to take chances, Hannah thinks.

"This isn't a game for me, Ethan. I've worked damn hard to establish my career."

"And it shows." He moves over to her bench. "I'm sorry, Hannah. I was just having a little fun. From now on, we'll keep things strictly professional. Although I won't lie. I'm crazy attracted to you."

She can't help but smile in response to his devilish grin. She's crazy attracted to him as well. But, for Gus's sake, she has to keep her eye on the prize. Her life is so different from

Ethan's. He's a playboy and she's raising a child. Hannah isn't sure she can be business partners with someone like Ethan. Someone who goes for drinks every night after work. Someone who parties and has promiscuous sex every weekend. Not that he's doing anything any different from other kids their age. Hannah made the choice to lead a different lifestyle when she became a parent. And, while she hasn't regretted her decision for a single minute, she admits to feeling a pang of jealousy for Ethan and Liza, for all the people she met today on the beach. They are free to live their lives to the fullest while she is burdened by schedules and responsibilities.

SEVEN

Max enters the cafe during the first lull in business on Saturday afternoon. "I need to load up. My guests are eating me out of house and home."

Birdie grabs a pen and a notepad. "Then you're in luck. We're fully stocked. But if you want the freshest of our menu items, I just finished a batch of key lime pies, and Sadie's in the back making donuts, the patriotic ones we do for Memorial Day."

"I'll take three pies and two dozen donuts." Max cuts her eyes at Cary, who is processing a customer's order. "I see you put him to work."

"He volunteered, jumped right in this morning as though he's been working here for years. I hate to admit it, but he's a pretty good salesperson."

Max turns up her nose as though she smells something rotten. "Most liars and cheats can sell sawdust to a lumber mill."

Birdie slams her pad and pen down on the counter. "Be nice, Max."

Max wags her finger at Birdie. "You're falling for him again."

Birdie sticks her tongue out at Max. "I am not. Now please stop saying that." She spins on her heels. "I'll be right back with your order."

Birdie assembles the baked goods and puts the credit charge through. "Do you need help carrying all this stuff to the hotel?"

"Sure," Max says. "I'll tell you about my date with Stan on the way."

"Deal." Grabbing the stack of boxed pies, Birdie comes from behind the counter, and they walk out together. "So? I'm dying to hear. How'd it go with Stan? I've been afraid to ask."

"It was a bust. At least for me. Stan talked about you the whole time."

Birdie furrows her brow. "Me? What do you mean?"

"His purpose for having drinks with me was to pick my brain about you. He wants to know if you're dating again. He doesn't frequent the MatchMade website and didn't know you'd joined."

Birdie holds the door open for Max, and they enter the hotel lobby. "What did you tell him?"

"That he should totally ask you out."

Birdie follows Max through the lounge to the commercial kitchen. "You didn't tell him Cary's back in town, did you?"

Max sets the donut boxes on the counter. "Actually, I did. I told him the two of you are shacking up."

Birdie's jaw drops. "You did not."

"Of course I didn't." Max snatches the pies from Birdie. "But it's only a matter of time before he hears. You're moving in a positive direction, Birdie. Don't let Cary ruin that for you, like he ruined your previous life."

"He's not ruining anything. I'm helping him get a fresh

start, so he can move on with *his* life." Birdie heads for the door. "I need to get back to the cafe."

Max calls after her, "Have fun on your date with Harold."

Harold. Birdie wishes she'd never agreed to go to dinner with him. Even though she told him the cafe doesn't close until six, he insisted on coming for her at five thirty. Only old people go to dinner so early.

She barely has time to change out of her uniform and into white jeans and a hot pink tunic before he arrives. She hopes he doesn't notice she smells of baked goods.

Standing outside the cafe, Harold gives her the once-over. "You look beautiful, Birdie."

"You don't look so bad yourself." Birdie doesn't consider Harold handsome. He's a little thick around the middle, but he's pleasant-looking and nicely dressed in a navy sport coat and khaki pants.

"Well then, shall we?" He offers his arm, and they walk the short distance to the Lighthouse restaurant.

Customers with fruity drinks occupy several tables on the deck. A gentle breeze is blowing off the ocean, and Birdie would prefer to sit outside. But Harold requests a table inside the empty restaurant.

Studying her menu, Birdie finds many of the offerings tempting. Goat cheese and arugula salad for a starter. Either crab cakes or sauteed scallops for the entrée. And fresh fruit on homemade cinnamon ice cream for dessert. Printed at the bottom of the menu is a notice about the early bird special they offer every evening between five thirty and seven.

That explains a lot, she thinks.

"Would you care for wine with your dinner?" Harold asks. "Pricewise, we're better off ordering a bottle."

"I don't care for wine. Thank you."

Harold appears relieved. Does he know she's a recovering alcoholic? Or is he glad he doesn't have to pay for her wine?

The waitress, an attractive young woman about Hannah's age, arrives to take their order. "We have several specials tonight," she says, and describes the list of entrée specials.

Birdie's face lights up when the waitress mentions soft-shell crabs, but before she can request them, Harold orders for her. "We'll both have the roasted rosemary chicken for our entrees."

Birdie can hardly believe her ears. Her eyes scan down the menu to the landlubber's section. What a cheapskate. Harold ordered the least expensive entrée on the menu.

The waitress scrawls their order on her pad. "Can I get you anything to start? Perhaps an order of fried calamari or oysters on the half shell?"

Birdie's mouth waters at the thought of oysters, but Harold shakes his head. "We'll just have the house salad that comes with it."

"And to drink?" she asks, a hint of irritation in her voice.

Harold takes Birdie's menu and hands both to the waitress. "I'll have a glass of the house red, and the lady would like sweet tea."

Sweet tea? Who said anything about sweet tea? Birdie gives the waitress a tight smile. "I'm fine with just water. Thanks."

When the waitress leaves, Harold launches into a discussion about his vegetable garden. Birdie has nothing against gardening, but she couldn't care less what he uses to get rid of aphids on his tomato plants. She considers excusing herself for the restroom and sneaking out the back door. But that would be rude, so she remains at the table and endures the boring conversation.

When the waitress brings their beverages, Birdie's eyes keep drifting to Harold's wine. As he goes on about his process for pickling cucumbers, Birdie's temptation to snatch his glass and gulp down the red liquid intensifies.

When her phone vibrates in her handbag, she slips the bag from the table to her lap. Harold's too busy talking about eggplant to notice. Removing her phone from the bag, she sneaks a glance at the text. *Hello, Birdie. This is Stan Morgan. I hope you don't mind me reaching out. I was wondering if you'd be interested in spending the afternoon on the water with me tomorrow.*

Max must have told him the cafe is closed on Sunday afternoons. Tingles of excitement flutter in her belly. A day on the water is Birdie's kind of date.

Harold denies Birdie the opportunity for dessert by requesting the check as the waitress is clearing their dinner plates. When he suggests a walk along the boardwalk, Birdie says, "I'm sorry, Harold. The cafe was bustling today, and I'm exhausted."

"I understand," he says and walks her to the front door.

When he moves in to kiss her, Birdie turns her head, and his wet lips land with a sucking noise on her cheek.

Harold straightens. "You're not going out with me again, are you?"

Birdie shakes her head. "Sorry. No chemistry. But thanks for dinner. Night, Harold," she says and closes the door on him.

Pulling out her phone, she quickly taps out a text to Stan. *I'm glad to hear from you. An outing on the water sounds lovely. The cafe closes at two. I'm free after that.*

His response is immediate. *Perfect. I'll pick you up at the marina dock at two thirty. Wear your bathing suit and bring sunscreen.*

Birdie's stomach does a somersault. Tomorrow afternoon can't get here soon enough.

She hears voices coming from the living room, and when she makes her way up the stairs, she finds Cary watching *On Golden Pond*. Saturday night was movie night when they were married. This oldie—with its all-star cast of Henry and Jane Fonda and Katharine Hepburn—was one of their favorites.

Birdie moves closer as the scene with Jane Fonda doing a backflip off the dock unfolds. When he notices Birdie standing near the sofa, Cary says, "How was your date?"

She pulls a face, and he laughs. "That bad?"

"Worse." She eyes a half-empty sleeve of Saltines on the coffee table. "I hope that's not your dinner."

"I'm not that hungry," Cary says, but Birdie suspects he doesn't have money for food.

"My dinner was less than satisfying, one bone-in chicken breast and a scoop of lumpy mashed potatoes. Wanna order a pizza? My treat."

His lips curl up in a grateful smile. "I've never been able to say no to pizza."

Retrieving her laptop from her bedroom, she sits down beside him on the sofa and places the order. They watch the rest of the movie, and when the pizza arrives, they choose another movie—*Rain Man*. The years fall away, and it's as if they're back in their beloved home on the inlet. Just an ordinary Saturday night, like so many others. Until he disappeared, and her world came crashing down around her. And she realized their life together hadn't been so perfect after all.

When the pizza box is empty and the second movie ends, Cary points the remote at the television, powering it off. "Early day tomorrow."

"Mm-hmm." Birdie slowly gets to her feet, stretching out her lower back.

Cary tosses the remote on the coffee table and stands to face her. "I enjoyed working behind the counter today. If you need me, I'm available the rest of the weekend. You don't have to pay me."

"That would be great. But I will not let you work for free."

"Why not? You're giving me a place to stay, and you just bought me pizza."

"I insist, Cary. You're a good worker. The customers like you."

"I've had zero luck with the law firms and reputable businesses in town. I'm thinking I'll apply for jobs at the retail establishments on Ocean Avenue like Freeman's Hardware. Or maybe Shaggy will hire me. At least I'd be able to earn some money while I'm waiting for something better to come along."

The unspoken hangs in the air between them. What if something better doesn't come along? "That's an excellent idea," Birdie says a little too enthusiastically. Eating pizza and watching movies with him brought back a lot of memories that confuse her. The sooner he leaves, the better.

"I didn't understand the impact my disappearance would have on my future. I got caught up in the moment. Melinda snared me into her trap. I got greedy. I wanted the white sandy beaches and hundred-foot yacht. Our marriage had grown—"

"Stale," she says, finishing his sentence.

Cary shakes his head. "Not stale. Comfortable. I should've been satisfied with that."

"I wasn't satisfied either, Cary. Our humdrum lifestyle drove me to drink. We let each other down. We should've tried harder, should've traveled, should've gone out more with friends."

He turns his head to look at her. "Are you saying you forgive me?"

"For abandoning me? Never. You took the coward's way out. But I understand why you made your choices." Her eyes well with tears. "My drinking drove you into the arms of another woman."

He thumbs a tear off her cheek. "Your drinking appears under control."

She sniffles. "Because I nearly drank myself to death after you left. With Max's help, I was able to quit."

"Why won't you give us another chance, Birdie? We were once so good together. We could have that again."

Birdie shakes her head. "No, Cary. Our marriage is over. I thought I made that clear."

She gathers her laptop and purse and flees to the safety of her room. Dropping her belongings on her bed, she goes to stand beside the window. The full moon reflecting off the water calms her. She tries to imagine a second chance with Cary. They were once so in love. At least she thought it was love. They were best friends. Being together was the only thing that mattered. Their sex life was . . . Was what? Birdie has little to compare it to. Before Cary, her experience with sex was limited to a few drunken encounters with frat boys in college. If she gets another chance at love, she'll settle for nothing less than burning passion.

EIGHT

Ethan makes an unexpected detour by his parents' house on the way to dinner. "I want to show you something," he explains as he turns onto a charming street with enormous homes.

"Okay," she says in a skeptical tone. What could he possibly want to show her at his parents' house?

He passes through the gates of a large estate that features a three-story home with double columned piazzas and a small, manicured side yard. Near the rear of the lot sits the original carriage house, built from the same old Charleston brick as the main house and the six-foot wall surrounding the property.

Hannah taps on the window. "I take it that's the carriage house you mentioned on the phone?"

"Yep. That's the one."

Clara and Hugh Hayes greet them on the lower porch. Hannah guesses them to be close to sixty. Both are nice-looking, physically fit, and casually dressed in knee-length shorts and polo shirts. When Hugh offers her a cocktail, Hannah turns him down. Despite the long naps she and Ethan took on the boat, her head is still fuzzy from the beer she drank on the beach.

Ethan also declines his father's offer of a drink. "We can't stay long. We have dinner reservations at eight."

"My son shared your work with me," Hugh says. "I'm impressed. You have quite the creative eye."

Hannah's face warms. "Thank you."

"Do you have a special someone in your life?" Clara asks.

Hannah immediately thinks of Gus. "No, ma'am."

"Mom, geez." Ethan says. "Give Hannah a break."

"Can't blame your old mom for trying, pretty girl that she is." A smirk appears on Clara's lips as she sips her vodka tonic.

Hannah smiles awkwardly. *What will Clara think when she finds out I'm a single mom with a three-year-old son?*

Ethan rolls his eyes at Hannah. "Ignore her. I brought you here for a reason, not to subject you to an inquisition." His gaze shifts to Hugh. "Dad has recently retired after forty years of practicing medicine." He gives his dad a fist bump. "They have several trips planned for the next few years."

"We're making up for lost time," Clara interjects.

Hugh adds, "And we're hoping to find someone to rent our carriage house and look after the property while we're gone."

"Small things like collecting the mail and watering plants," Clara says. "Nothing major. Since you're moving in from out of town, we thought you might be interested. I think you'll find the rent affordable."

When she says the amount, Hannah's eyes go wide. Not only affordable, but a steal.

"Would you like to see it?" Clara asks.

"Sure," Hannah says, and follows Clara down the brick sidewalk.

As they stroll together through the garden, Hannah imagines Gus running in circles around the fountain and climbing the sprawling oak tree.

The carriage house is bigger than her mother's apartment, but smaller than the house for sale on Summer Street. The one-story floor plan offers two bedrooms and a single bath. In the living room and adjacent kitchen, natural light spills in through curved windows that were once bays for the horses and carriages.

"Ethan has told us how hesitant you are to leave Palmetto Island. I don't blame you. I've been there many times myself, and I find the area quite lovely. My son thought this might help you make your decision. If you'd like, we can do a month-to-month lease. You can live here until you get more acquainted with Charleston."

"That is so kind of you." When Clara appears hopeful, Hannah quickly adds, "If I accept his offer."

"I understand." Clara locks the door, and they start back toward the house. "Our first trip isn't until October. I'm happy to hold it for you until the end of the summer. I'm sure we won't have any trouble finding a tenant if things don't work out for you. But I'd rather have someone I know taking care of my home."

"That makes sense. Your home is beautiful. Don't worry, Mrs. Hayes. I won't drag out Ethan's offer. It's not fair to him, and having a monumental decision hanging over my head stresses me out."

As they approach the porch, Ethan says, "Well? What do you think?"

"I think it's very nice," Hannah says. "Perfect, actually. I appreciate your parents giving me the opportunity."

"Great!" He steps down off the porch. "Let's go eat. I'm starving."

Clara gives Hannah her number in case she has questions, and Hannah thanks them again in parting.

Hannah is quiet, lost in thought, on the way to the restaurant. Ethan has told his parents a lot about her. Which must mean they have a close relationship. Like Hannah and Birdie.

"Are you an only child?" she asks as he's backing the Porsche into a parking space on a side street.

He takes the car out of gear and turns off the engine. "Is it that obvious?"

"Takes one to know one," she says, opening her door. "Where are we going to dinner?"

"Husk. If you've never eaten here, you're in for a treat."

"Good. Because I'm starving."

The hostess is young and beautiful and calls Ethan by his first name as though they are friends. "We have our best table ready for you on the upstairs porch," she says in a flirty manner to Ethan without so much as a glance at Hannah. He's handsome and successful, the kind of guy girls fall all over.

They follow the hostess up the stairs and through the dining room to a table for two on the porch. She waits for them to sit down before handing them menus. "Call me sometime, Ethan," she says and saunters off, giving her hips an extra shake for Ethan's benefit.

"Old girlfriend?" Hannah asks, her eyes on the menu.

"Childhood friend."

She waits for him to say more, but he doesn't.

Over the balcony, she watches the people wandering about on Queen Street below. "What's that?" she asks, pointing at the ancient brick building next door.

"They call it the Bar at Husk," Ethan says. "It's seriously cool, very authentic. We can go there after dinner for drinks, if you'd like."

"Oh! That reminds me." Hannah sets down her menu. "I forgot to tell you. My best friend Liza is dating your high school buddy, Stuart."

Ethan flashes his phone at her. "I heard. Stuart texted me earlier about getting together later."

Hannah squirms in her seat. This feels too much like a date. Couples getting together with other couples for drinks. She's relieved when their waiter appears, saving her from having to respond.

They both order shrimp and grits and a glass of rosé. "And can we please have an order of skillet cornbread to share?" Ethan asks as he hands the waiter the menus.

They focus their dinner conversation on business. Hannah grows more comfortable with her potential role in his firm and less comfortable with the thought of moving to Charleston. When she gives him the hard sell for working remotely from Palmetto Island, she can tell Ethan isn't buying into the concept.

The Hayes's property is spectacular, the carriage house charming. But it's not home. She'd have to find a new school for Gus and babysitters for nights when she's working late. For three years, she's relied on Max and Birdie and Sadie to watch Gus whenever she was running errands or during her sunrise trips on the inlet. She can't imagine not seeing Birdie every day. She's happy on Palmetto Island. She and Gus are safe there. Gus is thriving. Why rock the boat?

Their phones ping simultaneously with incoming texts. They drop their gazes to their phone screens. "Stuart," he says, and she nods. "Liza."

Ethan's tone is less than enthusiastic when he asks, "Do you want to meet them for a drink?"

"Not really. I've had enough alcohol for one day." While a noisy bar sounds miserable, she's not yet ready to go back to Liza's empty apartment. "I wouldn't mind taking a walk, though." She looks out over the buildings of downtown Charleston at the full moon on the horizon. "The moon is beautiful. I've photographed it many times, but my pictures never do it justice."

"Let's go for a walk along the seawall. I'll get the check," he says, and summons the waiter.

Fifteen minutes later, they park at his waterfront condominium building and walk down East Bay Street to the tip of the promenade, across from Battery Park. They lean against the railing, gazing at the moon beams shimmering off the water.

"I was an ass earlier today on the beach," Ethan says. "I hope I didn't scare you off. I am attracted to you, Hannah. Any man in his right mind would be. You're beautiful and talented and easy to be with. But I'm capable of remaining in the friend zone for the sake of our business relationship."

Friend zone. Hannah's feelings for Ethan confuse her. She enjoys his company. Being with him makes her feel all warm and cozy one minute and tingling with excitement the next. But she's never been one for casual hookups. The last time she had sex, with her then-boyfriend four years ago, she got pregnant with Gus. And the thought of being intimate terrifies her, yet every time he's touched her today, her stomach has flip-flopped. What if she accepts his offer? Will they always be fighting off this chemistry between them? If she turns down his proposal, they would be free to explore their feelings.

Ethan shoulder-bumps her. "So, how am I doing? Am I making headway in convincing you to move to Charleston?"

Perhaps if he knows about Gus, he would better understand her interest in working remotely from the island. "I'll be honest with you, Ethan. I'm leaning toward not accepting your offer. I'm intrigued by the prospect of working with you, but for personal reasons, I can't leave Palmetto Island." She inhales a deep breath. "I need to tell you something. I have a three-year-old son. I got pregnant my senior year in college, and I chose to keep the baby."

Ethan's face falls, and he drops his hand from her back. "Oh."

Hannah's heart pounds against her rib cage. He's upset. What did she expect? "Gus and I are comfortable living on the island. Being a single parent is hard, and my mom is a huge help. I'm not ready to leave."

Ethan rakes his hands through his sandy hair. "I don't understand. I checked you out. How did I miss a kid?"

"I work hard to keep him out of the public eye." She doesn't tell Ethan why. That Gus's father doesn't know he's alive.

She desperately needs to hear Ethan say it doesn't matter. That this doesn't affect his offer. Instead, he says, "Thanks for telling me." And what follows is even more devastating. "I should take you home."

NINE

S tan's sport fishing boat, *Island Daze,* is idling at the end of the marina dock when Birdie scrambles down the ramp with a hand clamped down on her sunhat and flip-flops flapping on wooden planks. Stan is waiting for her in the boat's cockpit amidst an assortment of inner tubes and paddleboards.

"I'm sorry I'm late," she says, slightly out of breath.

"Five minutes isn't late. We're on island time." Stan extends an arm, helping her on board. He pecks her cheek. "It's so nice to see you again, Birdie."

His genuine warmth sets Birdie at ease. "And you as well, Stan. Thank you for having me."

"So." He clasps his hands together. "I overheard some fishermen talking a moment ago. They spotted an enormous school of dolphin just offshore. Wanna go check them out?"

"Are you kidding me? Flipper? I would love that."

"Then what are we waiting for?" After untying the lines, he takes her bag from her while she climbs the ladder to the flybridge.

She hesitates when she reaches the top, not sure where to

sit. Stan joins her, tossing her bag on the bench in front of the console and motioning her to the swivel seat next to the captain's chair.

The tide is low, and when he puts the engines in gear, the propellers churn mud off the stern of the boat. "Busy weekend?" he asks as he guides the boat out of the marina.

She nods vigorously. "Very."

"We've been slammed at the store too. I barely got away myself." Stan's store, Island Water Sports, is a destination for Lowcountry boat owners and water sports enthusiasts. He carries everything from men's and women's apparel to medium-sized boats.

He settles back in his chair. "You're smart to close at two on Sundays. How did you come up with that idea? Is that an off-peak time for you?"

"I don't know, honestly. I adopted the hours when I bought the bakery from Amber several years ago. Our customers were already used to the schedule, so why change anything. Sunday afternoons have become sacred for me, the one time during the week when I can totally relax."

"That's important. When you're open seven days a week, you need a break now and then. I've been considering closing on Mondays, which are slow days for us."

Birdie considers this before answering. "That would give you the opportunity to reset the store after the weekend. And it would help with managing employees' time off. Mondays are busy for us. Our customers need strong coffee and comfort food to get them through the first day of the work week."

Stan chuckles. "I can relate to that." He places his right hand on the throttles. "I'm going to speed up. Hold on to your hat."

Birdie snatches her hat off her head and holds it tight in her lap as the engines rumble and the bow of the boat comes out of the water. She studies Stan as he navigates through the channel to the mouth of the inlet and out into the ocean. He's of average height and build, with salt-and-pepper hair and a scruffy beard. While his eyes are hidden by Costa sunglasses, visible laugh lines are a sign of his happy-go-lucky personality.

Birdie knew his wife, but they were never friends. Stan and Kim have been divorced for five or six years. Birdie often wonders if there's any truth to the unconfirmed rumors about Kim being gay.

They've only been in the ocean a few minutes when Stan yells, "Look! There's your Flipper. Off the starboard side." He slows the boat and puts the engines in neutral. "They're everywhere."

All around them, a sea of dolphin leap out of the water and dive back in. "They're amazing."

"Aren't they? Let's go down to the bow," he says, killing the engines.

They climb down the ladder, hugging the cabin as they make their way out to the bow. They sit down and stretch their legs out in front of them to watch the majestic sight before them. The ocean is as flat as Birdie's ever seen it. There's not a cloud in the sky, and the air is still and hot. Birdie is unfazed by the perspiration streaming down her back and dampening her armpits. She's used to the stifling summers in the Lowcountry.

"This is lovely," Birdie says. "I don't remember the last time I was in the ocean."

"We'll need to remedy that. It's criminal to live on the coast and not get out on the ocean."

When the dolphins move on, Stan and Birdie return to the flybridge. They cruise north up the coast several miles before turning back around.

Stan yells, "How about a swim?"

"Sounds good," she hollers back. "It's so hot. The water

will feel good."

Inside the mouth of the inlet, Stan anchors the boat near a sandy beach, and they strip down to their bathing suits.

"What's it gonna be, floating or boarding?" Stan gestures at the inner tubes and paddleboards in his cockpit.

"Considering I've never been on a paddleboard, I vote for tubing."

Stan places a hand on his chest. "Never been paddleboard-ing? You're missing out on one of the greatest pleasures in life. What about kayaking?"

Birdie shakes her head. "Kayaking was Cary and Hannah's thing. I didn't mind so much. I enjoyed watching them spend time together on the water."

Lines appear on his forehead. "More than two can kayak together, you know?"

"I know," Birdie chokes out past the lump in her throat.

Tossing the tubes in the water, Stan opens the transom door and they step out onto the swim platform. He cannonballs off the boat, and feeling like a kid again, she follows suit.

"Thatta girl." He offers her a high five. "There's hope for you yet."

Birdie and Stan climb into their tubes and float around in the water. They talk about their businesses, friends they have in common, and food. Stan enjoys cooking, and from the way he talks, he sounds like quite the gourmet chef. And they talk a bit about their children. She tells Stan about Hannah's web design business and her rambunctious grandson, who is constantly looking for mischief. And Stan talks about his daughter in Charleston—Jean, a successful interior designer with two teenage children—and his son, Blake, whom Stan is grooming to one day take over his business. Stan spends much of his free time with Blake and his daughter-in-law, Janie, who is expecting their first baby in November.

They exchange their inner tubes for paddleboards, and

Birdie is relieved to discover that keeping her balance as she paddles the board isn't as difficult as she'd anticipated. Gliding across the water to the beach, they sit in the sand for a while with their feet in the surf.

"I can't remember when I've enjoyed such a pleasant afternoon," Birdie says, relaxing back on her elbows and tilting her face to the sun.

Stan chuckles. "You need to get out more. If you're free next Sunday, we'll go on a wave runner adventure."

"I've never been on a wave runner," Birdie admits.

He palms his forehead. "Wave runners are my number one seller. I own three of them myself. They're parked at my dock. Why don't you come to my house and we'll leave from there?"

Birdie relishes the idea of spending another day like today with Stan. "Shall I pack a picnic for an early dinner?"

"As long as your picnic includes fried chicken," he says with a hint of mischief on his lips.

"I can arrange that. Along with all the fixings."

Stan inches closer to her until their thighs are touching. "I'm a straight shooter, Birdie. I hope that doesn't bother you."

Birdie sits up straighter. "Not at all. I appreciate directness. You can always be honest with me."

"Good! Because I've had a crush on you for the longest time, and I don't think I can wait a whole week to see you again."

Birdie giggles like a schoolgirl. She's as pleased as punch.

"Are you free for a cookout tomorrow night? What is Memorial Day without hamburgers and hotdogs?"

"I would love that. As long as you let me bring something."

"If you insist. How about one of your famous key lime pies for dessert? My daughter-in-law served one at my birthday dinner last month. We had half a pie leftover, and I ate every bit myself."

"I'm glad you enjoyed it. I plan to make a fresh batch in the morning. I will put one aside."

They sit on the beach a while longer, not talking but smiling at each other. Stan is a good guy, a normal guy with a big heart who enjoys life. And he has a crush on her. But the chemistry she feels between them scares her. It's been so long since she was intimate. Will she even remember how? What if she's bad at sex? What if she lets Stan down? What if he's disappointed at the sight of her naked body?

Stop, Birdie! You're getting way ahead of yourself.

Or is she? Whatever this thing is between them feels right. She's not getting any younger. Why not go for it? She has nothing to lose.

TEN

Hannah and Birdie have a standing date for Sunday afternoons. They usually take Gus to the beach, go for a walk on the boardwalk, and then out for an early dinner. Hannah can barely contain her irritation when she learns Birdie has a date with Stan Morgan. She doesn't blame Birdie for being excited. For an old man, Stan's pretty cool. But why does it have to be today, of all Sundays? When she's confused about what happened with Ethan and really needs her mom.

Hannah hasn't heard from Ethan since he dropped her at Liza's apartment last night. Learning she has a son had shocked him. Maybe once he's thought about it, he'll understand why she doesn't want to move and consent to letting her work from the island. Or maybe he assumes she's no longer interested. She told Ethan she was *leaning* toward not taking his offer. She didn't say her decision was final. Or maybe he doesn't want a single mom in a position of such high authority in his firm. What if he takes his offer off the table? Wouldn't that be discrimination?

Hannah tells herself not to worry. He's probably sleeping

in or at church services with his folks or doing chores to get ready for the week ahead.

To avoid her father, Hannah closes herself in her room. Gus, who is cranky from his sleepover with Robbie, puts himself to bed for a nap. Hannah works at her computer while he sleeps, checking her phone every few minutes for new texts. She spends an hour on the B&H website, trading her old camera and lens in for new equipment she can use without being reminded of her father.

When her phone vibrates the desk with an incoming call around four thirty, she's disappointed to see her Realtor's name on the screen and not Ethan's.

"A Realtor friend informed me the owners of the Summer Street house are getting an offer this evening," Shannon says. "Although, apparently, the offer is weak. The owners are closing on their dream home next week and may take it, anyway. If you're interested, Hannah, give them your best offer. There's a good chance you'll get it."

Great! Hannah collapses back in her chair. As if the moving parts in her life weren't already complicated enough. "I don't know, Shannon. I love the house. But I have some stuff going on that I'm trying to figure out."

"Would it help to see it again? I'm sure I can get you in."

"Sure. Why not? Another walk-through would be helpful. But I'll have to bring my son with me. Mom's not here to take care of him."

"That's fine," Shannon says. "I'll watch him while you look at the house."

"Okay. Text me when you confirm the time."

"Will do," Shannon says and ends the call.

Hannah hears Gus rustling around in bed, followed by his sweet voice. "I'm hungry, Mommy. I wanna snack."

Swiveling around in her chair, she gets to her feet and moves over to his bed. "Did you have a nice nap, little man?"

He bobs his head.

"Good. You needed it. Let's get you dressed." She helps him out of his pajama top. "We need to run an errand. We'll get a snack from the kitchen on our way out."

"What kinda errand?" Gus asks, holding his hands over his head while she slips on his T-shirt.

"We're going to look at a house."

He scrunches up his face. "Whose house?"

"Somebody's. No one you know."

"But I don't wanna look at somebody's house. Can't I stay here with Birdie?"

"Birdie's not here. She's gone out with her friend. I promise it won't take long. If you're a good boy, we'll stop at Scoops on the way home."

He folds his arms across his chest. "I don't want ice cream."

Usually the suggestion of ice cream does the trick. "Fine. I'll eat your share," she says and tickles him until he laughs and falls over on his side.

Her phone pings with a text from Shannon. *Owners are having guests for dinner. We need to tour the house now.*

Hannah texts back. *Be there in ten minutes.*

Cary is watching television in the living room. When Gus sees him, he sprints across the room and leaps into his lap. "Pops! Can I stay with you while Mommy goes to see somebody's house?"

"Of course, buddy," Cary says, mussing Gus's blond hair.

Hannah considers the arrangement. Touring the house without Gus in tow would be easier. But letting her father babysit will give Cary the impression she's softening toward him, which she definitely is not. "Sorry, Gus. You're coming with me." She picks up her son and carries him, kicking and screaming, down the stairs.

She retrieves a juice box and an individual-size package of

animal crackers from the kitchen. Gus is still sobbing when she straps him into his stroller, but he quiets when she hands him his snack. She jogs across Ocean Avenue and racewalks up Magnolia Street.

What is she doing? Why is she even thinking about making an offer on a house with her future so uncertain? She pauses on the sidewalk to check her phone. Nothing from Ethan. Why hasn't he called? Maybe he went deep-sea fishing with his father today. *Stop, Hannah! Quit making excuses for him. Ethan has made it clear. He doesn't want a twenty-five-year-old single mom as his creative director.*

Hannah pushes the stroller onward. Even if she never hears from him again, the experience has taught her a valuable lesson. She underestimated the importance of having a successful career. Being professionally fulfilled is the key to her happiness. Truth be told, her firm is the wrong fit for Ethan's. He all but admitted it himself. His clients are mainstream professionals like bankers and doctors while hers are authors and small business owners. She has a long waiting list of potential clients. Why not hire a web designer and grow her own company? In order to expand her business, she would have to use her house money. Would living at her mother's apartment a little while longer be the end of the world?

Hannah's Realtor is waiting for her on the sidewalk in front of the Summer Street house. "I'm sorry, Shannon. I've wasted your time. I can't make an offer on any house right now."

Shannon removes her oversized sunglasses, as though to get a better look at her. "What's changed, Hannah? You've been in the market for months now."

"I've decided to pursue other career opportunities. I need more time to think things through."

"I totally understand, hon. Buying a house is an enormous deal. You have to be absolutely certain." Shannon returns her sunglasses to her face. "You know where to find me if and when you're ready."

Hannah smiles. "Thanks for being so understanding."

"Happens all the time. It's part of my job."

Gus cranes his neck to see Hannah. "Is this somebody's house, Mommy?"

Hannah smooths her son's hair off his forehead. "Yes, sweetheart. Somebody lives here."

Shannon's face melts. "He's adorable. Love those baby blues. He's gonna be a lady killer when he grows up."

"Thank you. I'll be in touch," Hannah says, turning the stroller around and heading back the way she came.

Her steps are lighter on the return home. She'll start slowly by hiring another designer and work toward finding someone with an outgoing personality to bring in accounts. Why settle for being someone else's employee when she can be her own boss? Control her own destiny. Maybe one day, when Gus is older, she'll be in a position to move to another city. She can't see herself in a big city like Atlanta or New York. Maybe somewhere like Charlotte or Raleigh. Or maybe even Charleston. Ethan doesn't own Charleston. And it's only an hour away. She can come home on the weekends to get her island fix. While that may be years down the road, it's something for her to work toward.

By the time she reaches the waterfront, Gus has fallen asleep in the stroller. Still evading her dad, she drapes a blanket over the stroller to keep the sun off her sleeping child and sits down on a bench in the park. Tourists stroll past and a gentle breeze rustles the palm tree fronds.

Hannah is deep in thoughts of expanding her firm when her mom strolls up from the dock a few minutes later.

"How was your date?" Hannah asks and moves over to make room for Birdie on the bench.

Birdie drops her beach bag on the ground and plops down

beside Hannah. "Lovely," she says with a dreamy expression. "He invited me for dinner tomorrow night."

Hannah digs her elbow into Birdie's side. "Go, Mom."

"Stan is a genuinely kind person and fun to be around."

"I'm relieved you've found a new love interest. I admit I was worried you were falling for dad again."

"That chapter in my life is closed." Birdie lifts the blanket to peek at Gus. "Tell me about Charleston."

Hannah recounts the events of her trip, including the part when she told Ethan about Gus.

"Don't jump to conclusions, sweetheart. I'm sure there's a logical explanation as to why he hasn't called."

"Maybe. But I doubt it." Hannah yearns to tell Birdie about her business plan, but voicing her idea makes it more real. Is she ready to set things in motion? She draws in a deep breath. *Go for it, Hannah.* "I'm thinking of expanding my firm. I'll have to use my house money, which totally freaks me out. What do you think?"

Without hesitation, Birdie says, "I think you're the most talented person I know. I have absolute faith in you, and you can count on my support of you in all your endeavors."

"That means a lot, Mom. Thanks. So, you're okay with Gus and me living with you a while longer?"

Uncertainty followed by resignation crosses Birdie's face. "Yes, but only for a couple of months. Until you can find your own place. You don't have to buy. You can rent. Don't get me wrong. I love having you, and I'll miss you like crazy, but Gus needs his own room."

While not the answer Hannah is expecting, her mother is giving her the push she needs. She can afford a two-bedroom apartment. She may even find a rental house with an extra room she can convert into an office. The thought suddenly perks her up. "You're right. It's time."

Birdie pats her thigh. "We have a warehouse full of furniture leftover from the old house you can use to get started. I'll even help you decorate."

"That'll be fun." Off in the distance, Hannah spots a familiar figure gliding a kayak across the water toward the marina. "Looks like Dad found his kayak. I hope that means he'll be out of the apartment more. He's like the obnoxious houseguest in that old skit "The Thing That Wouldn't Leave.""

Birdie snickers. "That's mean, Hannah. I know the situation isn't ideal. But he's trying."

Hannah's mouth falls open. "Why are you so nice to him? I don't understand how you can forgive him after everything he put us through."

"I haven't forgiven him for abandoning me, and I probably never will. He knows that. I've told him as much to his face. But that doesn't mean you shouldn't forgive him." Birdie tilts Hannah's chin toward her. "Bitterness and resentment will eat you alive, Hannah. But forgiveness cleanses the soul. Your father left because of problems in our marriage that had nothing to do with you. You just got caught in the aftermath. He's your father. The two of you once shared a special relationship."

"So special he never once tried to get in touch with me during the three and a half years he was *missing*," Hannah says, her fingers in air quotes.

"We all make mistakes, sweetheart. But good things often come from those mistakes."

"True," Hannah says in a soft voice. "My biggest mistake brought me Gus."

"And your dad's disappearance forced me to face some stark realities about myself. Because of him, I quit drinking and bought a bakery."

"I've lost all respect for him, Mom. Will I ever be able to trust him again?"

"I don't know. But you owe it to yourself to try."

ELEVEN

Miss Daisy closes her day care for the Memorial Day holiday. With no one to care for Gus, Hannah is exempt from working in the cafe. She takes Gus to the beach for the morning. He loves the wide-open space. He chases birds and splashes in the surf. He fills buckets with sand to make sandcastles and then mows them down with his dump truck. Which is what he's doing when Liza calls.

"We missed seeing you on Saturday night. But I totally get it. You and Ethan wanted to be alone. So, how'd it go? Are you in love?"

"*Love*? Ha. We're not even in *like* at the moment." Hannah tells her best friend about the abrupt ending to her evening with Ethan.

"I'm sure there's a logical explanation," Liza says.

"There is. He wants nothing to do with a girl who has baggage. But forget about Ethan. I'm expanding my own firm."

Squeals of delight penetrate Hannah's eardrum. "That's fab, Han! Does that mean you're moving to Charleston?"

"Not now. But maybe one day."

"Bummer. I really think you'd love it here."

Hannah's chest tightens, and she suddenly finds it difficult to breathe. "I'm sure I would. But I have to think about Gus."

"Of course you do. I totally get it."

"Anyway, I'm going to hire another web designer. I'm looking for someone with a lot of creative ideas and not much experience. If you hear of anyone . . ."

"Definitely! I'll ask around. I'll do whatever I can to help."

Logistically, the designer she hires can live anywhere. But it would be nice to find someone close by. While Gus buries his legs in the sand, she searches LinkedIn for candidates, but she has little success.

When Gus whines for lunch, she gathers up their things and loads them into the car.

"Can we eat lunch in the cafe, Mommy?" Gus asks on the way back across the causeway.

She looks at him through the rearview mirror. "I don't think so, buddy. Today is a holiday and the cafe will be busy."

He kicks the passenger seat in front of him. "But I wanna grilled cheese."

Here we go, Hannah thinks. The hunger demons are showing their ugly heads. "I'll make you a grilled cheese in the kitchen."

"But I want one of Birdie's grilled cheeses. Hers are better."

"A grilled cheese is a grilled cheese, Gus." She makes a left-hand turn off of Ocean Avenue and drives down the short alley to the parking lot the cafe shares with Johnson's Pharmacy.

When she unbuckles her son from his car seat, he slips past her and takes off around the side of the building. Slamming the car door, she runs after him, calling his name. By the time she catches up with him, he's managed to get inside the cafe and is making a beeline to his grandfather, who is working behind the counter. Pops scoops him up and gives him a hug.

"Gus! Come here, you naughty boy." Hannah goes behind the counter and takes her son from her father. "You can't run away from me like that. You could've been hurt."

A voice on the other side of the counter behind her sends a chill down her spine. "Hannah? Is that you?"

She slowly turns to face the customer. He's changed since she last saw him in early March of their senior year in college. His blond hair has darkened from white to sandy, and he's wearing it shorter, his boyish waves now gone. But she would know that adorable face and dimples anywhere. "Hello, Ryan."

Ryan nods at the child in her arms. "Did you call him Gus? Is that my son?"

Hannah is aware of other customers watching them, including the attractive brunette glued to Ryan's side. Her knees go weak, and she leans against her father for support. Managing to sound flippant, she says, "Don't be ridiculous. Why would you think such a thing?"

"Because my middle name is Augustus. You know that. You once told me how much you like the name. Never mind he's the spitting image of me at that age." Ryan's eyes shift from Hannah to Gus. "How old are you, kid?"

Gus holds up two fingers. He won't be three until August.

Ryan's intense gaze unsettles her, and she shifts Gus from one hip to the other. "Sorry for interrupting. Please continue with your order." Gripping her son tight, she turns away from Ryan, heading toward the kitchen door.

Ryan calls after her. "Not so fast, Hannah."

She freezes, and her father whispers to her. "He's not going away. You need to take this conversation outside."

Hannah notices her mother hovering nearby. "Here." She deposits Gus in her arms. "Will you please make him some lunch?"

Coming from behind the counter, Hannah exits the front door with Cary, Ryan, and Ryan's assumed girlfriend on her heels.

The girlfriend tugs on his shirtsleeve. "What's going on, Ryan? How do you know this person? Is that little boy seriously your son?"

"He could be. Hannah and I dated for a while in college." Ryan thrusts his keys at his girlfriend. "Wait for me in the car."

She gapes at the keys. "But I'm your fiancée. I have a right to know what's going on."

"Danielle . . ." he says in a warning tone.

She takes the keys and scurries off.

"What're you doing here, Ryan?" Hannah asks. "I thought your family vacations on Pawley's Island."

"Danielle's parents have a beach house on the island. But that's beside the point." Ryan steadies his gaze on Hannah. "Tell me the truth. I have a right to know. Who is the kid's father?"

Fear clenches Hannah's gut. She could lose everything. "He doesn't have a father. He's *my* son."

"Don't be ridiculous. Unless he was miraculously conceived, he has a father." Frown lines appear on Ryan's forehead. "Wait a minute. It's all coming back to me now. I remember your roommates making fun of you for gaining weight. You stopped partying and started spending all your time with the Chinese guy."

"His name is Chris. And he was a friend to me when the rest of y'all turned against me."

"Nobody turned against you, Hannah. You shut us out. Because you were pregnant." He steps closer to Hannah. "We went to the mountains for our formal weekend in November. You were worried because you forgot to pack your birth control pills. That's the last time we were together."

"Right. We broke up the following weekend when you cheated on me."

"Gus looks older than two. If you got pregnant in November . . ." Ryan counts the months on his fingers. "He'll be three in August."

"Let it go, Ryan. You're getting married. You don't need a child complicating your life."

Her father leans in close. "Careful what you say, Hannah."

Ryan glares at Cary. "Who are you, anyway?"

"I'm her father."

"Oh, right. The man who mysteriously disappeared."

Cary's jaw tightens. "I'm also an attorney."

"Good for you. I'm a law student, and my father is attorney general of South Carolina." Ryan grips Hannah's upper arm. "That little boy is my child, my flesh and blood. And I'm not going away." He drops his hand. "I'll be in touch."

Hannah and Cary stand in silence, watching him go. When he disappears around the corner of the pharmacy, Hannah bursts into tears, and Cary takes her in his arms. "I really messed up, Dad. Can he take Gus away from me?"

Cary strokes her hair. "That depends. Who did you name as the father on Gus's birth certificate?"

"No one!" she cries into his chest. "I lied. I claimed father unknown."

"Why did you do that?"

"Because I didn't want Ryan to feel obligated to marry me." Hannah pushes her father away. "I told you all this when I confessed that I was pregnant, a week before you disappeared."

Cary frowns.

Hannah wipes her eyes with the hem of her T-shirt. "I guess you don't remember. You were too busy plotting your getaway." She pauses, letting her jab sink in. "Ryan and I had broken up. He cheated on me, and I wanted nothing to do with him. I found out a couple of months later that he was planning to go to law school. I assumed he'd want nothing to do with the baby."

"Maybe he didn't back then. But he clearly does now."

She sniffles. "Will I have to share custody?"

"That all depends on Ryan. We'll have to wait for his next move. His fiancée didn't appear too keen on having a toddler in her life. Every child needs his or her father, Hannah. Especially a child who is all boy like Gus. Would it be so terrible to allow Ryan visitation?"

She gawks at him. "I should've known you would take his side. Yes, Dad, it would be terrible. I didn't tell Ryan about Gus because I don't want to share him. He's *my* son. Do you hear me, Dad? *My* son. I won't let Ryan do to Gus what you did to me."

Cary's face falls. "What did I do to you besides love you?"

"You left me. You broke my heart." Turning her back on them, Hannah enters the cafe, leaving her father standing on the boardwalk alone.

That evening, after closing the cafe, Birdie finds Cary waiting for her in the living room. "I can't believe you let Hannah lie on her child's birth certificate."

His condescending tone reminds Birdie of arguments they'd had throughout their marriage. The old Birdie would've poured herself a vodka on the rocks. But the new Birdie refuses to let him get to her. "Believe me, I tried to talk sense into her. But she's as stubborn as you. Once she makes up her mind, there's no stopping her. Maybe if you'd been here, it would have been different. She listened to you more than she's ever listened to me."

He opens his mouth to respond and then closes it again.

Birdie glances at her watch. She's running late for her date with Stan. She crosses the room and taps lightly on Hannah's door. "Hannah, I'm going now. I hate to leave with you so upset. I can easily stay here. Stan will understand."

Hannah's muffled voice comes from within. "I'm fine, Mom. Have fun on your date."

"Okay, but call me if you need me."

Birdie leaves the apartment without saying goodbye to Cary. How dare he criticize her parenting. She resents his intrusion into their lives. The sooner he gets his own place, the better off they'll all be.

The short drive out to Stan's house is pleasant, with sprawling moss-draped oak trees lining both sides of the road. A long gravel driveway leads to a one-story Lowcountry-style house with wraparound porches and deep overhangs.

Stan, looking handsome in blue jeans and a short-sleeved plaid button-down, is waiting for her in a rocker on the porch. He rises to greet her. "Good evening."

"Hello there. I'm sorry I'm late."

"You're not late. Remember? We're on island time."

"Oops. I forgot." She hands him a bakery box. "Your pie, sir."

"Thank you, ma'am." When he leans in to kiss her cheek, she catches a whiff of his cologne that smells like summer ocean breezes.

He opens the screen door for her. "Come on in. Today is a fruity drink kind of day. I made a batch of virgin strawberry daiquiris."

"I hope you didn't leave out the alcohol on my account."

"Not at all. Max mentioned you weren't much of a drinker, but neither am I. I have an occasional beer after a long day or when I'm watching a football game. Other than that, I do my best to stay away from the stuff."

The interior is handsomely decorated with rich coffee-with-cream colored walls, seagrass carpets, and leather furniture. The open floor plan features a living room and adjacent kitchen with the dining area off to the side.

He sets the pastry box on the counter and fills two tall glasses with strawberry daiquiri. He hands one to Birdie. "To Memorial Day," he says, holding his glass out to toast.

She clinks her glass against his. "Cheers." She takes a sip of the daiquiri and licks her lips. "This is yummy. Not too sweet."

"I only used fresh ingredients."

"I'm impressed." She has a look around the living room. "Your home is lovely. Did you live here with Kim?"

He shakes his head. "Kim and I lived over on the ocean. I built this place after the divorce. I much prefer the inlet."

"The inlet is more scenic in my opinion."

"I agree." He takes her by the hand. "Come. Let me show you my favorite room." He leads her outside, across the porch, and down a set of steps to a covered bluestone terrace. A u-shaped wicker sofa with upholstered cushions is arranged in front of a stone fireplace. Mounted above the mantel is an enormous wide-screen television.

Stan notices her eyeing the television. "What can I say? I'm a huge football fan."

"You're the most outdoorsy person I know. You should totally have an outdoor living room."

He grins, as though relieved. "Let's walk down to the dock."

Hand in hand, they cut across the freshly cut lawn to the water. The dock stretches long against the bulkhead. The *Island Daze* is tied up front and center. To the right is a port for his three wave runners, and to the left is a covered section that offers shelter for two racks of paddleboards and kayaks.

"I know where to come when I need to borrow a boat," Birdie says.

He grins. "Are you hungry?" He gestures at two wooden Adirondack chairs. "Or do you want to relax for a while?"

"Let's relax for a minute and enjoy our beverages." She lowers herself to the chair, and he sits down next to her. She leans her head back. "This is nice after a long day." She misses not having a porch or private outdoor area.

He presses his lips thin. "Nice. But often lonely. Do you get lonely, Birdie?"

"Ha. I sometimes wish for lonely with my daughter and grandson living in my small apartment."

A comfortable silence falls over Stan and Birdie as they finish their daiquiris and watch the sun begin its descent below the horizon.

Birdie sets her empty glass down on the dock beside her chair. "I have a confession to make. Max made light of my drinking problem. The truth is, I'm a recovering alcoholic. I hit the bottom after Cary disappeared. I don't know where I would be if not for Max. She saved me."

If this surprises Stan, he doesn't show it. "Thanks for trusting me enough to tell me." He reaches for her hand. "Are you doing better now?"

"Much. I go to at least two meetings a week, and I try to avoid certain triggers like cocktail parties and restaurants."

"Then we're well suited for each other. I avoid cocktail parties like the plague, and I never go out to dinner."

"Really? Why? I thought I was the only one in the Lowcountry who doesn't enjoy eating out."

"Why be stuck inside a stuffy restaurant when I have this view in my own backyard?" He makes a wide gesture toward the inlet. "Besides, I can cook better than any chef in town."

Birdie laughs out loud. "You're awfully confident."

He flashes her a grin. "Modesty isn't one of my virtues."

"Clearly. What other flaws do you have?"

"I'm a tough businessman, although a fair one. And I'm

incredibly high strung. I have this constant urge to be doing something."

"That surprises me. I haven't noticed any of your body parts twitching while we've been sitting here."

"I do a good job of hiding it." He jumps up and pulls Birdie to her feet. He brushes a stray strand of hair out of her face. "I haven't been with anyone since my divorce. While the thought of having sex with another woman terrifies me, I can't stop wondering what it would be like to kiss you."

Placing his hands on the sides of her face, he presses his lips lightly against hers. The feathery kiss sends tingles down her body to her toes. When he draws away, she palms his soft cheek. "You shaved."

His face beams red. "In anticipation of kissing you."

She leans into him, kissing him back with more urgency. His arms circle her body, bringing her close as his tongue parts her lips.

When the kiss ends, he says, "You're as sweet as a Georgia peach, Birdie Fuller. Let's get dinner over with so we can kiss some more."

She touches the tip of her finger to his lower lip. "I would love that," she says, and they walk hand in hand back to the built-in grill on the terrace.

Stan wasn't lying about his culinary skills. The burgers are the best she's ever had, although messy with chili, sauteed onions, and cheddar cheese. They eat at the picnic table on the porch. Stan gobbles down his burger in anticipation of dessert. But Birdie savors hers, eating every morsel and forgoing the key lime pie.

Once they've put the dishes away, they return to the sofa on the terrace. They've no sooner sat down when Stan kisses her again. Even during their wildest sex, Cary never kissed her with such intensity. To his credit, Stan is a true gentleman. He keeps his hands to himself and makes no move to take things further.

Birdie's lips are swollen and her skin raw when she finally breaks away from him. "It's late." The sultry tone in her voice sounds foreign to her. "I should head home."

When she moves to get up, he pulls her back down on his lap. "I'll only let you go, if you promise to have dinner with me again tomorrow night."

Tomorrow night seems like light years away to Birdie. "Only if I can cook for you this time."

He hesitates a long minute. "How about if we cook together?"

"Fine," she says with a laugh and kisses him again.

TWELVE

The week after Memorial Day drags on at a snail's pace. Hannah assumes Ryan still has her cell number from college, and waiting for him to call is like watching a live hand grenade tumbling through the air toward her.

Hannah replays the scene with Ryan over and over in her mind. Was he angry or hurt? Both, she finally decides. Gus is Ryan's clone. There's no point in denying he's Gus's father. How does Ryan's fiancée fit in? Will Danielle go along with him if he pursues a custody agreement? Taking care of an almost three-year-old will put a crimp in their style as newlyweds.

Hannah's mom offers little comfort. Birdie works at the cafe during the day and goes out every night with Stan. Birdie wears a dazed expression, and more than once, Hannah catches her humming in the kitchen. Is her mom hooking up with Stan? Hannah can't bear to think about them having sex.

Little by little, her father insinuates himself back into their lives. She'd made the mistake of allowing him to comfort her during a moment of weakness, and now he acts like her new best friend. It's as if he thinks he could make up for his abandonment of her by standing up for her against Ryan. Cary is always around, either working in the cafe or watching TV in the living room. The only way she can get away from him is to spend more time in her room or out on the water in her kayak.

She's desperate to get out of her mother's apartment. And now that Ryan has discovered her, she no longer has to hide. She daydreams of living in Charleston. It's not that far. She can come home on the weekends to get her island fix. She considers the professional opportunities the resort city has to offer. The boutique hotels and countless food establishments would present an opportunity for her to break into the vacation industry.

By Wednesday, when she still hasn't heard from Ethan, she assumes his offer is off the table. She can't wait any longer. She's in control of her own destiny. She researches preschools in downtown Charleston and finds a small church school that offers year-round classes and an extended day program. On a whim, she contacts the director who informs her they have an opening beginning the first of July.

"I'll take it," Hannah says. "Send me the paperwork."

Hannah experiences a rush of adrenaline. This is really happening. She's venturing out into the real world again. She's as terrified as she is thrilled. But she's a survivor. As long as she has Gus in her life, she can accomplish anything.

She signs into LinkedIn and posts a job opportunity for a web designer with limited experience located in Charleston. Within an hour, she receives her first response. Ironically, Christine Cain is a recent graduate from Hannah's alma mater, Virginia Commonwealth University in Richmond.

Grabbing her phone, Hannah clicks on the number for her former advisor. When her call goes to voice mail, she leaves a detailed message. Professor Burgess calls her back thirty minutes later.

"Hannah! How wonderful to hear from you. I've been following your progress online. You're making quite a name for yourself."

"Thank you, Professor Burgess. Things are going really well. In fact, I'm hiring a designer. I'm curious if you know Christine Cain. She responded to my post on LinkedIn."

"I know Christine well. She writes code almost as well as you. And she's a brilliant illustrator. Coupled with your flair for photography, the two of you would make an excellent team."

Hannah's pulse quickens. *An illustrator. Think of the possibilities.* "She might be just the person I'm looking for. Thank you, Professor Burgess," she says and ends the call.

She messages Christine through the LinkedIn portal, asking to set up a networking call. After going back and forth with times, they set up a call for Thursday afternoon at two.

Hannah and Christine talk for a minute about VCU before Hannah explains her purpose for reaching out. "With your credentials, I'm surprised you haven't already found a job."

"I took some time off after graduation to travel," Christine explains. "I returned from Italy a few days ago. I'm starting to seriously look for jobs. Problem is, I have no clue where I want to live. I'm originally from Charleston, and I love it here, but most of my friends have moved away."

Hannah laughs. "You and I have a lot in common, Christine. I'm relatively new to the industry myself, and I'm looking for someone to grow with me. If you're interested, I'd love to grab coffee one day early next week."

"Sure! Would Monday work?"

"Monday is perfect." They discuss times before settling on eleven o'clock. "In the meantime, if you would forward me your portfolio, I'll send you links to some websites I've designed."

Hannah sits at her desk for a long time after the call. What does she have to offer Christine? No office space. No health-care benefits or retirement plan. But she has money in the bank. Taking out her calculator, she computes the projected costs of operating her business. If she's careful, she'll make it at least one year.

Friday rolls around with no word from Ryan, and she breathes a little easier. She's on her way to pick Gus up from Miss Daisy's a few minutes before five, when the dreaded text comes in. *I want to see my son.*

Hannah slows her pace as she considers how to respond. Ryan's life is complicated with law school and wedding plans. With any luck, he'll go away once he sees what's involved in taking care of a young child. Ryan will have to see Gus on Hannah's terms. She thumbs off a text. *I'll allow a supervised visitation. Tomorrow morning at ten. We'll take Gus to the beach.*

He texts right back. *Done.*

Birdie feels guilty for being so happy when Hannah is so stressed out, but she can't help herself. She's not certain she's in love. But she's deeply infatuated with Stan.

She's been to dinner at his house every night since Sunday. Their evenings have fallen into a routine. They cook dinner together in his kitchen with country music playing softly in the background. They walk around in bare feet. She sneaks glances at Stan's fine fanny in blue jeans, and he takes breaks from the stove to plant a trail of kisses on her neck. After dinner, they make out on the sofa for hours. They haven't moved beyond kissing, but they are both hot and bothered, and it's only a matter of time. Any lingering anxiety about having sex with someone new has long since passed for both of them.

After work on Friday evening, they go for a ride in the

ocean on the *Island Daze*. Stan mixes a pitcher of virgin margaritas, and Birdie brings along cold cut sandwiches. They cruise north for about twenty miles, and when they turn back south, the sky is black with an approaching storm.

Stan's face falls. "Uh-oh. Where did that come from? When I checked the weather earlier, there was zero percent chance of rain." Pulling his phone out of his back pocket, he accesses his radar app. "It's still way off. If we hurry, we might make it home before it hits. Hold on. I'm going to speed up."

He lays his hands on the throttles and the boat picks up speed. Streaks of lightning dance across the sky in the distance, raising the hairs on Birdie's neck and arms. She doesn't admit her fear to Stan. He appears concerned enough without her nagging him. They're passing through the mouth of the inlet when they hit a wall of rain. The rain stings her face and she ducks her head.

"Go down to the cabin," Stan yells.

She shakes her head. "I'm not leaving you up here alone. Did this boat not come with a windshield?"

He laughs. "I'm having new flybridge enclosures made. They took the old ones off two days ago."

She gives him a thumbs-up. "Impeccable timing."

Twenty minutes later, they arrive back at the dock. While Stan fights the boat against the wind, Birdie goes down to the deck. He hollers instructions to her. She fumbles with the lines but manages to tie the boat to the dock.

Stan shimmies down the ladder to the cockpit. A crack of lightning is followed by a boom of thunder. "That was close. Let's wait out the storm onboard," Stan yells, holding the cabin door open for her.

They stand just inside the cabin, dripping water onto the carpeted floor. Stan takes her in. "You're beautiful."

Birdie looks down at the thin cotton sundress, wet and

clinging to her curves, and back up at him. An understanding passes between them.

He places his hands on her slim hips. "Are you sure?"

"I'm positive," she says, her voice deep with lust.

He yanks the upholstered cushion off the sofa, tossing it to the other side of the small cabin, and tugs a hideaway bed out from within. There are no sheets on the bed, only a mattress pad.

Stan turns to her and closes the distance between them. He slips the dress over her head, and she stands in front of him, wearing only her bra and panties. When she shivers, he strips off his soaked shirt and presses his warm body against hers. He kisses her forehead. "I have protection. Do you think we need it?"

Biting down on her lower lip, she shakes her head. "Cary is the only man I've been with in nearly thirty years."

"Other than Kim, I haven't been with anyone either. And I had a vasectomy."

She laughs. "I'm too old to worry about getting pregnant."

Covering her mouth with his, Stan walks her backward to the bed, lowering her gently to the mattress. He steps out of his shorts and boxer shorts and stretches out beside her.

While the storm rages outside, they explore each other's body until they are both bursting with desire. When he finally enters her, she screams out as a wave of sheer ecstasy washes over her.

"Wow!" Stan exclaims as he rolls off of her onto his back. "That was incredible."

Birdie curls up beside him, draping a leg over his thigh. "I've been missing out all these years. I never knew sex could be that good. Was it this good for you with Kim?" Her face warms. "I'm sorry. It's inappropriate of me to ask that."

Stan chuckles. "I never kiss and tell. But that was pretty spectacular."

"Do you think it's because you've been deprived for so long?"

"No. I think it's you, Birdie." He repositions himself so he can see her face. "I have feelings for you. Strong feelings. This isn't a casual fling for me. I enjoy your company. I may be getting ahead of myself, but I'm a middle-aged man, and I don't take my time on this earth for granted. I want to build a future with you."

"I want that too, Stan," Birdie says in a soft voice.

He kisses the tip of her nose. "I'm glad we're on the same page."

Thunder rumbles outside. "And the storm rages on," she says.

"Looks like we're gonna be here a while. Might as well get comfortable." He leaves the bed and disappears deeper within the boat, returning a minute later with a blanket tucked under one arm and the other laden with candles. He covers Birdie with the blanket and lights the candles, lining them up on the window ledge behind the sofa.

When he rejoins her under the covers, Birdie asks, "How long do you think the storm will last? I can't stay here all night."

"Why not? How could you possibly leave when it's so cozy with the rumbling of thunder and waves lapping against the hull?"

Birdie likes the idea of waking in his arms after a night of passion. "I should at least text Hannah to let her know where I am." Birdie retrieves her bag from the chair beside the door where she left it hours ago when she first boarded the boat. "Ugh. My phone is dead. Do you have a charger?"

Stan sits up in bed. "No. Sorry. Not on the boat. Use my phone. It's in my pocket." He points at his shorts on the floor.

Birdie retrieves his phone from his soggy shorts. When she

presses the button to power it on, nothing happens. "Yours is dead too."

"No way. I had a full charge when we left the house earlier. Let me see it." She tosses the phone to him, and he fiddles with it a minute. "I think the rain ruined it. That sucks."

She clucks her tongue. "Too bad. I guess you'll have to buy a new one." She's been teasing him about his outdated phone. "The newer models are waterproof, you know."

A loud clap of thunder sends Birdie back to bed. "I hope Hannah isn't worried about me."

He pulls her close. "Why would she worry? Doesn't she know you're with me?"

"She probably *assumes* I'm with you. But I didn't see her this afternoon to tell her."

Stan kisses her damp hair. "You're a grown woman, Birdie. You have to cut the apron strings at some point. I know it's hard. I've done it myself with my own daughter. But it was the best thing that could've happened to her."

"My relationship with Hannah is complicated, Stan. Cary's disappearance drove us apart. And for a time, I thought Hannah might be lost to me forever. But then Gus came along and brought us closer together. Because we don't have any other family, we're very protective of each other."

"Of course, you are. I'm sorry, Birdie. I can't imagine what you went through after Cary left. Have you heard *anything* from him in all these years?"

Birdie is surprised Stan hasn't heard about Cary's return. Then again, Max would never have told him. She despises Cary. And Stan isn't the type to partake in gossip.

She opens her mouth to tell him the truth, but the words get stuck in her throat. There is no sane explanation as to why Cary is living in Birdie's apartment. "Not a word." As the lie slips off her tongue, she realizes what a terrible mistake she's making.

THIRTEEN

Hannah's anxiety mounts as ten o'clock approaches on Saturday morning. Where is her mom? Ryan will be here in a few minutes, and she needs Birdie to reassure her she's doing the right thing. Hannah clicks on her mom's number again, but the call goes straight to voice mail. Is Birdie's battery dead? Did something happen to her during the storm? This isn't like her mom. Birdie would never let Hannah worry like this. And she's never trusted Sadie to open the bakery on a summer Saturday.

When she hears the downstairs door open, Hannah rushes to the stairs. Air gushes out of her lungs at the sight of her mother's blonde head. "Thank God! Where have you been, Mom? I've been trying to call you."

Birdie climbs the stairs. When she reaches the top, she flashes her phone at Hannah. "I'm sorry, sweetheart. My battery died. It's a long story. Stan and I got caught in the storm. We spent the night on his boat."

Hannah steadies her gaze on her mom. "You could've called from Stan's phone."

"His phone got wet during the storm. I think it's ruined."

"Did it ever occur to you I might be worried?" Hannah says in an accusatory tone that brings back long-forgotten memories from her high school years. The tables have turned. Hannah is now the parent and Birdie the delinquent teenager.

Gus looks over from the sofa where he's watching *Curious George*. "Mommy, why are you yelling at Birdie?"

Hannah snaps at her child, "I'm upset, Gus. Watch your program."

"Now, Hannah. No need to take your frustration out on your son." Birdie drops her bag on the table and turns back to face Hannah. "I'll remind you, I'm a grown woman. I don't have to report my whereabouts to you."

"You're right, Mom. You don't *have* to report anything to me. But we're a family. We respect each other. Or we used to. I shouldn't have to remind you that Dad disappeared during the night. Not that you would ever do such a thing. But still, I was freaked out."

"Oh, honey. I never thought . . ." Birdie embraces her. "I'm so sorry. You're right. I should've tried harder to get in touch with you."

Hannah collapses against her mother's body. "Ryan's coming in a few minutes for his first supervised visit with Gus. I'm worked up about it, and I wanted to talk to you. Do you think I'm doing the right thing in letting him see Gus?"

"I don't think you have much choice." Her mother rubs circles on her back. "Play along with Ryan. See what he wants. Maybe he'll be satisfied with monthly visitation."

"That's best-case scenario." Hannah rests her head on Birdie's shoulder. If only she could stay in the safety of her mother's arms forever. "Can we get rid of Dad? He's driving me crazy. He's always hovering over me. He wants to make things right between us, but he can't do that overnight. If ever."

Birdie sighs. "I agree. This apartment isn't big enough for

the four of us. I'll give him until the end of next week. If he hasn't found a job yet, I'll loan him some money and send him on his way."

"Thank you!" Hannah draws away from her mom. "I need to go. Ryan is waiting for me." She scoops Gus up and starts down the stairs.

Birdie calls after her, "I'm plugging my phone in to charge. Call me if you need me."

Hannah hurries through the kitchen and out the front door to find Ryan leaning against a palmetto tree in the park.

"Hey." She lifts her hand in a tentative wave. "I hope you haven't been waiting long."

He throws a thumb over his shoulder at the Palmetto Hotel. "I got a room for the weekend. I figured it would be easier."

Weekend? Hannah was planning to limit the visitation to a couple of hours on the beach. Surely Ryan doesn't expect them to spend the entire day together? And what about dinner?

"Gus, this is . . ."

Ryan kneels down eye level to Gus. "Hey, buddy! I'm your daddy."

Gus hides behind Hannah's legs.

"Ryan, please. He's only two years old. He doesn't understand."

Gus peeks out from behind her legs. "I'm almost three, Mommy. Remember?"

She musses his white hair. "Of course you are." She looks over at Ryan. "Are you ready to go? You can ride with us. My beach chairs and Gus's sand toys are already in my Jeep."

Ryan steps in line beside her, and they go around the building to the parking lot behind the cafe. "I can't believe you're driving the same old heap you had in college."

"My Wrangler's not a heap. And it's not that old. It was new when my dad gave it to me for high school graduation, and I've hardly put any miles on it since college."

"Because you've been hiding out on your island with my son," Ryan says as he watches Hannah hoist Gus into his car seat.

Hannah doesn't respond. She can't defend herself against the truth.

They ride in awkward silence out of the parking lot and over the causeway. She finds a spot at her favorite beach access, and they pile out of the Jeep. When Ryan starts off down the boardwalk with Gus, she yells after him. "Not so fast! I could use a hand, please."

Reluctantly, he retraces his steps. She opens the rear door to reveal folding chairs, a cooler, and two canvas totes—one housing Gus's toys and the other packed with towels and an assortment of sunscreen.

"Are you kidding me? All that has to go down there?" he asks, pointing at the beach.

"Yep. Get used to it. Kids require a lot of stuff."

He slings the cooler strap over his shoulder. "What's in here?"

"Lunch. I picked up some sandwiches from the Sandwich Shack. I wasn't sure what you wanted, so I got you an Italian sub."

"Anything's fine." He grabs one chair, leaving the other and two beach bags for Hannah.

Down on the beach, Hannah is setting up their chairs when Gus struggles out of his T-shirt and makes a beeline for the water. She runs in after him, grabbing him seconds before a wave swallows him up. "Gus! How many times have I told you not to go in the ocean without me?" She carries her squirming son back up the beach, deposits him in the sand with his dump truck, and plops down in her chair.

"I'm exhausted from watching you," Ryan says, sitting down in the chair beside her.

"Children are hard work." Hannah removes a bottled water from the cooler and takes a long pull.

"Believe it or not, Hannah, I've thought about you a lot since college. We had something special back then."

"We *made* something special," Hannah says, her eyes on her child.

"Do you ever think about me?"

Every time I look at our son. "I think about how much you hurt me when you cheated on me."

He flashes her a wide smile. "Are you admitting you cared about me?"

She's relieved to find his dimples no longer work on her. "More than you cared about me. Otherwise, you wouldn't have cheated on me." She looks away, staring down the beach at a young family—a man and woman and their two small children. She wants that for her son. She wants that for herself. But it has to be the right man.

"Why didn't you tell me you were pregnant? I would've helped you."

"Right. Helped me into having an abortion."

His raised brows are visible behind Ray-Ban sunglasses. "Are you saying you never considered the option?"

"For about a second. The pregnancy was an accident, but my child was not. I love Gus with all my heart."

Ryan looks beyond her toward the ocean. "To be honest, I'm not sure how I would've responded to your pregnancy when we were in college. I was young and reckless back then, as evidenced by my cheating on you. But I'm a different person now. I want to do right by my son." His gaze shifts from the water to Hannah. "I broke up with Danielle, hoping you'd give me another chance."

"What? I thought the two of you were engaged."

"We were." He hangs his head. "Things haven't been right between us for a while. Seeing you on Monday was a sign, the kick in the butt I needed to end our relationship." Ryan buries his feet in the sand. "What do you say, Hannah? Can we be a family—you, me, and Gus?"

"Slow down, Ryan. You just broke up with the woman you planned to spend the rest of your life with. Besides, you and I haven't seen each other in over three years. Just because we have a son, doesn't mean we'd make a good couple."

"That's true. All I'm asking for is a chance. If you let me, I'd like to prove myself to you. I'm ranked in the top ten in my law school class."

Hannah remembers Ryan sweating about his grades when they dated. Maybe he has grown up and become more responsible. "Good for you, Ryan. That's awesome."

"I graduate next May, and I'll take the South Carolina bar exam in September. I'm hoping to stay in the state. Palmetto Island is too small for me, not enough professional opportunities. But I'm willing to consider other cities like Greenville or Spartanburg or Charleston. I'll be able to provide a comfortable lifestyle for you and Gus."

"Let's just see how the day goes, Ryan."

"Of course. Will you and Gus have dinner with me tonight?"

"Ryan," she says in a warning tone.

He raises both hands. "Sorry."

Gus pulls a plastic container of Matchbox cars out of his tote bag and shakes it at Ryan. "Wanna play cars?"

Ryan's blue eyes light up. "Are you kidding me? I love Matchbox cars."

Sliding out of his chair, Ryan crawls across the sand to Gus. "How many cars do you have in there, buddy?"

"I dunno," Gus says, and hands Ryan the container.

Ryan opens it and counts ten cars. "How about if you take your five favorites and give me the rest?" They count together as Gus picks out his cars, one at a time, and sets them on the ground. Once the collection is divided, they build a racetrack in the sand and drag their cars around and around, making louder zoom noises than one hears on a busy interstate.

When they tire of playing cars, they roll about on the ground, flailing arms and legs while giggling, until they're covered in sand. Hannah can't help but smile to herself. Ryan is like a kid himself, and Gus is eating up the attention.

Ryan jumps to his feet and throws Gus over his shoulder. "Hey, Mom," he calls out to Hannah. "Okay if we go rinse off? I promise not to let go of him."

"Be careful. He's slippery when wet."

Hannah watches Ryan carry a cackling Gus down to the water. True to his word, he grips her son tightly as they wade in. Ryan is falling for Gus. It's easy to do. He's a lovable little boy. Until Monday, he was *her* little boy. And now she must share him. She has more questions than answers. Does she still have romantic feelings for Ryan? Can they be a real family? What will this mean for her company and the life she's hoping to build in Charleston? From her observations today, she knows, deep down, Gus will benefit from having Ryan in his life. For the sake of their son, she should give Ryan another chance.

Birdie moves through the day with a mix of emotions. She's elated after a night of exquisite sex, feels guilty for scaring Hannah, and is remorseful for lying to Stan about Cary. She had plenty of opportunity to tell him the truth between bouts of lovemaking when they snuggled in each other's arms and shared their deepest secrets and dreams for the future. So why didn't she? Because she's afraid Stan will question her judgment for allowing Cary back into their lives. As he should. Birdie was a fool to let Cary stay with them. She remembers her conversation with Hannah from earlier. *Can we get rid of Dad? He's driving me crazy. He's always hovering over me.* It's true. Cary *is* always hovering. And he's driving Birdie crazy too.

Birdie can't bear the burden of the lie. She'll tell Stan about Cary at dinner tonight. She'll explain why she lied and pray he forgives her.

During a break in business around three o'clock, Birdie is replenishing baked goods in the showcase when Stan enters the cafe with an enormous bouquet of wildflowers. Spotting her behind the showcase, he smiles and waves the flowers at her. She smiles back at him, her mind racing. She needs to get him out of the cafe before he sees Cary. She slams the showcase door, but before she can make it around the counter, Cary comes through the swinging door from the kitchen with a tray of donuts.

"Birdie, we're almost out of the cherry almond donuts. Do you—"

Birdie's eyes are on Stan, whose jaw drops as his gaze shifts from Cary to Birdie and back to Cary. Spinning around, he tosses the flowers on the ground and flees the cafe.

Birdie hurries after him. "Stan! Wait! I can explain." She catches up with him in the parking lot behind the bakery. "I'm sorry. I was going to tell you tonight."

"Tonight?" Stan says, gripping the door handle of his pickup truck. "Why not last night when I asked you about him? You lied to me. You said you hadn't heard a word from Cary, yet here he is working behind the counter in your cafe. Are the two of you back together?"

"What? No! Never! I'm just helping him out until he gets back on his feet. You've gotta believe me, Stan. There's nothing going on between us. We're getting a divorce."

"How can I trust anything you say?" He jerks open the truck door. "I'm a private man, Birdie. I keep to myself, and I

rarely let people get close to me. I thought you were different."
He climbs behind the wheel and starts the engine.

Birdie tugs on his arm. "Please, Stan! Can't we talk about this?"

"There is nothing left to say." He pries her fingers from his arm and slams the door shut.

When he puts the truck in reverse, she steps out of the way, watching him speed off down the alley toward Ocean Avenue.

She fights back tears as she returns to the front of the building. She finally found happiness, and she ruined it. Inside the cafe, Cary is still behind the counter, transferring the cherry almond donuts from the tray in his arm to the one in the showcase.

"Trouble in paradise?" he asks, a smirk on his lips.

"None of your business." She snatches the tray from him. "You don't work here, Cary. I'm grateful to you for helping over the holiday weekend. But I don't need extra staff. Have you had any luck finding a job?" He shakes his head, and she asks, "Have you even tried?"

"Yes, I've tried. I've applied to every business on Ocean Avenue. They're either not hiring or they won't hire me, as is the case next door. Shaggy says I'm not good enough to wash his dishes."

Birdie winces. That's harsh. But not her problem. Cary brought this on himself. "I warned you this would happen, Cary. You have until next Friday. Then, job or no job, you'll have to find somewhere else to stay. There simply isn't enough room for the four of us in my apartment."

His hazel eyes widen. "Come on, Birdie. Are you seriously going to kick me out on the street?"

"Not at all. I'm giving you five days to work something else out." Turning her back on him, she takes the empty tray to the kitchen.

Sadie looks up from her mixing bowl. "What's wrong, Birdie? You're as pale as a ghost."

Birdie sets the tray in the sink. "I just fired Cary."

Sadie drags a rubber spatula around the inside of her mixing bowl. "I didn't know he was officially working here."

"I was paying him, even though he volunteered." Birdie drizzles liquid soap on the tray and lets warm water run over it. "I told him he needs to move out by Friday. I feel bad, though. He has nowhere else to go, and no one will hire him."

"You've got nothing to feel bad about. Men like that prey on women like you."

"What kind of woman is that, Sadie, a gullible old fool?"

Sadie jabs her spatula at Birdie. "Don't go putting words in my mouth. You're a good-hearted woman, Birdie. That's what kind of woman you are."

She may have a good heart, but she's also a liar.

FOURTEEN

Ryan is already seated at a prime table on the crowded porch when Hannah and Gus arrive at Shaggy's for an early dinner. "Nice job on the table. Did you flash your dimples at the hostess?"

He chuckles. "Works every time."

Ryan watches Hannah struggle with Gus's booster seat, but offers no help. He seems to enjoy the fun part of having a child, like rolling in the sand and playing Matchbox cars. Does he think the unpleasant parenting duties are beneath him?

When she orders chicken tenders and fries for Gus, Ryan asks for the same. "You're joking, right? You could have scallops or crab cakes, and you're ordering chicken tenders."

He grins. "I'm living vicariously through my child."

When the waitress brings their dinner, Ryan challenges Gus to a french fry eating contest. They are loud and obnoxious, and the people around them gawk at Ryan as though he's lost his mind. He allows Gus to win, and Gus claps his ketchup-covered hands.

While Ryan pays the check, Hannah takes Gus to the restroom to clean him up.

Ryan is waiting on the boardwalk when they return. "Ice cream, anyone? I hear Scoops makes a mean hot fudge sundae."

"Yay, ice cream!" Gus yanks his hand free of hers and throws himself at Ryan's legs.

"Ryan, no!" Hannah shakes her head vehemently. "Chocolate this time of night is a bad idea."

Gus looks up at Ryan. "Please, Daddy," he says in a pleading voice.

Daddy? Did Gus pick up on that when she introduced them this morning? Or did Ryan drive the point home while they were rolling around in the sand on the beach?

Hannah tosses her hands in the air. "I give up. You can see for yourself the effects sugar and caffeine have on a two-year-old."

"I'll take my chances." Ryan gives Gus a high five. "Let's go!" Gus takes Ryan by the hand, and they hurry ahead of her down the boardwalk. As they cross Atlantic Avenue, Hannah notices that both father and son walk with their toes turned slightly outward. How is it fair that she does all the work and Ryan gets the glory?

Ryan and Gus devour the hot fudge sundae while Hannah, still full from dinner, refuses to take a bite. Returning to the park afterward, Ryan and Hannah sit on a bench while Gus runs circles around them.

"Watching him is making me dizzy," Ryan says, his eyes on his son. "You were right about the sugar and caffeine. It appears I have a lot to learn about parenting."

"Yes, you do. But you'll learn a lot by trial and error. If you decide to stick around," Hannah says, fishing for clues about his intentions regarding Gus.

"I'm not going anywhere, Hannah. I will own up to my responsibilities. I'd like to think I would've owned up to them when you got pregnant if you'd given me the chance."

"After you cheated on me, I didn't feel I could trust you with my child. You have to earn back that trust, Ryan."

"I will. However long it takes." Ryan's gaze shifts to the cafe behind her. Squinting, he says, "Who's that woman in the window watching us?"

Hannah cranes her neck to see. "That's my mom. I want you to meet her." She motions for Birdie to join them. Birdie lifts her hand in a half-hearted wave, but she doesn't get up from her table. "Hmm. That's not like Mom. I hope nothing is wrong."

"I know what's wrong. Her little girl is on a date with the guy who knocked her up."

Hannah cast him a sideways glance. "I don't consider this a date, Ryan. Besides, Mom's not like that. She blames me for getting pregnant as much as she blames you. None of that matters to her anymore, anyway. She adores Gus."

Gus finally runs out of energy and crawls into his daddy's lap. Ryan kisses his sweaty forehead. "My mom is excited to meet you both."

"Yeah, right."

"I'm serious. She wasn't thrilled when I first told her about Gus, but she's come around. This coming week is our family's annual trip to Pawley's Island. I'm going straight there when I leave here tomorrow. My parents want you and Gus to spend next weekend with us."

Hannah jumps to her feet. "Whoa, Ryan. Meeting your parents is a big step. I'm not sure I'm ready for that."

With Gus in his arms, Ryan stands to face her. "Let's be fair here, Hannah. My parents have a right to know their grandchild. You've kept him from us for almost three years."

Hannah can't argue with that. "Will your sister be there?" When they were together, Hannah remembers Ryan speaking fondly of his older sister.

"Olivia's there now. Unfortunately, she has to leave on Wednesday to go back to New York."

"That's too bad. Let me think about it. I'll text you in the morning. I need to get this little one to bed," Hannah says, and takes a sleepy Gus from Ryan.

Ryan glances at his watch. "It's still early. Take care of him and let's go back to Shaggy's for a drink."

Hannah considers his invitation. She doesn't trust Ryan any more than she trusts her heart. Slow is the only way to go in figuring out their relationship. Hannah was once very much in love with Ryan. Which makes her vulnerable. And he just broke up with his fiancée. Which makes him equally vulnerable. She refuses to be his rebound person. "I don't think so. I'm pretty beat."

"Come on. Your mom's here. Can't she watch him?"

Hannah looks over in time to see Birdie dabbing her eyes with a tissue. She's definitely upset about something. "I'm sorry, Ryan. Not tonight. I need to go see about my mom."

Birdie hears the lock on the door click, followed by footfalls on the wooden floor as Hannah makes her way across the cafe to her table.

"Mom, what's wrong? You look so sad."

Tears blur her vision as Birdie looks into her cup of tea. "I lied to Stan, and now he's furious at me."

"But you're honest to a fault. What could you possibly have lied about?"

Birdie describes the scene in the cafe earlier with Stan discovering Cary and storming out.

Hannah shifts a sleeping Gus from one hip to the other. "Let me put him down. I'll be right back."

Hannah returns twenty minutes later with a cup of tea and the baby monitor. "Where's Dad?" she asks, sliding onto the chair opposite Birdie.

Birdie hunches a shoulder. "He went out. I'm not sure where he's gone. He's mad at me too. I gave him notice. I told him he has to get out by next Friday."

"Good for you. I don't know why you let him live here in the first place. Look at all the trouble he's causing."

More tears fill Birdie's eyes. "I did it for you, sweetheart. I was hoping you and your father would resolve your differences. I thought, when you heard his side of the story, you might feel some compassion for him. Have you even talked to him about what happened in Maui?"

"I don't care what happened to him. I'm grateful to have closure. But what Dad did to us is unforgivable." Hannah softens her tone. "Don't let Dad get in the way of your happiness. You and Stan have been spending a lot of time together. If he doesn't know by now what a huge heart you have, he's not good enough for you."

"He's too good for me." Her tissue now soggy, Birdie blows her nose into a napkin.

"Not true, Mom. If you explain why you lied, Stan will see you made a bad decision for the right reason."

Birdie picks at the balled napkin in her hands. "You don't think it's too late?"

"Not if he cares about you. Which I'm sure he does."

Birdie inhales an unsteady breath. "Okay. I'll go see him after closing tomorrow afternoon. Maybe he will have calmed down by then."

"I'm sure of it." Hannah sits back in her chair and sips her tea. "Ryan asked me to give him another chance."

Birdie frowns. "I thought Ryan was engaged."

Hannah shakes her head. "He broke up with Danielle."

"I see. But what about Ethan?"

"What does Ethan have to do with anything?"

"You tell me," Birdie says, a smirk playing on her lips. "Your pretty green eyes sure sparkle whenever you talk about him."

"I haven't heard from Ethan all week, which I interpret to mean he's no longer interested. Besides, Ryan is Gus's father. After seeing them together today, I should give him a chance."

Birdie levels her gaze on her daughter. "Because he's Gus's father? Or because you still have feelings for him? Don't confuse the issues, sweetheart. Every woman wants to provide a happy home with loving parents for her child. But no home is happy when the parents don't love each other."

"That's a valid point. I need to sort out my feelings for Ryan. And the only way to do that is to spend more time with him. This week is his family's annual beach vacation on Pawley's Island. They want Gus and me to come next weekend. I figure we'll go. What do we have to lose?"

"Nothing. And everything to gain. At least for Gus. He'll get to meet his paternal grandparents. And you get to see how they are with them. As the saying goes, the apple never falls far from the tree. Watching Ryan interact with his parents will give you a clue what kind of father he'll be to Gus."

"I haven't thought of that, but you're right." Hannah runs her finger around the rim of her empty teacup. "I'm done with putting my life on hold. I love the island and the inlet. But I've been living here for all the wrong reasons."

Birdie reaches for Hannah's hand. "The world didn't end when Ryan found you."

"Exactly. Even if we don't end up together, Gus will have a relationship with his father." Hannah looks away. "Dad scarred me for life when he left us. I thought that by staying close to you I could somehow protect you. I couldn't stand the thought of losing someone else I care about. When you didn't come home last night . . . well, it made me realize I can't control what happens to any of us. You're a fifty-three-year-old woman, perfectly capable of taking care of yourself."

"We all need to work harder to let go."

"I agree. The months after Dad's disappearance were the worst. But you and I grew closer because of those hard times. You're my best friend, Mom. And I will forever be grateful to you for helping me raise Gus these past few years. I've learned so much from you. But I lean on you too hard. I've decided to move to Charleston, Mom. I'm terrified at the prospect of being a single mother living in a strange city, but I need to get out of the rut I'm in."

Birdie narrows her blue eyes. "But you said you haven't heard from Ethan."

"Ethan isn't part of my plan. I'm going to use my house money to hire another designer and expand my own firm."

"Good for you, sweetheart."

"Wait? You're okay with this?"

"I'm fine with it. I will miss you and Gus something fierce. But I say go for it. Go make your mark on the world, Hannah Fuller." Birdie gives her hand a squeeze before letting go. "You're going to do great, sweetheart. I have so much faith in you. Never sell yourself short. You're talented and outgoing, and you have a special way with people. I'm convinced you can accomplish anything you set your mind to. Just look at what you've already accomplished. And no matter where you live, I will always be here for you."

"I'm counting on that." Hannah pushes back from the table. "What a day. I'm heading up. Are you coming?"

"Not yet. I need to figure out what I'm going to say to Stan tomorrow."

Hannah stands. "If you marry Stan, do you think he'll give me a deal on a wave runner?"

Birdie bursts into laughter. "Where will you keep it if you're living in Charleston?"

"Here. At the marina. For when I come home on the weekends." Hannah stuffs her phone in her back pocket of her white jeans and gathers her empty teacup and baby monitor. "I was livid when you sold our house on the inlet and bought this building. But our tiny apartment feels more like home than that house ever did."

A tender expression crosses Birdie's face. "We've shared a lot of laughs and tears in that apartment over the past three years."

Hannah kisses the top of Birdie's head. "We'll never forget those memories, but I look forward to making plenty of new ones."

Birdie waits for Hannah to leave before taking her mug to the kitchen for another cup of tea. She's waiting for the pot to boil when Cary stumbles in the back door.

She crosses the kitchen to him. "You're drunk?"

He closes one eye, as though trying to focus the other on her. "I may have had a few too many."

"I thought you were broke." She eyes him suspiciously. "Did you spend the money I paid you for working the cafe?"

Cary gripped the doorjamb to keep from falling down. "I met an old friend for drinks. He picked up the tab."

"What old friend?" When he avoids her gaze, Birdie knows he's lying. "I'm a recovering alcoholic, Cary. I won't tolerate drunkenness in my home."

"What happened to you, Birdie? You used to be so much fun. Let's dance." He takes her in his arms and waltzes her around the kitchen, banging her into the refrigerator and the work counters.

He slows long enough for her to shove him away. "Get off of me."

"Come on, baby. For old time's sake." He's all over her at

once with hands groping her breasts and mouth crushing her lips.

Rearing her arm back, she smacks the side of his head. "I said. Get off of me."

He rubs his head. "Geez, sorry. I don't remember you having such a mean right hook."

She jabs her finger at his face. "Because I let you walk all over me when we were married. But no more. If you ever lay a hand on me again, I'll call the police. Our marriage is over. The divorce papers will be ready any day now. I gave you until Friday to find somewhere else to live. And I'm a woman of my word. But if you try a stunt like that again, I will throw you out on your ear. Do you understand me?" She glares at him until he squirms.

"Okay. I get it."

Pushing past him, she locks the back door and stomps up the stairs to her room. So much has happened over the course of the past two weeks. Cary barged into their lives. She fell head over heels in love with Stan. Gus's father appeared out of the blue. And Hannah has decided to move to Charleston. For a woman who doesn't like change, this is a lot to stomach at once. She envies Cary his buzz. She relishes the idea of taking a break from the harsh realities of her life for just one night. To drown her sorrows about Stan.

Standing at her bedroom window, she watches the people spilling out of Shaggy's in various stages of drunkenness. Hannah has gone to bed. Cary will soon be passed out drunk on the sofa. No one will miss her if she sneaks next door for a glass of wine. She'll order Kris, her favorite Italian Pinot Grigio, so crisp and refreshing. And numbing. She'll only have one and then come home. The alcohol will help her sleep. She grabs her bag and is headed out of her bedroom when her inner voice stops her. *Don't do it, Birdie.*

She drops the bag on the floor and closes the bedroom door, leaning against it. That was close. And close is not good for an alcoholic. She needs to get rid of some of the stress in her life. She needs to make things right with Stan.

FIFTEEN

S tan's truck is in the driveway, but when Birdie rings the bell and bangs her fist on the door, he doesn't answer. She imagines him watching her from his bedroom window, hoping she'll go away. But she refuses to leave until she's had her say. Venturing around to the waterside of the house, she sees the *Island Daze* is missing from the dock. She waits in a rocker on the porch, out of the heat of the afternoon sun. Thirty minutes later, the rumbling of diesel engines grows closer and the *Island Daze* appears. She hurries down to the dock to help him tie up.

"What're you doing here?" he asks from the flybridge.

"If you can spare a few minutes, I'd like to explain why I lied to you."

Turning off the engines, he comes down the ladder and steps onto the dock. He leans against a piling, crossing his arms and legs. He doesn't offer her a seat in one of the Adirondack chairs. He doesn't intend for her to stay. "There is never a good reason to lie, Birdie."

"I totally agree, and I rarely stray from the truth. In fact, my daughter says I'm honest to a fault. But I'm also a sucker for someone in need. The woman Cary ran off with stole all his money and left him stranded in Maui with sixty bucks and a one-way airline ticket back to South Carolina."

Stan removes his baseball cap, smooths back his salt-and-pepper hair, and returns the cap to his head. "Serves him right, if you ask me."

"He got what he deserves. But I felt sorry for him, and in a moment of weakness, I agreed to let him stay with us until he finds a job."

Stan tucks his chin and peers at her from behind his sunglasses. "You mean he's living with you too?"

"Unfortunately." She sighs. "He can't find a job. No one will hire him."

"Because everyone in town knows how badly he mistreated you. Everyone except you, apparently."

Experiencing a surge of anger, she brings her body to her full height. "I'll never forget what he did to me, Stan. He nearly destroyed my life. But he's still Hannah's father. They were once close, and I was hoping they could rekindle that relationship."

"And have they?"

Birdie shakes her head. "Hannah won't even talk to him. I regret letting him stay with us. I told him he has until Friday to find somewhere else to live. If he doesn't find a job, I'll have to give him money to get rid of him. Regardless of what he did to me, I'm not heartless enough to just put him out on the street."

She waits for Stan to say something. When he remains silent, she continues, "I've fallen hard for you, Stan. I didn't tell you about Cary because I didn't want you to know what a foolish thing I'd done by allowing him back into our lives."

Stan pushes off the piling. "I don't judge people, Birdie. Except when they lie to me." He motions her to the chairs. "You may have heard that my wife cheated on me. You may also have heard that she cheated on me with another woman. A fifty-year-old woman doesn't suddenly decide she's gay. She confessed that she was bisexual in college. That's an important little tidbit she forgot to tell me when we got married. Our twenty-five-year marriage was based on a lie."

"I'm sorry, Stan. I can't imagine how difficult that must have been for you."

He shrugs. "I'm over it now. And I'm finally ready to let it go." He takes Birdie's hand. "I've fallen hard for you, too, Birdie."

Birdie's pulse quickens. "Does this mean you forgive me?"

He nods. "If you promise never to lie to me again."

She draws an *X* across her heart. "I promise. I will always be truthful with you no matter what."

"And I will with you. Like right now when I tell you I think we're moving too fast. And that's my fault. I've been pushing things along at a rapid rate because I enjoy your company. And I want to be with you. But seeing Cary behind the counter with you at the cafe reminded me of the painful part of being in a relationship. I realize now it's best if we ease into it."

He's putting me on probation, Birdie thinks. *To make certain I won't lie to him again.*

"I understand," she says. "And I agree. I think we should slow things down. Hannah freaked out when I didn't come home on Friday night, as I worried she might. Cary's disappearance traumatized her. When she couldn't get in touch with me, she assumed the worst."

Stan frowns. "That's also my fault. I coerced you into staying."

"Not at all. I should have trusted my instinct and gone home. It looks as though Hannah is moving to Charleston, and I want to support her as she makes this transition. She and I are closer than most mothers and daughters because of what we've been through together, losing Cary and Hannah having a baby. I will miss her like crazy, but this move is what she needs."

"Lucky for you, Charleston is nearby." He gets up and pulls Birdie to her feet. "We were supposed to go out on the wave runners this afternoon. Did you bring your bathing suit with you?"

Birdie gives him a sheepish grin. "Actually, I did. It's in the car. I was hoping you'd find it in your heart to give me another chance."

"I'd be a fool not to." Twirling her around, he smacks her bottom. "Now go change while I get the wave runners ready."

Birdie floats on air up to the house. He's giving her another chance. This time, she won't blow it.

When she returns to the dock, Stan whistles at the sight of her in her bathing suit. After a quick tutorial on the wave runner, they take off with Stan in the lead and Birdie following at a safe distance.

They ride for more than an hour before taking a break at a deserted beach. They're alone with no other boats in sight. Stan looks hot in his board shorts, and she desperately wants him to take her in his arms and make love to her in the sand. But he doesn't touch her. Not even a kiss. And later, when he walks her to her car, he pecks her cheek in parting.

He opens her car door for her. "Tell Cary to come see me in the morning. I'll give him a job."

Birdie narrows her eyes. "Why would you do that?"

"To guarantee he moves out of your apartment on Friday. Besides, I had a salesperson quit last week, and I'm short staffed."

Birdie stuffs her key in the ignition. "Honestly, Stan, I'm not sure that's a good idea. Remember, he embezzled funds from his law firm."

"Which is why I won't let him near the cash register. Let me worry about it. I can handle Cary."

Birdie drives off with a sinking feeling in her gut. She's relieved Stan agreed to give her another chance, but something has shifted in their relationship. There's an awkwardness between them that didn't exist before. He's the same Stan, yet he's somehow different. She senses he's waiting for her to make another mistake.

And what about Cary? Nothing good will come from him working for Stan. Cary made it clear last night he wants her back. He's proven in the past he'll do whatever it takes to get what he wants. Would he stoop so low as to sabotage her relationship with Stan?

SIXTEEN

Hannah takes an immediate liking to Christine Cain. When Hannah enters the Brown Dog Deli on Broad Street in Charleston, Christine embraces her in a warm hug. She's striking with medium brown hair, doe eyes, and a heart-shaped face.

"I've been so excited to meet you," Christine says. "Professor Burgess speaks so highly of you."

Hannah smiles. "He speaks highly of you as well."

"Let's sit outside." Christine leads her through the restaurant to an umbrellaed table on the open-air terrace where they make small talk until the waitress brings their coffees.

"I've been studying your portfolio," Hannah says. "I'm impressed. Your choice of colors for your feminine designs are so unusual. The romance authors I work with will appreciate your style. In contrast, your mainstream illustrations are bold and eye-catching. I admire your versatility."

Christine beams. "Thank you."

After talking for a while about the technical aspects of design, Christine says, "I have plenty of geeky friends, but you're the coolest computer nerd I've ever met."

Hannah laughs out loud. "We're a rare breed." Christine's energy and determination match Hannah's. She's exactly the type of designer Hannah's looking for, and she's tempted to hire her on the spot. But to do so would put things in motion. There would be no turning back. She would have to spend her house money. She's eager to move forward. Yet she's scared to death. "On the phone, you mentioned you have reservations about staying in Charleston. Have you given that any more thought?"

Christine laughs. "For a millisecond, I was freaking out because all my high school friends have moved away. But I'm over it. I'll make new friends. The most important thing is to find the right career opportunity. Which leads me to my next question." Christine moves to the edge of her chair. "Would you consider taking on a partner? I don't have any start-up cash, but I've lived in Charleston all my life, and I have a ton of contacts. My parents are real estate brokers here. They know everyone in the city. They own a building across the street." She tosses her thumb over her shoulder. "The second floor has been vacant for years. They'll let us set up our offices there, rent-free. If you're interested, I can show you the building. I can live at home to save money, and I've convinced my parents into letting me stay on their health insurance plan through the end of next year." She pauses to take a breath before continuing. "I interviewed a ton last spring, and I was offered a bunch of jobs. But I turned them all down, because none of them excited me. Not the way the prospect of being your partner excites me."

"I can see you've given this a lot of thought." Hannah pauses as she considers Christine's proposal. Going into business with a virtual stranger is nuts. Although, while they've only just met, they have much in common—age, educational background, drive to succeed. Hannah has a gut feeling this is the right move. To have someone share the burden of the risks takes the edge off her fear. "What the heck? Let's go check out your parents' building."

Christine and Hannah jump to their feet and make their way back through the deli to the sidewalk. At the corner, they wait for the light to change before crossing Broad Street. They enter the real estate office, and Christine waves at an attractive man who is speaking intently with someone on the phone.

"That's my dad," she explains. "Mom's not working in the office today. She has a bunch of showings."

Hannah follows Christine up the open staircase that runs the length of one side of the building. Aside from a pair of restrooms, the entire second floor is a large open space with hardwood floors and windows overlooking Broad Street.

Christine knocks on the wall separating the main room from the restrooms. "We could paint this wall a dramatic color with our logo front and center. We can come up with a catchy name. Something like Chris Hannah Studio."

Hannah repeats the name. "It has a certain professionally trendy sound. Do you go by Chris?"

She shrugs. "Most of my friends call me Chris."

"I consider that a good omen. I had a close friend in college named Chris."

Chris circles the room. "We'll need rugs on the floor to absorb some of the sound. I'm thinking Lucite desks and white lacquer credenzas on the walls for storage. If we find we need privacy, we can create screens by hinging shutters together to section off the room."

Hannah envisions the setup. "A female powerhouse."

"Exactly." Chris offers Hannah a high five. Then her face falls. "I'm overwhelming you. My mom says I come on too strong sometimes. I understand you need to think about this. You may not even want a partner."

Hannah moves to the window and looks down Broad Street toward the harbor. The building's location is ideal, close to

Gus's school and to where she hopes to find an apartment. "I definitely need to think about it. But I'm open to the idea of a partnership. I recently turned down a similar opportunity, actually. While that situation wasn't the right fit for my company, I think you and I will blend well together. We will highlight our individual strengths and develop a brand based on the model we come up with."

"That sounds perfect." Chris joins her at the window. "When are you moving to Charleston?"

"Soon. My son starts preschool on July first. I have a three-year-old child, Chris. I hope that's not a problem for you." Out of the corner of her eye, Hannah watches for Chris's reaction.

Her face lights up. "Are you kidding me? I think that's so badass! I love kids. What's his name?"

"Gus." Hannah turns her back to the window. "Thanks for showing me the space. If we move forward with our partnership, I'd like to take your father up on his offer of free rent until we get our feet on the ground." Checking her watch, Hannah starts toward the stairs. "I better be going. I have an appointment to look at an apartment in twenty minutes."

"Cool! I'll walk out with you."

They wave to Chris's father, who is still on the phone, before exiting the building. On the sidewalk out front, Hannah says, "If you're free this afternoon, I'll call you when I head back to Palmetto Island, and we can talk some more."

Chris bounces on her toes. "Yes! I'll be waiting to hear from you. In the meantime, I'll come up with some more ideas."

"I can't wait to hear them. Does your brain ever stop spitting out ideas?"

"No!" Chris presses her hands against the sides of her head. "It's like a curse sometimes. If only I could flip a switch and turn it off."

Hannah laughs. "Don't you dare do that."

She gives Chris a quick hug and walks on air toward her car. Fate brought Chris and Hannah together—two young southern girls charting their paths toward success.

Birdie is in the kitchen making corn bread when Hannah arrives home with Gus. "How was Charleston?" she asks as she spoons sour cream into her batter.

"Interesting. Let me fix Gus's dinner, and I'll tell you about it." Hannah sets Gus down and goes to the refrigerator for the leftover container of chicken hash.

Gus throws his arms around Birdie's legs, burying his face in her apron. "Pick me up, puh-lease, Birdie."

Birdie turns off the mixing bowl and lifts her grandson into her arms. She cherishes these moments. When they move away, not seeing him every day will be hard. She nuzzles his neck, inhaling his funky little boy odor. "Somebody's tired. Did you have a big day, sweet boy?"

"Mm-hmm. I miss my daddy."

Birdie locks eyes with Hannah over the top of his head. "You'll see him soon."

Hannah heats a heaping spoonful of hash in the microwave and transfers it to Gus's plastic Thomas the Tank Engine plate. "Come here, you." Taking Gus from Birdie, she deposits him in the chair at the small table Birdie set up for him in the back corner.

Hannah grabs an apple from the refrigerator and leans back against the kitchen counter. "Chris and I really hit it off. She's amazingly talented, and has the most creative ideas. She suggested a partnership, and I think it's the perfect solution for both of us. Her parents own a building on Broad Street. They will let us have the second floor rent-free. It almost seems too good to be true."

Birdie looks up from greasing foil pans. "In my experience, when things seem too good to be true, they usually are."

"Not with Chris. Wait until you meet her, Mom. She's down to earth and hardworking. I checked her out with my old advisor at VCU. Professor Burgess gave his stamp of approval."

"Sounds like you've made up your mind."

"I'm getting there. I talked on the phone with her all the way back to the island. I don't have any serious reservations. But I'm going to sleep on it and talk to her again tomorrow before making my final decision."

Birdie removes the bowl from the mixer and pours batter into the foil pans. "Did you have any luck with your apartment search?"

"I found the perfect apartment on Queen Street. You would love the landlord. Her name is Heidi Butler. She owns Tasty Provisions, that popular gourmet shop on East Bay."

"I've heard of it!" Birdie says.

"Unfortunately, the rent is more than I can afford. The apartment, which occupies the second floor of a single house, has two bedrooms, an updated kitchen and bath, and a small yard for Gus. I met Hope, the woman who rents the apartment on the first floor. She's a single mom too. Her adorable daughter, Sally, is a year older than Gus."

"Since you don't have to pay rent for office space, maybe you can afford the apartment."

"That's a good point." Hannah takes the last bite of apple and chunks the core in the trash can. "We'll see. I may look at some other apartments on my way to Pawley's Island on Friday."

The back door swings open, and Cary saunters into the kitchen. "Birdie, I owe you one. The new job is working out well."

"You got a job?" Hannah says in an incredulous tone. "Who hired you?"

"Stan Morgan. I sold three kayaks and two wave runners today. According to Ron, the sales manager, that's a record for a Monday. Patty Dunn, the woman who bought the wave runners, is new in town. She just moved into the old Hitchcock Estate. She's also interested in purchasing paddleboards and a small Key West center console."

Birdie notices the gleam in his eye. Is Cary interested in Patty? Should Birdie warn the woman that she may be his next prey? *Nah*. His love life is no longer her business.

Gus leaves the table and runs to his grandfather, staring up at him with unadulterated admiration. "Pops, will you take me to the marina? I wanna see the fishing boats."

Cary looks over at Hannah. "If your mom says it's okay."

Hannah sighs. She can't compete with any of the men in her son's life. "I guess. But hold tight to his hand. And only go to the marina. No i-c-e c-r-e-a-m," she spells out.

Birdie watches them go. "It's almost pathetic how much that little boy needs a permanent male figure in his life."

Hannah frowns. "Don't I know it. You heard Gus when he first came in. He misses his daddy. But he barely even knows Ryan. I hope I'm doing the right thing in going to Pawley's this weekend. What if Ryan lets him down?"

"He'll survive." Birdie cups her daughter's cheek. "The way you did when your father let you down."

Hannah places her hand on Birdie's. "I take it you and Stan made up. I hope he knows what he's getting into by hiring Dad."

"He forgave me for lying, but we've agreed to slow things down. Our relationship was moving too fast for both of us. But I'm grateful to Stan for giving your dad a job. He wants to make certain Cary has enough money to move out of my apartment on Friday."

"Good!" Hannah rests her head on Birdie's shoulder. "Mom, will you be okay here alone once Gus and I leave?"

"I've been thinking about that a lot lately, actually. I may buy a small house of my own on the water. Our apartment has been our refuge these past few years. But I'm ready for a change too."

Hannah pushes away from Birdie. "What will you do with the apartment?"

"Rent it." Birdie crosses the kitchen to the coatroom. "I was thinking of adding a door here, so my tenant would have access to the apartment stairs but not the kitchen. I would need to add a stove and a full-size refrigerator to the kitchenette. The waterfront location should bring a handsome rent."

When Birdie turns away from the coatroom to face her daughter, she catches Hannah swiping tears from her eyes. "What's wrong, sweetheart?"

"I'm afraid. I'm ready for the change, but everything is happening so fast. How will I live day to day without you in my life?"

"You're going to adjust beautifully. You are stronger than most young women your age. I've done you a disservice by allowing you to stay under my wing for so long. There's a big world out there. Go with confidence! Make a name for yourself. You've worked so hard, you deserve success."

Hannah sniffles. "Thanks, Mom. Your faith in me means so much." She kisses Birdie's cheek before heading up the stairs.

Birdie's throat swells as she watches Hannah go. Her daughter is her pride and joy, and she will, without question, miss Hannah and Gus every day. But Charleston isn't that far away. And Birdie will manage her own life, just as she's managed every other change in her life. By putting one foot in front of the other and taking each day as it comes.

SEVENTEEN

The first rays of dawn are breaking through a layer of clouds when Hannah takes her kayak out on Tuesday morning. The tide is almost high, the water covering much of the marsh grass. With no camera to photograph wildlife, Hannah navigates her kayak down the inlet creek to their old house. The new owners have built an addition off the kitchen, and a large sport fishing boat is tied to the dock. All the good times spent here with her dad flood her memories. Cannonball contests off the dock. Floating down the creek in inner tubes. Playing flag football in the yard on Thanksgiving Day.

Her dad was her playmate while her mom was the one she turned to with skinned knees and friend problems. Birdie ran the household on a tight schedule, made sure Hannah's homework was done every night, and attended every single one of her events at school. Mother and daughter had drifted apart when Hannah went off to college. When Birdie's drinking became a problem.

Squeezing her eyes tight, Hannah tilts her head heavenward and asks God to give Birdie the strength to stay sober when she moves to Charleston.

Hannah turns the kayak around and heads away from the house. As she paddles against the incoming tide, she reminisces about digging for clams, string crabbing, and fishing for flounder. She'd wanted this inlet life for her son. Will their weekend visits to the island be enough?

Hannah is almost back at the dock when her cell phone rings in her shorts' pocket. *Who's calling so early? Did something happen to Gus?* She tugs her phone free of her pocket and accepts the call without looking at the screen. The sound of Ethan's voice on the other end surprises her.

"Good morning, Hannah. Are you out on the water?" Ethan says, sounding perfectly normal.

"I'm returning to the marina. What do you want, Ethan?"

"Ouch. Hostile. I guess, I deserve that. I want to explain why I haven't been in touch, and I'm curious what you're thinking about my offer."

"I'm no longer interested," she says and hangs up.

Furious, she rams the kayak into the dock and hoists it out of the water. He has some nerve leaving her hanging for more than a week and then reaching out to her as though nothing had happened. She waits for him to call her back, but she's not surprised when he doesn't. Ethan has proven unreliable. Which disappoints her. She had higher expectations of her ability to judge character. Is she wrong about Chris too? She seems like a genuine person. Then again, so did Ethan in the beginning.

After taking Gus to preschool, Hannah spends over two hours on the phone, grilling Chris about her work ethic and accomplishments to date. Chris answers all the questions to Hannah's liking. With her reservations resolved, they agreed to proceed with the development of Chris Hannah Designs.

"My godfather is an attorney," Hannah explains. "I'll have him draw up the papers to form our LLC."

"Awesome. I'm eager to get to work," Chris says. "I'll come up with some options for our logo. You mentioned a waiting list of potential clients."

"Yes! I can send it to you, if you're ready to reach out to them."

Hannah explains her steps for developing a website. Chris has suggestions on ways to improve it, and by the time they end the call, they have a process in place.

Thirty minutes later, Hannah is at her desk, having yogurt for lunch, when her mom calls up to her. "Hannah! You have a visitor."

Hannah barrels down the stairs to find her mom cutting out biscuits in the kitchen. "Who is it?"

Birdie smiles. "He didn't give me his name, but he's tall with sandy hair and lovely brown eyes."

Ethan. Hannah finds him sipping coffee at a table by the window in the cafe. As she approaches the table, she sees the dark semicircles underlining his eyes. "What're you doing here, Ethan?"

He stands to greet her. "I needed to see you in person. To explain." He gestures at the chair opposite her. "Can you give me five minutes?"

"Sure," she says reluctantly and drops down to the chair.

"You blindsided me when you told me about your son. Not because I disapprove. But because I didn't expect it. Like I told you, I'd checked you out. I don't know how I missed something so important. If anything, I think even more highly of you for being a single parent."

"Then why—"

He raises a hand to silence her. "I don't know why I was rude to you that night. I guess I needed time to wrap my mind around the idea of you having a child. I was planning to call you the next day to apologize. But during the night, my father had a massive heart attack."

Hannah gasps, and she brings her fingers to her lips. "Is he okay?"

Ethan's shoulders slump, as though he's bearing the weight of the world. "He will be. He's recovering from quadruple bypass surgery. My mom was so freaked out. We were both terrified we would lose him. I dropped the ball on everything at work. The surgery was Friday. When I finally came up for air, I realized I'd totally left you hanging."

"I'm so sorry, Ethan. I don't know what to say."

He holds his empty coffee mug out to her. "Say you'll get me more coffee."

"I can do that. I could use some too." She leaves the table with his empty mug and returns with two full ones.

Ethan continues, "Dad's prognosis is good, and my parents are more eager than ever to travel. Mom keeps asking about you. She wants to know if you're interested in living in the carriage house."

"Did you tell her I have a child?"

"Of course. But that doesn't matter. My parents love children. Dad will be thrilled to have a young boy around. Mom's afraid to be alone. I've been staying at the house since Dad's heart attack. She needs someone nearby she can trust. Someone she can call in an emergency."

"When I didn't hear from you, I thought you'd changed your mind about wanting to buy my company, and I pursued other opportunities." Hannah tells him about meeting Chris Cain and their decision to become partners.

Ethan nods his approval. "I don't know Chris personally. She's a few years younger than I am. But I know her family. The Cains will be a good networking source for you."

"Truth be told, Ethan, I don't think my company is a good fit for yours."

Ethan thinks about this. "You're right. I was trying to force a square peg into a round hole because I was so impressed with you." His expression lightens. "But hey, you're moving to Charleston, anyway. The offer of the carriage house still stands."

"Let me give it some thought. I've been looking for apartments. But I haven't found anything yet."

Ethan moves their mugs out of the way and reaches for her hands. "I've been thinking a lot about what you said on the boat that day. Given a choice between a business and romantic relationship with you, I pick romance." He runs his thumb across her fingers. "I have feelings for you, Hannah. Will you give us a chance? We don't have to work together to be a power couple."

A tingling sensation travels through her body as she stares down at their clasped hands. She imagines them married and living in a charming house on the Battery. They'll hire a nanny to take care of their brood of children while they run their highly successful web design firms.

The thought of Ryan brings her daydream to a screeching halt. When she looks up again, she realizes Ethan is waiting for her response.

"I have feelings for you too, Ethan." But she has feelings for Ryan as well. And she's suddenly overwhelmed by her feelings for both.

Ethan's lips part in a warm smile. "I'd like to meet your son. Is he here?"

"He's at day care." But Hannah needs to see how Gus interacts with Ethan. "If you have time, we can go get him and take him for a ride in the boat. I'd like to show you my inlet."

"I'll make time. That's an offer I can't refuse."

While Gus is thrilled by Hannah's untimely appearance at Miss Daisy's, he's skeptical about the tall man with her. But Ethan breaks the ice by offering Gus a piggyback ride back to the waterfront. At the marina, Ethan helps her untie the boat, and with Gus perched on the leaning post between them, she navigates away from the dock.

Ethan nudges Gus. "Tell me, little man. Do you have a girlfriend?"

Gus sticks out his tongue. "Girls are yucky. Robbie's my best friend. He didn't come to school today. He's sick." Gus tugs on Hannah's shirt sleeve. "Mommy, do I have to go back to Miss Daisy's?"

"Yes, sweetheart. I have work to do."

Ethan whispers in Gus's ear, loud enough for Hannah to hear. "Tell her you'll take a long nap if she lets you stay home."

"I'll take a long nap if you let me stay home." Gus presses his palms together. "Please, Mommy, please."

Hannah cuts her eyes at Ethan. "We'll see."

Ethan leans against the post and crosses his legs. "Do you like sports, buddy?"

"I watch baseball sometimes with Pops. But I wanna be a professional football player when I grow up."

"Oh, really?" Ethan winks at Hannah. What little boy doesn't want to play NFL when he grows up?

For the rest of the way to the mouth of the inlet, Ethan and Gus talk about football. Her son's knowledge of the NFL teams surprises her. Hannah knows little and cares less about sports. Did he learn this stuff from Robbie?

On the way back in, Gus falls asleep against Ethan's shoulder. "He's a great kid, Hannah. You've done an excellent job raising him."

"Thank you for saying that. But you can see he needs a male figure in his life." Hannah angles her body toward Ethan. "My life is a lot more complicated than it was a week ago. Gus's father appeared suddenly in our lives."

"You mean reappeared?"

"No. Appeared. I never told Ryan I was pregnant. I've been hiding out on the island, hoping he wouldn't find us. Then, out of the blue, Ryan stopped in the cafe on his way home from the beach on Memorial Day. Ryan wants to be a part of Gus's life. He wants to be a part of both our lives, actually."

"Oh. I see. So, I have competition. Talk about bad timing." Ethan stares off across the water. "If you don't mind me asking, why didn't you tell Ryan you were pregnant?"

"We'd broken up because he cheated on me."

"One strike against him."

"A big one," Hannah says. "I was angry and hurt, and I didn't want to share my child with him. I thought I could get away with him not knowing. And I did for three years." She looks away from Ethan. "For Gus's sake, I've agreed to give Ryan another chance. He's invited us to Pawley's Island to spend the weekend with his family."

"Selfishly, I hope it doesn't work out," Ethan says in a low voice.

They ride the rest of the way to the marina in silence. Ethan carries a sleeping Gus to the cafe before placing him in Hannah's arms. "Thanks for hearing me out and for introducing me to Gus."

"Thanks for coming down here. I'm sorry about your father, Ethan. I hope his health continues to improve."

He kisses her cheek. "The ball is in your court, Hannah. I hope to hear from you soon."

Her heart shrinks to the size of a pea as she watches him disappear around the building toward Ocean Avenue.

Her inner voices argue with each other.

"Go after him!"

"No! You owe it to Gus to give Ryan a second chance."

"Ethan is your guy. You felt something for him the first time you met."

"But you barely know Ethan. And you were once in love with Ryan."

"Were you, though? You were in college. Did Ryan ever make your heart do somersaults like Ethan does?"

"Oh, shut up!" she says out loud to the voice. Entering the cafe, she avoids her mother's curious gaze as she carries Gus through the kitchen. Upstairs, she tucks him into his toddler bed. How will Gus adapt to having his own room? What about the carriage house? Ethan didn't mention it again after she told him about Ryan. Is that because the lease has a strings-attached clause? Will his parents only rent to her if she's involved with Ethan? The location, the rent, the yard are all ideal. But what if she starts dating Ethan, moves into the carriage house, and they break up? That would make for an awkward situation whenever he visits his parents.

Hannah stretches out on her own bed. While she's sorry about his father's heart attack, she's relieved to know he had a legitimate reason for not calling her. She thinks back on their conversation.

I have feelings for you, Hannah. Will you give us a chance? We don't have to work together to be a power couple.

The voices return, but this time they agree. "Put Ethan out of your mind and keep your heart open for Ryan for now."

"Your weekend with Ryan will be very telling."

EIGHTEEN

On Wednesday afternoon, Birdie is manning the coffee bar for Amanda while she's at the dentist when Max comes barging through the door.

"Thank goodness you're here." Max collapses on top of the counter. "Give me a large coffee with an extra shot of caffeine."

"Think of the fortune I'd make if I *could* add extra caffeine." Birdie studies her friend's disheveled appearance as she pours the coffee. Max's cropped hair is sticking up straight, and mascara is smudged under her eyes. Birdie slides the cup across the counter. "You look awful. What happened?"

"A burst pipe. I was up half the night dealing with the flood. I'm so angry with Daniel for leaving me to deal with his dilapidated hotel." Max gestures at the row of empty tables along the banquette. "Can you take a break? You need to talk me off the ledge."

Birdie looks around the cafe. Customers occupy three tables, but no one is waiting in line for service. "I'm covering for Amanda until she returns from the dentist." She comes out from behind the counter. "But I can sit with you for a minute."

Birdie sits down next to Max on the banquette so she can monitor the coffee bar. "How bad is the water damage?"

"Really bad. My two best rooms are ruined. I'll have to hire a contractor to gut them, which means they are out of commission for the rest of the summer. I'm seriously considering selling that albatross. The land is worth a fortune. I could buy an oceanfront cottage and live out my life in peace." Max plants her elbows on the table and buries her face in her hands.

Birdie massages Max's shoulder. "Then what would you do? You love running the inn. You'd be bored sitting on the beach all day."

Max peeks at Birdie through parted fingers. "Who said anything about sitting on the beach all day?" She drops her hands and falls back against the bench. "I'll meet a wealthy man who owns his own private plane and travel with him around the world."

Birdie considers her fantasy. "That sounds lovely. And you may enjoy traveling. For a while. Until you grow restless. I know you, Maxine Summers. You're not happy when you're not productive."

"You have a valid point. But I've been putting Band-Aids on that hotel long enough. I have half a mind to close it down after the summer and renovate the entire building. Reconfiguring some of the suites will allow for more guest rooms. Which I definitely need. My business continues to grow. We're booked nearly year-round now. My guests love the beach in the fall and spring and even in December when they come from all over for the Boardwalk Festival of Lights."

"Then what're you waiting for?"

"Borrowing the money from the bank terrifies me. The economy is strong now, but travel is usually the first thing people cut out of their budget during a recession."

"I've never known you to talk yourself out of anything. You're usually full steam ahead when you come up with an idea. *And*, as you just pointed out, waterfront property in the center of a town as charming as ours will demand top price regardless of the economy. Selling the hotel is always an option if you get in over your head."

"That's true," Max says with a faraway look in her eyes.

Birdie leaves the table to wait on a customer. When she returns, Max says, "I haven't seen you in a week. Have you been hanging out with Stan, your new stud man?"

Birdie touches her fingers to her lips. "He is quite the stud." Her face warms. "We slept together, Maxie. Can you believe it?"

Max's brow hits her hairline. "Shut up! How was it?"

"Lovely." Without going into detail, Birdie tells Max about getting caught in the storm and their night of lovemaking on the boat. "We were ready for it. After a considerable amount of heavy making out, sex was a natural progression. Being with him felt so right. Like we were meant to be, however corny that sounds. And then I made a colossal mistake." She explains about the lie, and her subsequent argument with Stan.

A grave expression crosses Max's face. "That's not like you, Birdie. We've been friends since childhood, and I've never known you to tell a lie. Except that one time when we were really little."

"What time was that?"

"I was spending the night with you, and you told your mama we'd brushed our teeth when we hadn't. She washed your mouth out with soap for telling a lie."

Birdie shakes her head. "I don't remember that. Must have been some nasty tasting soap, though."

"Does any soap taste good?"

"You have a point." Birdie hangs her head. "I should've told Stan the truth when he asked about Cary, but I was afraid he'd think I was crazy for giving Cary a place to live after what he did to me." She watches her friend chew on her lower lip, fully expecting her to say her usual, "I told you so." Birdie is relieved and grateful when she doesn't.

Max drains the last of her coffee instead and slams the empty cup on the table. "I need more coffee."

Birdie's gaze shifts to the coffee bar. Amanda, who has returned from the dentist, is behind the bar replenishing napkin dispensers.

"You don't need more caffeine. You need fresh air." Birdie gets up and pulls Max to her feet. "Come on. Let's go for a walk."

Outside, a cool breeze blows off the water, a break from the humidity of the past few days. The two friends walk through the park and past the hotel.

Birdie pauses on the railing to look out over the marsh. "Stan says he wants to slow things down between us. I admit things were moving quickly. But it feels like he's pushing me away. We used to have a continuous stream of texts going. But I've heard from him only once since Sunday, a very formal text inviting me to come for dinner on Friday night."

"He just got scared, Birdie. He'll come around."

"Maybe. But I'm not sure I want him to. He's fun to be around with all his boats and water toys. And I enjoyed the companionship. But I feel like he's playing games with me, scrutinizing my every move with a microscope. I'm beginning to think no man is worth the heartache."

"I hear ya, girlfriend," Max says, giving Birdie a high five. "I've had a couple of dates this past week. They were both disasters."

"Why didn't you tell me?"

"Because I was embarrassed. I was the one who invited them out for drinks. One of the guys excused himself to go to the restroom and never came back."

Birdie leans in close to her friend. "Oh, Maxie. I'm so sorry. That's just awful."

"Not really. I was glad when he didn't come back," Max says with a chuckle. "The entire fifteen minutes we spent together, he talked about himself. And believe me, Kent is not nearly as exciting as he thinks he is." Max lets out a sigh. "Anyway, I've deleted my profile on MatchMade. If the right man comes along, great. If not, I have myself to keep me company. And myself is way better company than Kent."

Birdie digs her elbow into Max's side. "You have me."

"Ha. If you don't end up marrying Stan."

"I doubt I'll ever remarry. I value my independence." Turning her back to the water, Birdie says. "Look! That house is on the market." Crossing the boardwalk to the charming Cape Cod, she waves at the Realtor who is standing on the front porch looking anxiously at her phone.

Shannon steps down from the porch and cuts across the small green lawn. "Hey there, Birdie, Max. What're the two of you up to?"

"Just out for a walk," Birdie says. "I'm curious. How much are the owners asking for this house?"

Shannon hands Birdie a flyer. "Here's some basic information. But didn't Hannah call off her house search?"

"She did," Birdie says. "But I'm asking for me. I've always loved this house."

Shannon glances at her phone again. "Would you like a tour? My three o'clock appointment is ten minutes late."

Birdie shrugs. "Sure! Why not?"

"So, you're buying a house now?" Max asks, as she follows Birdie up the sidewalk.

"Maybe. I'm exploring my options. I feel the need for a change."

The interior of the house is nowhere near as charming as the exterior. Shannon babbles on about simple ways to improve the appearance, but Birdie isn't interested in paying above market value for a house that needs renovating.

Shannon's three o'clock appointment is waiting on the front porch when they exit the house. Birdie thanks Shannon for her time, and then heads off with Max down the boardwalk.

Max, struggling to keep up with her, asks, "What was that all about? I thought you loved your apartment."

"I do. But I miss not having a yard, and I'm tired of eating my meals in a commercial kitchen."

"Why not redo your kitchenette?" Max suggests. "You have the room in your apartment to add a small kitchen with an eat-in counter."

Birdie slows her pace as she considers her suggestion. "That's not a bad idea."

"There's nothing you can do about a yard, but you have amazing views of the inlet."

"True." Birdie surprises herself by bursting into tears. "Now that Hannah's moving to Charleston . . ."

Max embraces her. "Oh, honey. Hannah's only moving to Charleston, not California."

Birdie nods into Max's shoulder. "And I'm grateful for that. But I'm afraid of being alone. What if I start drinking again?"

Max hugs her tighter. "You won't! You'll go to meetings, and you'll lean on me. Like you did last time. You'll get through this. We'll find a new hobby or learn a new craft."

Birdie sniffles. "We can take up paddleboarding."

"Exactly. Think about how toned our bodies will be."

Birdie pushes away from Max, and they walk the rest of the way in silence. When they reach the hotel, Max gives Birdie another quick hug. "You're gonna be fine. I promise," Max says and disappears inside.

Her best friend means well. Birdie has always been able to count on Max. But it's not the same as having her daughter and grandson living with her.

Birdie thinks about what Max said earlier. *I have myself to keep me company.* Birdie failed miserably the last time, after Cary disappeared and she was left with only herself for company. But she has a business to run now. And Max and Sadie and Stan in her life. Well . . . maybe not Stan.

———

Hannah bounds down the stairs into the kitchen. "Sadie, have you seen my mom?"

"She was out front with Max. But they left a little while ago. Not sure where they went."

"Okay. Thanks." She passes through the cafe and out the front door where she finds Birdie on the boardwalk, looking out across the inlet with a faraway look in her eyes.

Hannah joins her at the railing. "Mom! I need to talk to you."

Birdie ignores her. "Hannah, will you teach me how to drive the boat?

"You mean now? But I—"

"Yes, now. I'm getting the boat in the divorce settlement, and I want to learn how to drive it. We can talk while we're out on the water."

"Okay. Let me run and get the key." Hannah hurries up to the apartment and is back in a flash with the boat key. With Hannah in the lead, they walk single file down the ramp to the dock. Over her shoulder, she says to her mom, "I can't believe you don't how to drive the boat."

"I never needed to. Your father was usually at the wheel."

They board the boat, and Hannah hands Birdie the key. "Always start the engine before you untie from the dock."

"Right. In case it doesn't start." Birdie turns the key in the ignition, and the engine comes to life.

"Now we can untie from the dock. You get the stern lines, and I'll get the bow." After the boat is free of the dock, Hannah shows her mother how to move the throttle forward to put the boat in gear. "Now steer out of the slip like you would a car, careful not to ram the stern into the dock. Driving a boat is easy. You just need to get a feel for it. Go slow until we're out of the marina."

Once they reach the creek, Hannah places her hand on top of Birdie's and eases the throttle forward, increasing the speed a tad. She drops her hand. "You're the captain. The inlet is yours."

"I'll just putt-putt around for a few minutes," Birdie says with arms straight and fingers gripping the steering wheel.

Hannah nudges her. "Relax, Mom. Boating is meant to be fun."

"Right," Birdie says, relaxing her shoulders. She looks over at Hannah. "What did you want to talk to me about?"

Hannah sinks back against the leaning post. "Ryan texted me. He wants us to come to Pawley's tomorrow instead of Friday. He says his parents are dying to meet us. I have a bad feeling about this, Mom."

"A bad feeling about what, exactly? Ryan? Or his parents? Or does it have something to do with Ethan's visit yesterday?"

Hannah considers her answer carefully before responding. "All the above. Ethan's father had a heart attack. He needed open heart surgery. That's why he hasn't called. I turned down his offer. We agree our firms aren't a great fit. But he has feelings for me, and me for him."

"I thought so," Birdie says. "Why don't you compromise and go to Pawley's on Friday morning? As much as you're dreading it, this trip will help you see things clearer."

"You're right. That's what I should do." Hannah pulls out her phone and types a quick text to Ryan. *Can't come until Friday morning. Looking forward to seeing you then.*

He texts back right away. *Darn. I was hoping for a moonlit stroll on the beach tomorrow night.*

Hannah gawks at her phone. Is he joking? A moonlit stroll on the beach? Who's gonna watch Gus? She doesn't respond.

"I think I'll take up fishing," Birdie says, interrupting Hannah's thoughts.

Hannah stuffs her phone into her back pocket. "Why fishing? What's with this sudden obsession with water activities?"

"I need to find a new hobby to occupy my time when you and Gus leave." Tears glisten in Birdie's eyes behind her sunglasses.

Hannah rests a hand on Birdie's shoulder. "I'm sorry, Mom."

Birdie shakes her head. "Don't be. Moving to Charleston is the right thing for you and Gus. I'll be fine. I just need to stay busy."

"Now's the perfect time for you to focus your attention on the cafe."

"What do you mean?" Birdie asks, her brows pinched. "Is something wrong with the cafe?"

"You've always said you want the cafe to be more restaurant than bakery. But you only have a few sandwiches on the menu. And customers still have to wait in line to place their orders. You could hire some servers and expand your hours into the evening."

Birdie lets out a grunt. "Fishing sounds simpler. And less risky. In order to serve dinner, if I want to be successful, I would need to get a liquor license. And storing alcohol in the cafe is too close for comfort."

Hannah narrows her green eyes. "But you've stayed sober for almost three years."

Birdie white-knuckles the steering wheel. "That doesn't mean I haven't wanted to drink in three years."

"Really? Why haven't you ever said anything?"

"I've said plenty at my AA meetings." A distant look settles over Birdie's face, as though lost in thought. "I admit I like the concept of serving dinner. I could keep the liquor locked up after hours."

Hannah gives her arm a shove. "That's the right attitude."

While Birdie navigates the boat through the small creeks around the marina, Hannah launches suggestions on ways to grow the business. "You could continue to staff the baked goods and coffee counters, as you do now. You have plenty of room to add more tables inside, and you could put a few umbrellaed tables on the boardwalk. The kitchen can easily handle the additional food preparation."

Birdie lets out a sigh. "This sounds like an enormous undertaking."

"Not really. Not in terms of capital. You could even do it a little at a time." When they round the bend and the marina comes into view, Hannah sweeps her arm at the buildings along the boardwalk. "Palmetto Island is growing. It's only a matter of time before a developer expands the boardwalk and builds on the land north of Ocean Avenue."

"You're right. I'll give it some thought. But for now, I need to learn how to dock this boat."

"I'm not sure you're ready for docking. Backing into the slip can be tricky."

When Hannah tries to hip-bump her out of the way, Birdie holds tight to the wheel. "Let me try. If I can't handle it, you can take over."

"If you insist," Hannah says in a skeptical tone.

She coaches Birdie as she maneuvers the boat into position with the stern facing the slip. "Okay, now put the boat in reverse and slowly ease in."

"Reverse is the opposite direction of forward, right?" Without waiting for Hannah to show her, Birdie moves the throttle into reverse and speeds up.

"Mom! What're you doing?" Hannah grabs the wheel and throws the throttle into neutral. She tries to grab hold of a piling, but the boat has momentum, and the stern crashes into the dock, cracking the engine's cover.

Birdie's hand flies to her mouth. "Oopsie. Maybe I should learn to kayak first."

Hannah laughs out loud. "You did fine. You just need to work on docking."

They secure the lines and survey the damage to the cover. In response to Birdie's long face, Hannah says, "Don't worry, Mom. I'm sure Stan can fix it for you or order a new one."

Birdie looks at Hannah as if she's lost her mind. "That would mean confessing to Stan that I wrecked the boat. I'll figure out something else."

Hannah and Birdie walk with linked arms up the dock to the boardwalk. "I admire your spunk, Mom. You're gonna do great. Your drinking problem is in the past. Only smooth sailing ahead for you."

"Sailing! That might be a better choice for me than a motorboat."

Hannah laughs. She loves being with her mom. But she's excited about the prospect of a new life. Of making new friends and discovering new hangouts. Of no longer having to hide.

NINETEEN

G us is keyed up over the prospect of seeing his dad. He exhausts himself from talking about Ryan and falls asleep before they cross the Ashley River into Charleston. As Hannah drives through downtown, she envisions Ethan at work in his office near the harbor. She yearns to stop in for a visit. To walk with him hand-in-hand along the seawall. To have coffee with Liza, followed by a working lunch with Chris. She's ready for her new life now. July is three weeks away, which feels like an eternity. She needs to find somewhere to live. The house on Queen Street would be ideal if the rent weren't so high.

Hannah glances at the clock on the dashboard and then over at her sleeping son. They got an early start, and she has plenty of time. What harm is there in driving by the house? Making a hard right onto Rutledge Avenue, she drives through the MUSC campus and across Calhoun Street, turning left onto Queen Street at Colonial Lake.

A little voice from the back seat says, "Are we at Pawley's Island, Mommy?"

"No, sweetheart. We're in Charleston. I need to make a quick stop. It won't take long."

Hannah parks on the curb in front of the gray single house. Hope is sitting on the porch steps reading a magazine while Sally plays in the sandbox in the side yard.

Hannah gets out of her Jeep and approaches the waist-high fence. "Hey there!"

Hope looks up from her magazine. "Hey, Hannah! Are you back for another look?"

She shakes her head. "I'm just driving by on my way to Pawley's Island for the weekend."

Hope gets up and walks over to the fence. "Are you still interested in renting the apartment? Sally would love to have a neighbor friend."

"I love the apartment. But I can't afford the rent. Do you think there's any chance Heidi would negotiate?"

Hope's smile lights up her face. She's pretty in a soft way that hints at a genuine soul. "You never know. She might. She's upstairs now. Why don't you ask her?"

Hannah frowns. "Is she showing the apartment to someone?"

"She might be getting ready for a showing, but she's alone right now." Hope notices Gus in the back seat. "Aww. Is that your little boy? Why don't you let him play with Sally while you talk to Heidi?"

"Really? That'd be great," she says and helps Gus out of the Jeep. "I want you to meet some friends of mine. Gus, this is Miss Hope and her daughter, Sally."

Hearing her name, Sally leaves the sandbox and runs around the fence to Gus. "Wanna play trucks with me?" She points at three large earthmovers in the sandbox.

Gus wrinkles his nose. "But you're a girl."

"So?" Sally gives him a sassy head shake, her blonde

ponytail bouncing on her shoulders. "Girls can play trucks too."

"Okay," Gus says in a shy voice. Is he intimidated by this adorable creature who looks like a girl but acts like a boy?

"Come on." Sally takes him by the hand and drags him to her sandbox.

Hannah watches them go. "I think Gus may have met his match."

Hope nods toward the house. "Good luck with Heidi. And take your time. We'll be right here."

"Thanks." Hannah retrieves her bag from the car and climbs the steps to the second-floor apartment. The door is open and she wanders in, admiring the open floor plan with large living room and adjacent kitchen.

Heidi looks up from wiping down the kitchen counter. "Hey, Hannah," she says, blowing a strand of bleached blonde hair out of her face. "This is a surprise."

"I was on my way through town, and I thought I'd drive by. I was hoping to see the apartment again, if it's still available."

"Oh. Gosh." Heidi sets her sponge in the sink and comes from behind the counter. "I took a verbal commitment on the phone this morning from a young couple moving to the area from Chicago. I was just sprucing things up for them. They're planning to move in on Sunday. I'm sorry. If I'd known you were serious about it . . ."

"The rent is more than I can afford, but thanks, anyway." Tears sting Hannah's eyelids as she turns to leave.

Heidi follows her out onto the piazza, and placing a hand at the small of her back, she walks Hannah to the railing. "I'm sorry. You'll find something else. Houses and apartments come up for rent all the time around here. If I hear of anything, I'll be sure to give you a call."

"I'd appreciate that."

They stand at the balcony, watching the kids play in the sandbox. "He's adorable," Heidi says. "I love the blond curls. What's his name?"

"Gus. We should get going. We're on our way to Pawley's for the weekend. Have a good day, Heidi. And sorry for barging in."

Hannah feels Heidi's eyes on her as she descends the stairs, claims her son, and says goodbye to Hope and Sally. Gus sobs as she buckles him into his car seat. "I wanna play with Sally."

"We're going to see your daddy, remember? He's waiting for us." Swallowing past the lump in her throat, she retrieves her iPad from her bag, accesses the *PAW Patrol* episodes she downloaded, and places it in his lap.

Tears stream down Hannah's cheeks as she pulls away from the curb and makes her way through downtown. Serves her right for being so indecisive. While the rent is higher than she'd budgeted, she probably could have made it work. She was afraid to commit for fear of . . . for fear of what? Something better coming along? Her deal with Chris falling through? Leaving Birdie's nest?

She wipes her eyes and steadies her breath, collecting herself for the drive across the intimidating Ravenel Bridge. She's on the descent into Mount Pleasant when her phone rings. The sound of Chris's voice perks Hannah up. "I found matching fake Oriental rugs in my parents' attic. Mom says we can have them for our office. They're beautiful, Hannah, in shades of pinks and grays. Envision this. The rugs will go under our desks, which will face away from the windows. Screens painted a high-gloss pale gray will separate our work-spaces. We'll have pendant lights and credenzas against the wall with floating shelves above them. What do you think?"

Hannah smiles. Chris's enthusiasm is contagious. "Love it."

"Awesome! There's more. Our conference table will go in

the center of the room, and in front of our logo wall, we'll stage the waiting area with a sofa, chairs, and a fluffy rug. Oh, and we'll have stacks of hip magazines like *Garden and Gun* on the coffee table. I know it sounds like a lot, but we don't have to do it all at once."

Hannah thinks about her life savings, sitting in her bank account, waiting to be spent. She already missed out on her dream apartment. She can't let her fears hold her back any longer. "We can probably do a lot now if we make smart purchases."

"Yay! I was hoping you'd say that. I created a Pinterest board with some ideas. I'll go through my parents' attic again. My mom has excellent taste. I'm sure I can find some more odds and ends. Please tell me you're moving to Charleston soon. I'm dying to get started."

"As soon as I find an apartment," Hannah says and tells Chris about losing out on the Queen Street house.

"Bummer. That's a great location. But there are plenty of others. Why don't you come to Charleston early next week? I'll help you find something."

"That would be great. How about Monday?"

"Monday works," Chris says, and for the rest of the ninety-minute drive to Pawley's, they discuss ideas for decorating their office.

Despite stopping in Charleston, Hannah and Gus arrive at the beach cottage a few minutes before eleven. The three-story oceanfront house is built on stilts with tan siding and a red tin roof. Gus runs ahead of her up the front brick steps. She rings the doorbell and bangs the knocker. When no one answers, they go around to the ocean side of the house. The screen door is unlocked, and a set of french doors are open to allow in the ocean breeze.

Taking a tentative step into the living room, Hannah calls out, "Hello! Is anyone home?"

Ryan, with bedhead and bloodshot eyes, emerges from a hallway off to her right. "You're here. I didn't expect you so early."

"Early? I told you we'd be here by lunchtime. Are you just waking up? I haven't slept this late since . . ."—Hannah pauses to think—"since Gus was born."

"Daddy!" Gus throws himself at Ryan's knees, knocking him off balance.

"Hey there, buddy. I missed you." Ryan picks Gus up and twirls him around. "Are you ready to have some fun?"

Gus tosses his hands in the air. "Yippee!" He wraps his arms around Ryan's neck. "Will you always be my daddy?"

"You betcha." Ryan tickles Gus's tummy. "Are you ready to go to the beach?"

"We need to change first," Hannah says. "Our bags are in the car."

"Why don't you get those while Gus and I swing in the hammock?" Ryan carries Gus to the hammock and falls in backward. The two burst into fits of giggles.

Hannah glares at Ryan. Is he seriously making her get her own bags?

Ryan points up at Hannah. "Look at the mean mommy."

"I'm warning you, Ryan, I'm raising my son to be a gentleman. Don't you dare teach him bad habits." She storms off the porch before he can respond.

Hurrying out to the car, she returns laden down with their suitcase, beach totes, and a gift bag of edible goodies for his parents. "Are your parents here?"

"No, they're playing golf in Litchfield."

Golf? She thought his parents were excited to meet her. She holds up the gift bag. "Where should I put this?"

"Just set it down anywhere." His indifference to her gift irritates her. Never mind that she spent nearly eighty dollars at Corks and Nibbles on cocktail nuts and a nice bottle of wine.

She places the bag on a nearby table. "Where should we change?"

"I'll show you the upstairs." Ryan untangles himself from the hammock, and tossing Gus over his shoulders like a sack of potatoes, he carries him up to the second floor. "You have the entire floor to yourself. Sleep wherever you like."

Hannah drops their bags in the hallway and takes Gus from him. "We'll be down in a few minutes."

She waits for Ryan to leave before setting Gus down. "Would you like to sleep in your own room, buddy? I'm sure we can find two that connect."

Gus shakes his head vehemently. "I wanna sleep with you."

Hannah has her work cut out for her when they move into their own place. "Okay then. I'll let you pick which room."

Racing up and down the hallway, out of the five other bedrooms, Gus chooses the largest oceanfront room with an en suite bath featuring a gigantic soaking tub and a glass shower. Changing into their bathing suits, they wait for Ryan in the rockers on the screened porch. Fifteen minutes later, he saunters out with coffee in one hand and a piece of jellied toast in the other. "Ready?"

Hannah eyes the toast. How rude of him not to offer them anything. She's not hungry, but Gus will be soon. Why didn't she think to bring snacks? "Maybe we should pack a picnic for the beach."

Gus nods. Looking up at Ryan, he says, "I'm a growing boy. I need lots of food."

Ryan stuffs the last of his toast in his mouth. "How about we have a snack now, and I'll take you out for a late lunch later?"

Hannah rises out of the chair to face him. "Children have schedules, Ryan. Gus eats breakfast around seven. Lunch at noon. And dinner at five thirty or six."

"That's fine when he's with you. When he's with me, he'll need to be more flexible."

When he's with me? A flash of anger hits her like a bolt of lightning. "I made a mistake in coming here." Hannah lifts Gus from the chair and starts toward the stairs.

Ryan hurries after her. "Please don't go, Hannah. I'm sorry. I didn't mean to make you mad. It's just that . . ." He grabs her arm, preventing her from going up. "This is my family's one vacation a year. We value our beach week. We stay up late talking and watching fireworks on the porch. We sleep late in the mornings and take naps in the afternoons. And we eat when we get hungry."

Hannah softens as the tension leaves her body. She doesn't remember the last family vacation she took with her parents. "That's fine for you and your parents. You are adults. But Gus gets cranky when he's hungry. Once you witness the meltdown, you'll never let it happen again."

Ryan laughs. "Understood. Let's go pack a lunch. I know we have peanut butter and jelly, and I'm pretty sure Mom bought sandwich meat at the store."

Hannah loses herself in the summer's hot new romance novel while Ryan and Gus swim in the ocean and play in the sand. If Ryan is going to be a father to their son, he needs to be all in. And that includes allowing Hannah time to relax.

Around three o'clock, Hannah looks up to see dark clouds overhead. "Looks like rain. We should go up. Gus needs to take a nap, anyway."

Upstairs in their room, she gives Gus a bath, puts on his pajamas, and tucks him into the king-size bed. After a long hot shower, she dresses in jean shorts and a pink sleeveless top, and takes her novel and baby monitor down to the porch. She's no sooner settled into the hammock when Ryan comes out onto the porch with his hair still damp from the shower.

When he drops into the hammock beside her, she stares at him with one brow raised. "What do you think you're doing?"

"Snuggling with you." He throws his leg over hers. "Nap time for the kids means playtime for the grownups."

"If *playtime* means what I think it means, it's not happening."

"Come on, Hannah. Doesn't the rain make you horny?" When he moves in closer, she feels his erection against her thigh.

She knees his leg off hers. "Forget it, Ryan."

"Geez, Hannah! I don't remember you being such a buzzkill in college."

"Because I didn't have a child in college."

A rustling sound catches Ryan's attention, and he sits up in the hammock, looking around for the source of the noise. Spotting the monitor on a nearby table, he says, "Are you kidding me? You brought a monitor with you? The kid is right upstairs. You can hear him crying if he needs you. Stop pampering him, Hannah. And toughen him up."

"You stop telling me how to parent my child. You've been a father for less than two weeks, which hardly makes you an expert."

She moves from the hammock to a rocker, sticking her nose in her novel. A few minutes later, Ryan sits down beside her. "I'm sorry. We're getting off on the wrong foot, and it's my fault. We have a lot of catching up to do. Why don't you tell me about your life?"

His tone is genuine, the Ryan she remembers from college. Hannah closes her novel.

As the rain beats steadily on the roof, she tells him about the stormy night Gus was born and everything that's happened to her in the three years since. When she tires of talking about herself, she questions him about law school and the type of law he wants to practice. Hannah imagines what life might be like as the wife of a prominent attorney. She was crazy in love with Ryan in college. But that spark no longer exists. Her heart doesn't pitter patter when he flashes those dimples. Perhaps, over time, she'll develop new feelings for him based on their mutual love for Gus. But is that what she really wants? Why should she settle for anything less than true love? Ethan comes to mind, his warm brown eyes that melt her heart. Should she sacrifice happily ever after with Ethan in order to give Gus a nuclear family with both his biological parents?

Ryan's parents return home around four. Sylvia and Patrick Stevenson make a striking couple. He has strong facial features with dark hair, graying at the temples, and she's a platinum blonde with Gus's and Ryan's crystal blue eyes. Sylvia speaks in a sugary tone, but the slight curl of her lip suggests she's not as sweet as she sounds.

Sylvia looks around the porch. "Where's the babe?"

"He's taking a nap," Ryan answers.

Sylvia clasps her hands together. "Wake him up! I'm dying to meet him."

Hannah has no intention of waking Gus before he's ready to get up. "He won't sleep much longer."

Sylvia consults her Cartier watch. "I hope not. It's already four o'clock. I need to get ready for dinner soon. We have drinks with the Pattersons at six, and then a seven o'clock reservation at Frank's Outback."

Drinks? Dinner? Hannah thought Ryan's parents were eager to spend time with their grandson.

Sylvia continues, "I took the liberty of hiring a babysitter. Rebecca is a darling looking girl. I met her on the beach yesterday. Her family is staying a few doors down."

Irritation crawls across Hannah's skin. She's not used to

people making plans for her without consulting her first. "I'm sorry, but I'm particular about babysitters." She only trusts four people to keep Gus—Birdie, Max, Daisy, and Sadie.

Ryan places a reassuring hand on Hannah's arm. "Don't worry. We'll stay home. We'll order a pizza or something. Hannah's a little overprotective of our son," he says to his parents.

Hannah cuts her eyes at him. "Because Gus is a rambunctious little boy. He needs to be watched every single second."

Through the monitor comes the sound of Gus's little voice calling for her.

"Speak of the little devil. I'll be right back." When she moves to get up, Ryan pulls her back down to the chair. "Let me go."

After Ryan leaves, an awkward silence settles over the porch as voices spill out from the monitor.

"Hey there, buddy," Ryan says to Gus. "Did you have a good nap?"

"Yes. Where's my mommy?"

"She's downstairs. Come on. I want you to meet *my* mommy and daddy."

A minute later, Ryan exits the house with Gus in the crook of his left arm and a beer in his right hand. When Sylvia casts a disapproving glance at the beer, he holds up the bottle. "It's five o'clock somewhere."

Ryan's parents bend over to speak to Gus. "Aren't you adorable," Sylvia says, close to Gus's face.

"The resemblance is uncanny," Patrick adds. "He's the spitting image of Ryan at that age."

Gus holds his stuffed alligator in front of his face.

"Isn't that cute?" Sylvia says. "Does your alligator have a name?"

"Atticus." Gus wiggles out of Ryan's arms and climbs onto Hannah's lap, burying his face in her chest.

"Aww, look." Sylvia clutches her husband's arm. "He's shy."

Patrick grunts. "I don't remember Ryan being timid."

"He's neither shy nor timid," Hannah says in a defensive tone. "He's not used to strangers crowding him."

Sylvia straightens. "Make yourself at home while you're here, dear," she says to Hannah. "If there's anything you need, Ryan can get it for you."

"Yes, ma'am. Thank you for having me."

"You're welcome." She gives Gus a pat on the head. "Well then, I'm off to take a long hot bath."

"And I'm going to close my eyes for a few minutes," Patrick says, following his wife off the porch.

Ryan guzzles the remainder of his beer and goes to the kitchen for another. He returns with two bottles, but instead of offering one to Hannah, he stuffs the second in the pocket of his board shorts. "Looks like it stopped raining. Let's go for a walk on the beach."

"Yes! Let's!" Gus says, sliding out of Hannah's lap to his feet.

The rain drove vacationers to their cottages, and they have the beach to themselves. But instead of racing about, chasing birds and skipping through the surf, Gus sticks close to Hannah's side. They walk for close to an hour, and when they return, Hannah is relieved to see Sylvia and Patrick have already left for the evening. Ryan orders the pizza, pours himself a scotch on the rocks, and they go out to the porch to wait for the delivery man. Sticking his thumb in his mouth, Gus curls up in Ryan's lap.

"Is he always so clingy?" Ryan asks. "He's been kinda whiny too, since he woke up from his nap."

"He's just overwhelmed. This is all new for him. Big house and new people," Hannah says, despite being worried. Gus has seemed off all afternoon. When he refuses pizza, her concern mounts.

"Do you feel okay, sweetheart?" She presses her cheek against Gus's forehead. "You're burning up. I think you have a fever."

Seated at the breakfast room table, Ryan slides his chair away from Gus. "Is he contagious?"

"Probably not. Kids get all kinds of summer viruses. His friend Robbie missed school earlier in the week."

"What do we do?" Ryan asks, his eyebrows pinched together into one.

"Give him some Advil to lower the fever."

Ryan jumps to his feet. "I'll get it. My parents have some in their bathroom."

"We need liquid Advil, Ryan. For children. He's too young to swallow pills."

"Then I'll go to the store," Ryan says, grabbing a set of car keys out of the bowl in the center of the table.

"No, wait! You've been drinking all afternoon. I'll go." She retrieves her purse from her bedroom.

Ryan calls after her, "There's a Walgreen's just up the road before you get to Highway 17."

Gus runs after her, sobbing and hugging her legs. "Don't go, Mommy! Please, don't leave me."

She looks over at Ryan. "I need some help here. I can't take him with me."

"Why not? Can't you leave him in the car for a few minutes?"

Hannah's jaw hits the floor. "Are you out of your mind?" She kneels down in front of her son. "I'll be right back, sweetheart. I'm going to the store for some medicine to make you feel better." She picks Gus up and places him in Ryan's lap. The sounds of her son's screams follow her out.

Leave him in the car for a few minutes? One doesn't have to be a parent to know how dangerous that would be. After such a comment, she may never feel comfortable leaving Gus in Ryan's care. She doesn't wish her son ill, but his virus may be a convenient excuse for cutting short their weekend.

TWENTY

W hen Birdie arrives at Stan's for dinner, she finds him in the kitchen preparing the baby back ribs for grilling. He's so focused on sprinkling rub mixture on the meat, he doesn't notice when she enters the room. Her gaze shifts to the ribs, which are coated in an excess of seasoning.

"Stan! What're you doing? That's way too much." She drops her bag on the floor and takes the condiment bottle from him.

With a dazed expression, he looks from the ribs to her and back to the ribs. "I guess I ruined dinner."

"No, you didn't." Transporting the ribs to the sink, she rinses off the rub, pats the meat dry, and returns the rack to the platter. "Let me do it this time."

"Have at it, if you think you can do a better job," he says in a snippy tone.

Birdie frowns. "What's wrong, Stan? You don't seem like yourself."

"Did Cary move out today?"

Her skin prickles. *Cary again. Be cool, Birdie. You've done nothing wrong.* "Yes. Thank goodness, he's gone. He made friends with the new owner of the Hitchcock Estate. He's renting her garage apartment." She snickers. "Poor woman. I hope she knows what she's getting into." She sprinkles rub on the ribs. "There. Now. That's better." She looks up at Stan and their eyes meet.

"Birdie, are you sleeping with Cary?"

Her mouth falls open. "What? No! Why would you ask that?"

"Because Cary hinted that the two of you are . . . you know, being intimate."

"Cary is a liar and a cheat! He's just trying to cause trouble. I warned you about him when you hired him. You should fire him."

"I can't. He's too good of a salesperson." The lines in Stan's forehead deepen as he studies her. "Are you sure you're not sleeping with him?"

Birdie squirms under his intense gaze. "Of course, I'm sure. I would know if I'm sleeping with someone, Stan."

"I'm sorry. But I have a hard time believing you after you lied to me."

"That's your problem." Birdie slams the condiment bottle down on the counter. "This isn't working for me. Last week was blissful. But you're a different man this week. I feel like a lovesick teenager whose boyfriend can't decide whether to break up with her. But you know what, Stan? You don't get to make all the decisions about our relationship." She jabs her thumb at her chest. "*I'm* deciding I don't want to be with *you*. Not like this. Not unless you trust me. I understand that trust is earned, and once broken, it's difficult to repair. But you won't even give me a chance."

Birdie waits for him to say something, but he remains silent, staring down at the seasoned raw meat.

"I have a lot going on in my life. I need someone who will

support me. Not someone who is watching and waiting for me to make a mistake." Crossing the kitchen, she retrieves her purse and swings open the back door. "Goodbye, Stan." She hesitates in the doorway, waiting for him to call her name or come after her. When he doesn't, she kicks the door shut and runs to her car.

Tears blur her vision as she pulls out of his driveway and heads back to the waterfront. She was doing fine on her own. Until Max convinced her to join MatchMade. She slows down as she passes the liquor store. She can almost taste the vodka. Stomping on the accelerator, she circles the block and parks in the liquor store parking lot.

Don't do it, Birdie. She throws the car in reverse, peels out of the parking lot, and speeds home.

Back at her apartment, she paces the floor with her phone gripped in her hand. Why doesn't Stan call? Why is he taking Cary's word over hers? Why does she even care? *Grow a spine, Birdie. You don't want him if he's going to treat you this way.*

Her stomach is in knots, and she's afraid she might vomit. If only she had a drink. One teensy glass of Pinot Grigio to take the edge off. She stares at the phone. *A watched phone never rings, Birdie.* She hurls the phone across the room. It lands on the rug and tumbles beneath the coffee table.

When live bluegrass music drifts up from next door, she moves to the window and observes the crowd on Shaggy's porch, enjoying their Friday evening happy hour. She longs to join them. *Don't go there, Birdie.*

Birdie lets out a series of screams, her howls echoing throughout the building. The exertion depletes her, zapping her negative emotions and leaving her feeling somewhat calmer.

"Good riddance, Cary," she says out loud to the empty living room. At least she has many wonderful memories from the past three years to comfort her during sad times. This tiny apartment is her home. She's comfortable here. So what if she doesn't have a yard? She has an inlet, which is even better.

Grabbing a tape measure and notepad from her junk drawer, she measures the kitchenette and space around it. Max was right. She has ample room to create a small kitchen with an eat-in counter. Seated at the table with her laptop, she pins photos of space-saving kitchens to a Pinterest board.

When she looks up from her computer, she's surprised to see the room has grown dark. She retrieves her phone from under the coffee table. There are no texts or missed calls from Stan. A heaviness overcomes her. He's throwing their chance at happiness away because of Cary's lie.

When cheers erupt outside, Birdie grabs her bag and hurries down the stairs, out the back door, and around the building to Shaggy's. The crowd on the porch is thinning. Only a few tables are occupied. She claims an empty stool at the bar and orders wine. When the bartender sets the glass in front of her, Birdie's mouth salivates, but she doesn't take a sip. To break sobriety means losing control. And Birdie is no longer weak and vulnerable, despite how Stan makes her feel. She's been strong for Hannah these past few years. She'll continue to be strong for herself after Hannah's gone.

Max appears suddenly at her side. "What're you doing?" she asks, snatching the wineglass away.

Birdie shifts on the barstool toward Max. "I was having a moment. But it passed. What're you doing? Are you here alone?"

Max's eyes travel the porch. "No. Yes. Both. I was supposed to meet someone, but he's thirty minutes late, which I assume means he's not showing up."

Birdie frowns. "Meeting someone? As in a date? I thought you deleted your MatchMade account."

"I did. I met this guy on Facebook."

"You're a glutton for punishment." Birdie laughs and adds, "Takes one to know one."

Max plops down on the empty barstool next to her. "What happened? More trouble with Stan?"

Birdie sighs. "Yep. It's over between us. He has too many trust issues."

"Stan's a fool!" Max takes a gulp of Birdie's wine. "This dating business is for the birds. I'm lonely sometimes, but I'm not unhappy being alone."

"I wouldn't know. I haven't been alone for three years. The last time I was alone, after Cary disappeared, I fell apart. And now, ever since Hannah decided to move to Charleston, the temptation to drink has been growing stronger." Birdie looks down at the wineglass. "But, hey! I ordered wine, and I didn't drink it. I didn't even want it."

"Because you're stronger than you realize, Birdie. You're one of the strongest women I know. You're also beautiful, on the inside and out. When the time is right, you'll make some guy damn lucky."

"So will you, Maxie. But for now, we have each other for company, and I say we focus on ourselves and our businesses. I'm taking your advice and converting my kitchenette into a kitchen with an eat-in bar. Since you know more about construction than most men, I could use your opinion."

"I'm your girl. Tell me what you're thinking."

"If you have time, I'd rather show you."

"I have nothing but time," Max says, sliding off the barstool to her feet.

They're on their way out when Max suddenly stops dead in her tracks. "That's him. That's the guy from Facebook."

Birdie follows her gaze to a middle-aged man sitting alone at a table on the railing. "He's kinda cute."

Max bites down on her lip. "He is, isn't he?"

Birdie nudges her. "Go talk to him."

Max lifts her chin and holds her head high. "No thanks. I'm done with men for now. It's just you and me, Birdie."

"Are you sure? I realize he was late, but at least, he came."

"You're right, I guess. But wait for me on the boardwalk. I'm just going to speak to him, tell him I'm not feeling well."

Birdie exits the porch and waits for Max in front of the cafe. When Max joins her a few minutes later, she's wearing a sheepish grin. "Okay, so he seems like a nice guy. He got tied up at work. We're going to try again for dinner next week."

"Why? He's already here. Don't you want to have dinner with him now?"

Max loops her arm through Birdie's. "No thanks, I'd rather be with you."

They spend an hour in Birdie's apartment, measuring and discussing her options. Max and Birdie have been friends since childhood. Never has she enjoyed anyone's company more, not even Cary's during their happily married years. She'll take friendship over romance any day.

TWENTY-ONE

Gus sleeps peacefully, and when he wakes at seven o'clock the next morning, he's raring to go. Hannah wraps her arms around him, drawing his soft body close to hers. "How do you feel?" She places her hand on his forehead. His skin is cool to the touch. "You had a fever last night. Maybe we should go home today."

"No!" He clambers to his feet and bounces on the bed. "I wanna see my daddy."

She presses her finger to her lips. "Shh! I doubt your daddy's awake yet."

Gus drops to his knees. "I'm hungry, Mommy."

"I'm sure you are. You hardly ate any dinner. But it's still early. We have to wait awhile. Why don't you play one of your games while I read my book?" She hands him her iPad and settles deeper beneath the covers with her romance novel.

By eight o'clock, Gus is starving, and she can no longer hold him off. Mother and son pad in bare feet down the stairs to the kitchen. Hannah pauses in the doorway. Ryan and his father are seated at the breakfast table—Ryan wearing athletic shorts and a T-shirt, and his father dressed for golf. Hovering over them with a coffee carafe is Sylvia, fresh as a daisy in plaid Bermuda shorts and a pink top with her platinum blonde hair pinned in a bun at the nape of her neck.

Ryan notices Hannah and Gus and motions for them to join him. "There's a coffee cake on the counter. Or eggs in the refrigerator if you feel like making them."

If you feel like making them, she thinks. *Who's the guest and who's the host here?* Hannah helps Gus into a chair at the table and goes to the refrigerator for milk, butter, and a carton of eggs.

"Would you like coffee, dear?" Sylvia asks Hannah, holding the carafe over an empty mug at the table.

"Yes! Please," Hannah says. "How was your dinner last night?"

"Wonderful," Sylvia says.

"But it was a late night," Patrick adds in a grumpy voice.

Ryan comes to stand beside Hannah at the stove. "One of dad's friends invited Dad and me to play golf today at Caledonia. I realize the timing sucks, but Gerald Wagner is the senior-most partner of one of the largest law firms in the state. I'm hoping he'll consider hiring me after I pass the bar. This is an important opportunity for me, Hannah. You don't mind, do you?"

Hannah hides her irritation as she scrambles eggs. "Of course not."

"You could run errands with Mom," Ryan suggests.

Hannah glances up in time to see a look of horror cross Sylvia's face. "That's okay," Hannah says, forcing a smile. "Gus isn't great at running errands. We'll be fine on the beach."

Ryan gives her a half hug. "Thanks for understanding. We'll be back early afternoon." He drops his arm from around her. "I'd better get changed."

Hannah scoops eggs onto a plate and sits down next to her

son. Sylvia and Patrick exchange a look, a private communication between the two.

Sylvia returns the carafe to the coffeemaker and joins them at the table. "Mr. Stevenson . . . Patrick and I would like to have a word with you, dear. We have some concerns about your relationship with our son."

Patrick adds, "Not about you specifically, Hannah. You seem like a nice girl."

Sylvia gives her a tight smile. "It just happened so soon after Ryan's breakup with Danielle. He's on the rebound, you know."

Tears sting Hannah's eyes and she lowers her gaze. "Ryan told me he broke up with Danielle. But it's none of my concern. I'm here because of Gus. Ryan wanted you to meet your grandchild."

"Which is true," Patrick says.

Hannah leaves the table with Gus's empty plate and her mug. Dumping the rest of her coffee down the drain, she rinses the dishes and places them in the dishwasher. She's cleaning the egg pan when she hears Patrick talking to Gus in a hushed voice. He says something that makes Gus giggle, but Hannah doesn't look over at them for fear they'll see her tears.

From another part of the house, Ryan calls for Gus, who runs off to find him.

Sylvia crosses the room to Hannah. "We didn't mean to hurt your feelings, Hannah. We only want what's best for our son. Patrick and I were shocked when you and Gus came crawling out of the woodwork."

Dropping the pan in the sink with a loud thunk, Hannah turns to face Ryan's mother. "We didn't come *crawling* out of the woodwork, Mrs. Stevenson. I'm not sure how much you know about my relationship with Ryan. We dated during the fall of our senior year in college. I was very much in love with him until he broke my heart by cheating on me. I never told him I was pregnant, and I never wanted him to find out about Gus."

Sylvia's face registers surprise. "Are you saying you're not romantically interested in Ryan?"

"I'm not sure. Ryan asked me to give him another chance. For Gus's sake, I agreed to try."

Sylvia presses her lips thin. "There's no denying Gus is our grandson. If he weren't the spitting image of Ryan, I'd insist on a DNA test. Is it money you want? Because we can work out a deal. A monthly allowance, perhaps. But a family like ours . . . well, we have to protect our interests. Ryan will have other children one day. Legitimate children who will be entitled to his inheritance."

A sob escapes from Hannah's throat. She's never once considered Ryan's inheritance. Angry tears stream down her cheeks, and when Ryan enters the kitchen with Gus on his shoulders, she rushes over to them. "Put him down, Ryan. Before he gets hurt."

"What's wrong, Hannah?" Ryan gazes past her at his mom. "What did you say to her?"

Through gritted teeth, Hannah says, "Put. My son. Down."

Ryan lifts Gus off his shoulders and sets him on his feet. Hannah scoops her son into her arms and brushes past Ryan on her way out of the kitchen.

Ryan follows her upstairs to their room. "Hannah, wait! What's going on? What did Mom say to you?"

Hannah finds a movie for Gus on the iPad and places headphones over his ears.

"You lied to me, Ryan. You told me you broke up with Danielle."

His mouth falls open. "I *did* break up with Danielle. My mom doesn't know what goes on in my relationships."

"Your *mom* basically called me a gold digger." Hannah

jabs her finger at Ryan's chest. "I don't want your money, Ryan. And I never wanted you to be a part of Gus's life."

He appears wounded. "You don't mean that. I'm crazy about that kid. I've already missed three years of his life. I don't want to miss another minute."

"You'll have other children, as your mom just pointed out." Hannah hooks her fingers in air quotes and adds, "Legitimate children who will be entitled to your inheritance."

Patrick's voice booms out from downstairs. "Come on, Ryan. We've gotta go. We're gonna miss our tee time."

Casting a nervous glance at the door, Ryan says, "Look. This golf outing is important. Otherwise I wouldn't go. I hate leaving you upset like this. We tee off at nine. I should be back no later than two. We'll spend the afternoon together. And we'll talk."

Hannah shakes her head. "I don't know, Ryan. I can't promise I'll still be here."

"For Gus's sake, I hope you are." Ryan walks toward the door, stopping before he reaches the hallway. Without looking back, he says, "I intend to have a relationship with my son. We can either do this in a congenial manner, or we can get the lawyers involved."

Hannah watches his retreating figure disappear down the hallway. How dare he threaten her? She's Gus's biological mother. He'd never win in a custody battle. Would he? Then again, his father is attorney general of the state of South Carolina. He has the power to take Gus away from her.

When her legs wobble, she sits down on the bed beside Gus. She can't let that happen. She must try harder with Ryan. Even if she feels nothing for him romantically, organizing visitation and making decisions for Gus will be easier if they're on friendly terms.

Hannah stays in her room until she hears the front door close and Sylvia's engine start in the driveway. Dressed for the beach, Hannah and Gus go down to the kitchen where she packs cheese sandwiches and snacks in a cooler along with several bottles of water. She plans to avoid Sylvia by staying at the beach until Ryan returns from golfing.

Gus is in a low-key mood today, content to play quietly in the sand while she reads. When two o'clock rolls around with no word from Ryan, she takes her son up to the house for his nap. She's relieved to find Sylvia's car still absent from the driveway. Ryan's mom must have had a lot of errands to run.

While Gus is sleeping, Hannah showers, blow-dries her hair, and dresses in a floral sundress. At three fifteen, she's reading in a comfortable chair by the window when she hears Sylvia return. A few minutes later, she receives a text from Ryan. *Sorry. Gonna be a while longer. Wagner insisted we have lunch with him after golf.*

Hannah packs their belongings. When Gus wakes with a fever around four o'clock, she gives him a dose of liquid Advil, and they leave the cottage, careful not to disturb Sylvia who is sleeping in the hammock.

Gus begins to sob as they pull onto Highway 17, and he doesn't stop until he finally falls asleep forty-five minutes later. When her phone rings, she declines the call from Ryan and sets the volume to silent. As she nears Mount Pleasant, the sky darkens with an approaching storm. The rain pours down in torrents, and even with the windshield wipers set on full speed, she can see little in front of her. She's on top of the Ravenel Bridge when her engine sputters. She glances at her dashboard. A light on her gas gauge beams red. *Empty.* She'd been too angry at Ryan and distracted by Gus's crying and the approaching storm to pay attention to her gas gauge. The engine sputters again and then dies.

Please, no! Not now. Not on top of the bridge.

Turning on her hazard lights, she eases the Wrangler to the far right lane. Panic grips her chest. She's heard tragic stories of people being killed in such situations. *Chill, Hannah. You can't fall apart on top of the bridge.* Her immediate thought is to call Birdie. But her mother is more than an hour away. She needs someone closer. Liza is probably at the hospital. Which leaves Chris and Ethan. And she doesn't want her new partner to know she's so irresponsible she let her car run out of gas.

Removing her phone from the cup holder, she ignores the twenty-two missed calls from Ryan and clicks on Ethan's number. He answers on the second ring. "Hannah. This is a surprise. Where are you?"

"I ran outta gas," she blurts. "On top of the Ravenel Bridge. I'm scared, Ethan."

"Take some deep breaths," he says calmly. "Is Gus with you?"

"Yes. He's asleep in his car seat. Should I call the police?"

"Yes. But in this storm, it may take them a while to get there. I'm on my way. My parents keep gas in their garage for the lawn mower. I'll swing by there and pick it up. Hang in there. Are your hazard lights on?"

"Yes. I'm in the southbound lane." She hangs up and calls 9-1-1 to request roadside assistance.

She shrinks away from the window as a tractor trailer speeds past her. Rain pounds the roof, and streaks of lightning dance across the sky in the distance.

Gus wakes up. "Where are we, Mommy? Is my daddy here?"

"No, sweetheart. We ran out of gas. Ethan's coming to help us."

Gus tries to wiggle free of his car seat. "But I have to go pee."

She angles her body toward him. "You'll have to hold it, sweetheart. Ethan will be here in a minute."

Gus squirms some more. "But I'm hungry."

"Once we get gas, we'll find somewhere to use the restroom and get food."

Gus begins crying again. She retrieves Atticus from the rear floorboard and hands him to her son, which only makes Gus cry harder. Hannah is on the verge of tears herself when headlights pull up behind her. Seconds later, Ethan taps on her window.

She rolls the window down. "I'm so glad to see you."

Rivulets of rain stream off the hood of his black raincoat as he holds up a red gas can. "There's three gallons in here, which will get you to my apartment."

She gives him a grateful nod. "Thank you!"

As Ethan is pouring gas into her tank, a police cruiser pulls up alongside of them. Ethan has a word with the police officer and he drives on. Ethan returns to his car, and Hannah follows him closely as he drives slowly through the downtown streets of Charleston to his condominium building. Parking in the first-floor garage, Ethan helps Gus from his car seat, and they ride in the elevator to the third floor. "Gus needs to use your restroom, and then we'll be on our way."

"Seriously? In this weather? Have you seen the radar?" Ethan removes his phone from his coat pocket and shows her the blob of yellow, orange, and green sliding across coastal South Carolina.

"But I have to feed Gus, and I'd rather not get home too late."

"Why don't you eat dinner with me? I can make grilled cheeses with bacon or we can order pizza, although the delivery might take a while in this storm."

"We had pizza last night," Gus says.

"Then, grilled cheese and bacon it is."

Ethan unlocks his door and steps out of the way so they can enter. He holds his hand out to Gus. "Come on, buddy. I'll show you the bathroom."

Hannah roams around the living room while they're gone. Ethan's home, much like his office, is handsomely decorated in masculine colors and furniture with mounted wildlife, ducks and geese and fish, on the walls.

When Gus and Ethan return, the three of them gather in the kitchen. Ethan lifts Gus up to the marble countertop and fills a small bowl with Goldfish.

Gus's blue eyes grow wide. "You like Goldfish?"

Ethan grins. "I mean, ye-ah. Who doesn't like Goldfish?"

"I love them!" Gus grabs a handful of the crackers and stuffs them all into his mouth at once.

Ethan pops the cork on a bottle of red wine. When he offers Hannah a glass, she shakes her head. "I can't. I'm driving."

"Do you really want to drive home in this weather? I have a spare bedroom. Why don't you stay the night and leave early in the morning?"

Gus's fanny comes off the counter. "Please, Mommy! Can we have a sleepover with Ethan?"

Hannah consults her radar app again. There's no end in sight to the long line of storms. "We're probably safer spending the night. If you're sure you don't mind having us."

"It would be my pleasure." He hands her the wine, and this time she accepts it with a smile.

Ethan moves about the upscale kitchen with the ease of a man who spends a lot of time here. After cooking thick slices of bacon in an iron skillet, he enlists Gus's help in assembling cheese and bacon between slices of grainy bread.

As she watches them work together, Hannah can't help but compare the way the two men in her life interact with her son. Ethan is patient and gentle, whereas Ryan, in many ways, is like a child himself. One is Gus's teacher and the other his playmate.

When the sandwiches are ready, Ethan adds a spoonful of

potato salad to each of their plates, and they eat on barstools at the island. Throughout dinner, Ethan and Gus carry on an in-depth discussion about Gus's friends at Miss Daisy's.

When they're finished eating, Hannah takes care of the dishes while Ethan and Gus go down to the car for their bags. Ethan helps Gus into his pajamas, and after brushing his teeth, the threesome watches *Blue's Clues* on television until Gus falls asleep between them on the sofa. Ethan carries him into the guest bedroom and Hannah tucks him in tight.

"Would you like more wine?" Ethan asks when they return to the living room.

"A little, please."

He goes into the kitchen and comes back with two half glasses of wine.

"Your home is lovely," Hannah says, standing at the window, looking into the inky darkness.

"The view is spectacular on clear nights." He opens the french doors, and they step out onto a covered balcony.

He motions her to wicker chairs tucked in a corner, out of the rain. "How was your weekend at Pawley's?"

"A disaster. I was supposed to stay until tomorrow, but I left early." She walks him through her brief visit with Ryan's family, including Sylvia's insults and Ryan disappearing for the day to play golf.

When she tells him about Gus's fever, Ethan says, "Really? He seems fine to me."

"That's the way viruses are sometimes. The fever comes and goes. Hopefully, he's over the worst of it."

"I'm sorry Ryan's mom was so rude," Ethan says. "You deserve better than that."

"Thanks." Hannah kicks off her flip-flop and tucks her foot under her leg. "I'm glad I went, though. I'm no longer confused about my feelings for Ryan. I thought I still cared about him when what I really wanted was for Gus to have his mother and father living under the same roof."

"Families come in all shapes and sizes, Hannah."

"I'm realizing that." Hannah sips her wine. "Anyway, I'm thrilled about starting my new life in Charleston."

Ethan touches his wineglass to hers. "You're gonna love it here. The carriage house is still available if you're interested."

"I appreciate the opportunity. The rent is generous, and the house is ideal. Gus would love running around the grounds. However, after living with my mom for three years, I'm looking for a no-strings-attached living situation. Gus and I need a fresh start. We need to be completely on our own."

"I don't blame you for that." Ethan takes her wineglass and sets it on the ground. He stands up and pulls her to her feet. "I hope this no-strings-attached mentality doesn't include our relationship. What do you say, Hannah? Will you give us a chance?"

Hannah hesitates before answering. "I'm falling for you, Ethan, and I'm powerless to do anything about it. Even if I wanted to, which I definitely do not. But I have Gus to consider. I won't always be free to go for drinks after work. Or take off on a whim to the beach for the weekend. My son and I are a package deal."

"I understand that." Cupping her cheeks, he brings her face close to his, kissing her softly on the lips.

"Do you? Because I'm not sure you can until you've experienced parenthood." Turning away from him, she moves to the edge of the porch where the rain has slowed to a drizzle. "You haven't seen him when he's sick or grumpy or having a tantrum. I would like to give us a chance. But I'm not sure I'm ready yet."

He comes to stand behind her, his breath near her ear. "I'll give you all the space you need. We'll start out as friends."

Hannah leans into him. "Friendship, I can handle. I'm scared, Ethan. The last time I had sex, I got pregnant."

"We'll take it slow. You'll call all the shots. You can trust me, Hannah. You may not believe that now, but you will in time."

She wants to trust him. But, thanks to Ryan and her father, she has trust issues with men. Hannah doesn't want Gus to grow up to be untrustworthy like his father and grandfather. Which makes her even more determined to find an honest and dependable father figure who loves Gus like his own. Is Ethan that guy? He could be. He dropped everything when his father had a heart attack and stayed by his side until after his surgery. Only time will tell. For now, where Ethan is concerned, she'll keep an open heart and mind.

TWENTY-TWO

Max circles the crowded parking lot at Home Depot several times before finding an empty space. She takes the car out of gear but doesn't turn off the engine. "What are we doing at Home Depot on a Saturday night?"

"Checking out their kitchen section for remodeling ideas," Birdie says. "This was your idea, remember?"

Max drums her fingers on the steering wheel. "Of course I remember. But we should be having fun."

"Didn't we determine last night this *is* our fun?"

"This is old lady fun. I'm not ready to give up my youth yet."

Birdie's eyes grow wide. "Your youth? You're not twenty, Maxie. At fifty-three, you're middle-aged."

"You know the saying, Birdie. You're only as old as you feel." Max reverses out of the parking space.

"Where are we going?" Birdie asks, bracing herself against the door when Max whips out of the parking lot in the direction opposite the waterfront.

With a naughty glint in her eye, Max says, "On a road trip."

"A road trip to where?"

"To Charleston. There's an oyster bar there I've been dying to try."

Birdie groans. "Come on, Max. You know I don't do restaurants."

Gripping the steering wheel, Max steps on the gas pedal. "That all changes tonight. We're going to practice cognitive behavior therapy. By refusing to eat in restaurants, you're not only forgoing the chance to socialize with friends, you're missing out on the opportunity to eat delicious food. How're you going to open a cafe when you don't know what your competition offers?"

Birdie tilts her head to the side as she considers this. "You have a point. But the temptation to drink is too great."

Max risks a glance at Birdie. "Hence the reason for the cognitive behavior therapy. Tonight, you're going to order a nonalcoholic beer or a virgin cocktail, something besides water."

"Max—"

"I'm not taking *no* for an answer."

Birdie lacks the energy to argue with her. Besides, maybe she's right. Where's the harm in trying it? "Fine. I'll give it a shot," she says, shifting in her seat as she settles in for the ride.

"Tonight, our dining experience is about the food, not the beverage."

Birdie removes her phone from her purse. "All right, already. Tell me the name of the restaurant so I can pull up their menu."

"Leon's. On Upper King Street."

Birdie accesses the website and scans the menu. "This does sound good. Besides raw and grilled oysters, they have several small plates I'd like to try. You may regret bringing me here."

"Not a chance. I'm starving. We'll order one of everything on the menu." Max tunes into a classic rock station, and they sing along, loud and off-key, to songs they remember from their youth.

Birdie's phone vibrates in her lap with a text from Stan. "Guess who just texted me?"

"Stan. What does he have to say for himself?"

She reads the text aloud. "I'm so sorry for doubting you, Birdie. Can you come over so we can talk?"

"Bastard," Max says, palming the steering wheel. "Don't respond to him."

"Don't worry. I'm not."

They're approaching Charleston when raindrops splatter the windshield. Seconds later, it begins to pour.

"Where did this come from?" Max asks. "I didn't know it was supposed to rain."

"It wasn't." Birdie pulls up the forecast on her phone. "Sixty percent chance of a thunderstorm. Typical unpredictable summer weather in the South. Hopefully, it passes quickly."

Leon's parking lot is located down the street from the restaurant. They find a space, but with no raincoats or umbrellas, their clothes are soaked through by the time they sprint down the block. To make matters worse, the hostess informs them of a twenty- to thirty-minute wait.

They add their name to the list and go in search of the restroom where they remove smudged mascara from their cheeks and stick their wet heads under the hand drier. They return to the front entrance and wait in the crowded space just inside the door. Birdie feels claustrophobic with so many bodies pressed close together. When the color drains from Max's face, she asks, "What's wrong, Max? Do you feel okay? It's awfully stuffy in here. Do you need to get some fresh air?"

"I'm fine. But that woman over there looks like Amelia."

Max inclines her head at a couple making their way through the swarm of people to the front door.

Birdie follows her gaze to the striking blonde. "You mean our Amelia? Amelia Fairchild?" She looks from the woman to Max and then back at the woman. "How would we even know what Amelia looks like when we haven't seen her in almost thirty years?"

"She has that look about her, the classic Carolina girl turned middle-aged woman—thin with long legs, sun-bleached hair, and a golden tan."

"Remember, we used to call Amelia's mama the Southern Belle Barbie. I wonder if Amelia grew up to look like Miss Dottie."

Max chuckles. "Probably." She squints at the blonde woman's partner. "I remember little about the guy she married, except that he was an ass. I wonder if that's him. What was his name?"

Birdie shrugs. "I have no clue. But that's not him, because that's not Amelia."

Max tears her eyes away from the couple. "I've tried to find Amelia through social media. But she appears to have disappeared off the planet."

Birdie lets out a humph. "She's probably hiding from us. And I don't blame her, after the way we treated her."

"We tried to save her from making the biggest mistake of her life," Max says.

"Amelia loved that guy, what's his name. She was determined to marry him regardless of what we thought."

When the hostess calls Max's name, they follow her to a table for two in the center of the restaurant. "Nothing like being in the limelight," Birdie says.

Max looks around at the other tables. "These people are enjoying their dinner. They aren't paying any attention to you."

"You're right," Birdie says, and sucks in a deep breath.

The waiter, a handsome young man with a broad chest and muscular arms, arrives to take their order. "Evening ladies. Can I get you started with a beverage?"

Birdie smiles up at him. "I'd like a nonalcoholic beer." When he lists three, two that she's never heard of, she says, "Beck's, please."

Max bats her eyelashes at the waiter while she quizzes him about craft beer. When he suggests the Holy City, she jumps on it. "That's what I'll have."

Birdie waits for him to leave the table. "You're shameless. You were planning to order the Holy City all along."

"So, what if I was?" She looks away, toward a group of young women seated at the bar. "Do you remember that time in college when the three of us drove down to Mardi Gras?"

"How could I forget it? I did most of the driving while you and Amelia stayed drunk the whole time. How ironic that I ended up being the drunk."

"You're not a drunk, Birdie. Don't talk like that," Max says in a scolding tone.

"Excuse me. I'm an alcoholic." She corrects herself. "A *recovering* alcoholic."

The waiter brings their beers in frosty mugs. Birdie takes a sip, and the refreshing beer hits the spot. For the first time in three years, Birdie feels like a normal person, enjoying a cocktail in a restaurant. Whoever said cocktails must contain alcohol?

Wrapping her hands around her mug, Max says, "Do you remember in high school when we snuck out of the house to go to the Rolling Stones concert in Columbia?"

"How could I forget it? I got grounded the longest. An entire month while you and Amelia only got two weeks. What's with the nostalgic mood tonight?"

Max sips her beer. "I've been thinking a lot lately about

how fast our lives are passing us by. Like I said in the car, I'm not ready to be old yet. I don't want the fun to end."

"Me either. And you're right. I need to get out more, to stop being so anxious about my drinking problem."

Max holds her mug up to Birdie's. "The more you go out, the easier it will get."

"I'll become a food connoisseur." Birdie picks up her menu. "And speaking of which, let's order. I'm starving."

Signaling for the waiter, Birdie says, "We'll have the raw and grilled oysters, a dozen of each." Dragging her finger down the menu, she chooses several small plates and a basket of hush puppies to share.

The waiter furrows his brow. "The plates are small, but that's a lot of food."

"We're sampling," Birdie says, but when the food arrives, they polish off nearly every morsel.

Max leans across the table to Birdie. "Don't look now, but the men at the table behind you are watching us."

When Birdie shifts in her seat, Max kicks her under the table. "I told you not to look."

"They're kinda cute, if you don't mind the hair loss."

"Shh! Here they come."

The two men approach the table. They look enough alike to be brothers. The taller of the two says, "Evening, ladies. You appear to be having a good time. Do you mind if we join you for a drink?"

"Don't worry," the other guy says. "We're harmless. I promise."

Max and Birdie exchange a look of indifference. "Sure," Birdie says, and Max adds, "Why not?"

Introducing themselves as Mark and Tim, they slide their chairs up to the table with Mark beside Birdie and Tim next to Max.

"Are you celebrating a special occasion?" Mark asks.

"Birdie is expanding her restaurant business," Max explains. "We've been sampling the menu offerings."

Mark and Tim exchange a look. "We were wondering how you stay so thin with such healthy appetites," Mark says.

Max laughs. "We don't normally eat like this. I promise."

The waiter clears the table, and when the others order another round of drinks, Birdie asks for a cup of hot tea. "I'm driving," she explains. "But I'm also an alcoholic."

Mark and Tim take this information in stride, as though it doesn't bother them at all.

For once, Birdie isn't embarrassed about her disease. She has a problem. She will always have a problem, but she's proud of the hard work she's done to get her problem under control.

"We're real estate developers," Mark explains. "We live in Spartanburg, but we do a lot of business in the area."

While Mark and Tim claim to be divorced, neither makes a sexual advance toward Birdie or Max. They share some great laughs, a discussion on world affairs, and a respectful debate about politics. They are four friends enjoying drinks on a Saturday night. Mark picks up the tab for the drinks, and they exchange phone numbers, promising to stay in touch, although Birdie doubts they will.

The rain has stopped, and a light drizzle is falling as they walk to Max's car. Birdie gets behind the wheel and navigates through town toward the Ashley River.

As they're crossing the bridge, Max reaches over and grips Birdie's thigh through her white jeans. "I was proud of you for admitting you're an alcoholic. And see, they didn't even bat an eye."

"Thank you for saying that, Max. I feel like I made a giant breakthrough tonight. And I had a really great time. Kudos to you for suggesting an impromptu outing. We should be sponta-neous more often."

"I totally agree." Max rests her head against the back of the seat. "It restores my faith in humanity to know that nice guys like Mark and Tim still exist."

Birdie chuckles. "Isn't that the truth?"

"Are you going to call Stan?"

"I'm not sure. I think I'll let him stew for a few days."

Birdie hasn't thought about Stan all evening. She'll probably go out with Stan again at some point. But she wants to be on her own for a while before committing to a serious relationship. While she sees Max nearly every day, they haven't had nearly enough quality time together—which gives her an idea.

She looks over at Max. "Would you like to take a trip with me?"

"Sure! Where do you wanna go?"

"I don't know. Maybe California or Hawaii."

"Or maybe we could eat our way through Italy," Max says, and for the rest of the way back to Palmetto Island, they discuss all the places they'd like to visit.

There's nothing like having a true friend, that special someone who loves you for you, despite your flaws. When Max goes off on a tangent about Iceland, Birdie's thoughts drift to Amelia. She didn't just disappear off the face of the planet. Is she still alive? Did she ever have children? Get divorced? Birdie would love to see her again. Wouldn't they have fun reminiscing about old times?

TWENTY-THREE

Hannah wakes to the smell of frying bacon. Beside her, Gus sits bolt upright in bed. "Bacon!" Scrambling from beneath the covers, he disappears out of the room, and returns seconds later. "Come on, Mommy." He gives her a shove. "Ethan is making bacon and pancakes for breakfast."

Hooking an arm around his neck, she pulls him closer, pressing her cheek against his forehead. "Yay. No fever."

"I'm not sick anymore." Gus tugs on Hannah's arm. "Hurry, Mommy."

"I'll be there in a minute, Gus. Let me get dressed."

Hannah changes out of her pajamas into shorts and a T-shirt and goes across the hall to the bathroom to wash her face and brush her teeth. Smoothing her hair into a ponytail, she joins Gus and Ethan in the kitchen.

"You have a thing for bacon," she says, standing beside him at the stove.

A big grin spreads across his face. "Bacon, bacon, bacon," he says the words in quick succession. "I can never get enough bacon."

She watches him flip pancakes. "I'm seriously impressed with your culinary skills. I should hang out with you more often."

He leans into her, nudging her with his elbow. "Consider me your friend with benefits."

"As long as those benefits don't include sexual favors," she says under her breath so Gus can't hear. "All kidding aside, who taught you to cook?"

"My parents. They cook together all the time. I've picked up a few skills from hanging out with them in the kitchen."

"Have you always been close to your parents?"

"As an only child, my parents treated me more like a peer instead of their kid."

"Ha. As an only child, my parents treated me like their kid, especially when I misbehaved."

He stacks pancakes onto three plates and adds two slices of bacon each. Hannah transfers the plates to the island, which he has set with utensils, napkins, and glasses of orange juice.

Once they sit down, Ethan asks, "So what's on your agenda for today? Can you hang out for a while? We can go out in the . . . b-o-a-t."

Hannah hesitates. The thought of spending the day on the water with Ethan appeals to her. Seeing him in his board shorts again appeals to her even more. "We really should get home. I have chores this afternoon, and I'm coming back to Charleston tomorrow to look for a place to live."

"How about a quick walk on the seawall before you go?"

Gus's blue eyes get big. "Please, Mommy. Can we? I wanna walk on the sea."

Hannah smiles at her son. "It's a seawall, sweetheart. Like the boardwalk down by the marina, except it's built of concrete instead of wood."

Gus scrunches up his face as he thinks about this. "Okay. But can we do that?"

"All right. I guess a short walk won't hurt. You can burn off some of your energy, and I can burn off all the bacon I've eaten in the past twelve hours."

After cleaning up from breakfast, the threesome set out for their walk. The sky is hazy and the air heavy with humidity. Even though it's early on a Sunday morning, local folks with dogs on leashes crowd the sidewalks. Gus asks the owners if he can pet their dogs. Some are nicer about it than others.

"I envision a puppy in your future," Ethan says, watching Gus drag his tiny fingers through a golden retriever's thick coat.

She glares at him from under furrowed eyebrows. "No way! A puppy is the last thing I need."

"You might change your mind once you're settled in Charleston. When do you think you'll move?"

Hannah kicks at a pebble on the ground. "As soon as possible. I have to find somewhere to live by July. Gus starts preschool on the first."

"You're welcome to stay in the carriage house until you find permanent housing," Ethan says.

"I may take you up on that offer if I get in a jam. I'm worried the transition will be difficult for Gus. I'd hate for him to have to move twice."

Gus stops suddenly, sticking his head between the railings as he watches a large powerboat speed across the water.

"He seems like a tough kid. I'm sure he'll adjust fine," Ethan says, placing a hand on her shoulder.

The warmth of his touch is reassuring. It would be so easy to lean on him. But she can't let him get too close. Not until he's proven himself. She starts walking again, forcing Ethan to drop his hand.

"I really screwed up," she says when he steps in line beside her. "I passed on the perfect apartment because I thought the rent was too high. It would have been a stretch, but I could've made it work. Gus really hit it off with Sally, the little girl who lives in the downstairs apartment. Sally's mom seemed nice as well. They would've made great neighbors."

"That's a bummer. But something else will come along. I'll take a drive around downtown this afternoon and let you know if I come up with anything."

"That'd be great, Ethan. Thanks."

"I'd like to help you move when the time comes."

She'd planned on hiring professional movers, an expense she'd rather not incur. "Does your Porsche have a trailer hitch?" she asks in a teasing tone.

"No, but my dad has a pickup truck for times like these."

She laughs. "Of course he does. Then I accept your offer. You're turning out to be a friend with *many* benefits."

He beats his chest. "Me Tarzan. Me like Jane."

She sends an elbow to his ribs. "You're incorrigible."

He's also funny and resourceful and so damn adorable. Not to mention kind and considerate. Hannah wonders how long she'll have the strength to fend off his advances.

Gus, who's been walking a short distance ahead of them, suddenly turns and runs back to them. "Ethan, can I ride on your shoulders?"

Ethan looks over at Hannah. "If your mommy says it's okay."

Hannah remembers how freaked out she got when Ryan carried Gus on his shoulders. She realizes with a jolt that she already trusts Ethan. Way more than she ever trusted Ryan.

———

Gus jabbers on about Ethan for the entire drive to Palmetto Island. But he doesn't mention one word about Ryan. Hannah almost feels sorry for Ryan. But not enough to answer his calls or texts.

Despite eating a huge breakfast, Gus is begging for lunch by the time they arrive home at eleven thirty. Hannah is eager to tell her mother about her weekend. But Birdie and Sadie are busy behind the counter. The cafe is slammed with customers. Are they short-staffed? Where are Amanda and Melissa? She wishes she could help them. If only she had someone to watch Gus.

Hannah makes Gus a peanut butter and jelly sandwich and carries it upstairs to the living room. She's relieved to find her father gone and to have the apartment to herself again.

She unpacks while Gus eats, and when he's finished, she tucks him into bed with a few of the books from their last visit to the library. As she's emerging from a long hot shower, she hears her mother calling her from downstairs. Wrapping herself in a towel, she goes to the top of the stairs. "What's up, Mom?"

A harried-looking Birdie says, "Is there any way you can help work the counter? Amanda and Melissa both called in sick, and Sadie and I are swamped. Tie Gus up in a corner if you have to."

Hannah laughs. "He's napping. I'll be down in a minute."

Back in her bedroom, she drops her towel and dresses in shorts and her yellow Birdie's Nest polo. Grabbing the baby monitor, she secures the baby gate at the top of the stairs and hurries down to the cafe.

The line extends out the front door. Hannah loses track of time as she waits on one customer after another. Business finally slows a few minutes before closing at two o'clock.

"I need to check on Gus," she tells Birdie and darts up the stairs, straddling the baby gate at the top. Her heart stops when she discovers her son's bed empty and the sheets cool to the touch. "Please, no. Not again."

Dropping to her knees, she crawls around on the floor, searching under the beds. She checks the bathroom and closets, anywhere a small person could hide, before flying back down to the kitchen. Sadie and Birdie are side by side at the sink with their backs to her.

"Gus is gone, Mom! He's gone!" Hannah's green eyes bounce wildly around the kitchen. "I can't believe this is happening again. Where could he be?"

Birdie turns to her. "Calm down, sweetheart. He's here somewhere. Did you search thoroughly in the apartment?"

"Yes! Maybe he's out front."

It takes the three women less than five minutes to check under the tables and counters in the cafe.

Hannah's mind races as she thinks back over the last two hours. "The three of us were working the counter. He couldn't have gotten past us without us seeing him. He must have left through the back door."

Sadie and Birdie follow Hannah through the kitchen to the coatroom. Hannah turns the doorknob. "The door is unlocked. I'm certain I locked it when I got home."

The color drains from Sadie's face. "I took the trash out earlier, during that mad rush of customers. I may have forgotten to lock it when I came back in."

Hannah marches across the room to Sadie. "When was that?" When she hesitates, Hannah snaps. "Think, Sadie. This is important. Was it after I started working the counter?"

Sadie's chin quivers as she nods. "The trash can was overflowing. I had to take out the trash."

Birdie rests a hand on Sadie's back. "It's okay, Sadie. It was an accident."

An accident that could cost Gus his life, Hannah wants to scream but bites her tongue at the sight of Sadie's tormented face.

"Call Max, Mom! See if Gus is over there." Hannah squeezes her eyes tight while Birdie places the call. *Please, God, let him be there. Please, oh please.* But she can tell by the disappointment in her mother's voice that Gus is not with Max.

Birdie ends the call. "Max hasn't seen him. But she's on her way over to help us look."

Hannah imagines her three-year-old son letting himself out the back door and walking around the building to the board-walk. "The inlet." Her hand covers her mouth. "If he falls in, he'll drown."

TWENTY-FOUR

Hannah has no sooner gone out the front when Max explodes through the back door, body tense and blue eyes wide. "What do we do? Is he lost? Should we form a search party? Surely someone didn't kidnap him. Not on Palmetto Island."

The bottom falls out of Birdie's gut at the prospect of someone abducting Gus. "Stop talking and let me think."

Her thoughts bat around her brain like steel balls in a pinball machine. *Take deep breaths, Birdie. Stay focused.* "Okay. Max, you call your nephew while I try to reach Cary. It would be just like him to take Gus out for ice cream and not tell us."

"Right. Good thinking. I'm on it," Max says, and retreats out the back door to make the call to her nephew, the chief of police.

Birdie searches for Island Water Sports on her phone and clicks on the contact information. When she reaches the automated answering service, she impatiently taps numbers on her keypad until she reaches an irritated sounding saleswoman in women's apparel. "I need to speak with Cary Fuller, please."

"I'm sorry. Cary is with a customer at the moment. Can I take a message?"

How does she know Cary is with a customer when she's inside in the women's apparel department and Cary is outside helping customers in the boatyard? "This is an emergency. Please, get him to the phone. This is his wife."

"His wife?" the woman says in a suspicious tone. "Cary told me he's divorced."

"Not that it's any of your business. We've signed the papers, and we're in the waiting period. We have an emergency with our three-year-old grandson. I need to speak to Cary now. Either put him on the phone or I'm calling Stan."

"One moment, please."

Birdie hears a click, and Jimmy Buffet's voice fills the line. She notices Sadie standing behind the commercial mixer, crying silently into her apron. Birdie goes to her, placing her free arm around Sadie's waist and pulling her in for a half hug. "This is *not* your fault, Sadie. If anyone's to blame, it's me. I'm the one who asked Hannah to help us in the cafe."

Sadie sobs, "But I know better than to leave the back door unlocked."

"You were distracted. We were crazy busy today." She hugs her tight before letting Sadie go. "Now, try to get yourself together. We need you to help look for Gus."

"Okay. You're right." Sadie wipes her eyes one final time and smooths out her apron.

Birdie waves her phone in the air. "Why am I holding? If Cary is helping a customer, Gus is obviously not with him."

Sadie sniffles. "But he needs to know Gus is missing."

"True. I'll give him another minute." Birdie is getting ready to hang up when Cary comes on the line.

"What's up, Birdie?" he says, sounding out of breath. "Did something happen to Gus?"

"He's missing. I was hoping he was with you."

Cary sighs. "I wish he was. I've been with customers all day."

Birdie quickly explains about their grandson's disappearance.

"Poor Hannah must be beside herself. I'm on my way," Cary says and hangs up.

Birdie wonders how he'll get from the store to the waterfront without a car. When he was living in her apartment, Cary either took Birdie's car to work, or she dropped him off. Is he carpooling with a coworker now? Or is Patty Dunn chauffeuring him around?

Not your problem, Birdie.

"Come on, Sadie. Let's go outside. We know Gus isn't in here." Taking Sadie by the hand, they exit through the back door and join Max in the park.

"Toby's on the way. He should be here any second. I've enlisted some of my guests to help search," Max says about the crowd gathering nearby.

"Good thinking," Birdie says.

Blue lights flash and a loud siren sounds. "There's Toby now," Max says. The crowd moves out of the way as the patrol car drives down the wide brick sidewalk toward them.

Chief Toby Summers, Palmetto Island's police chief who is also Max's nephew, emerges from the patrol car and waddles over to them. He's plump with a thick neck and a jolly smile. Despite his general happy-go-lucky personality, Birdie has seen the chief's serious side and makes a point never to cross him.

"What happened, Birdie?" Summers asks. "Max says Gus is missing."

"Let's find Hannah. She can give you the full story." Birdie scans the boardwalk for her daughter, finally spotting her as she stands by the railing and looks down into the water. "There she is."

Birdie leads the chief over to Hannah, who hears them coming and turns to face them. "Chief Summers! Thank goodness you're here. You've gotta find my son. I'm so scared. He barely knows how to swim. He's only had a few lessons."

Summers pats Hannah on the back. "I know you're upset, Hannah. But try to calm down and tell me what happened."

Hannah inhales an unsteady breath. "Okay. So, Gus was taking a nap. I went downstairs to the cafe to help Mom and Sadie behind the counter. I had my monitor with me." She unclips the monitor from the waistband of her shorts and hands it to him. "I heard nothing."

Summers holds the monitor to his ear. "I hear crackling, so we know it's working. Have you used this monitor in this situation before?"

Hannah nods her head vigorously. "All the time."

"Are you certain you would have heard him if he'd cried out or called for you?"

Hannah thinks before answering. "The cafe was pretty noisy today with so many customers. But I was listening for him. I'm always listening for him. Isn't that a mother's job?"

Summers smiles. "That's what my wife tells me." He shifts his weight to the other foot. "What if Gus woke up from his nap and you weren't there? Would he have tried to come down to the cafe to find you?"

"He couldn't have gotten past the baby gate." Hannah palms her forehead. "Why didn't I think of that? Gus knows not to climb the baby gate. And even if he tried, he would've fallen down the stairs on the other side. Which means someone took him. Someone kidnapped my son!"

"Let's not jump to any conclusions yet." Summers removes a pen and notepad from the pocket of his uniform shirt. "But we need to rule out all possibilities. If we can identify a probable threat from a potential suspect, we can issue an Amber Alert." His gaze shifts to Birdie. "Where's Cary?"

"On his way here from work," Birdie says. "Which is where he's been all afternoon."

Hannah narrows her olive eyes at Birdie. "Are you sure, Mom?"

Birdie's fingers graze her daughter's arm. "I'm positive, sweetheart. I spoke to your father myself. He was both surprised and concerned about Gus."

"Think hard." Summers looks from Hannah to Birdie and back to Hannah. "Who else might have taken your son?"

"Ryan." Hannah mouths but no sound comes out.

Summers jerks his head toward Birdie. "What did she say?"

"Ryan. He's Gus's father. He only recently came into Gus's life." Birdie steps closer to her daughter. "Sweetheart, did anything happen over the weekend to make Ryan want to kidnap his son?"

Hannah nods. "A lot happened."

"Talk to me," Summers says with pen poised over notepad.

"Gus and I went to Pawley's Island to spend the weekend with Ryan's family. On Friday night, Gus started running a fever. I gave him medicine, and he was fine the next morning. I wasn't that worried. Gus's friend, Robbie, had been sick earlier in the week, and I assumed it was just a summer virus. The fever was gone on Saturday morning, but at breakfast, Ryan's mother accused me of using Gus to get Ryan's money."

Birdie gasps. "How dare her? I hope Ryan took up for you."

"He didn't seem to care, honestly. He was too busy getting ready to go play golf with his dad. He promised to be back by two, but he texted at three thirty, informing me they were going to lunch. When Gus woke up from his nap, his fever had returned. I gave him some medicine, and we left Pawley's Island. I was on my way home when my car ran out of gas on top of the Ravenel Bridge. My friend Ethan came to my rescue, and because of the storm, Gus and I spent the night with him in Charleston."

Summers looks up from his notepad. "We'll need to talk to Ethan. What's his last name?"

"Hayes. But he wouldn't do something like this." Hannah removes her phone from her pocket and clicks on a number. "Ethan! Gus is missing. He may have been kidnapped. The police want to talk to you." She thrusts the phone at Summers, who steps away to talk to Ethan.

"Mom!" Hannah collapses into Birdie's arms. "I can't believe this is happening."

"I know, sweetheart." As Birdie strokes Hannah's hair, out of the corner of her eye she watches Max's minions searching up and down the boardwalk, in and around the landscape bushes.

Summers rejoins them, handing the phone to Hannah. "Ethan wants a word with you."

Birdie studies her daughter while she's on the phone. Hannah's face softens in a way that tells Birdie she cares deeply for this young man.

"Be careful on the drive," Hannah says and ends the call.

"Ethan's driving down here," Hannah says. "He's been working at his office all afternoon."

"Right," Summers says with a nod. "Security cameras can easily prove his whereabouts. Not that I have any reason to question his word. He's not our guy." He raises his pointer finger. "But Ryan may very well be. You mentioned his family has money. Is he from around here?"

"No. Columbia. His father is Patrick Stevenson, the state's attorney general."

Summers's face falls. "Oh boy! We'll have to toe the line on this case. Have you had any communication with Ryan since you left Pawley's?"

"No, sir. Ryan tried to call a gazillion times, and sent a

bunch of apology texts, but I ignored them. The last call came in around midnight."

"Let's try to call him now." Summers nods at the phone in Hannah's hand. "If you can get him on the phone, I'll talk to him."

Hannah's call to Ryan goes immediately to voice mail, as do her three subsequent attempts.

"Do you have either of his parents' numbers?" Summers asks.

"No, sir. I only met them for the first time this weekend."

Summers unclips his walkie-talkie from his belt and barks orders to someone on the other end. "Get Attorney General Patrick Stevenson on the phone for me. Tell him it's a personal matter relating to his son and grandson."

"We're wasting time, Chief," Hannah says, her arms wrapped around her midsection. "What if it wasn't Ryan? What if Gus managed to climb over the baby gate and sneak out the back door?"

"I think that's highly improbable. But I'm one step ahead of you. Given your close proximity to the waterfront, I summoned the coast guard when I received Max's call. Here they come now," he says, his gaze fixed on the fleet of boats approaching the marina. "I need to give them some instruction. I'll be right back."

Summers has no sooner left Hannah and Birdie standing alone on the boardwalk when Stan arrives on the scene, followed shortly thereafter by Cary and an attractive brunette he introduces as Patty Dunn.

"Birdie, I'm so sorry," Stan says. "Cary told me what happened. What can I do to help?"

Birdie shakes her head. "There's nothing anyone can do except pray and wait."

"I've been praying, but I'm not great at waiting." Stan runs down to the dock, pulling the chief aside. Summers nods at something Stan says, and he hustles back up the ramp. "Summers gave me permission to help in the search. I'm recruiting two members of my staff to go out with me on my wave runners."

"Thank you, Stan," Birdie says. "We'll be here if you need anything, or if we can help in any way."

Cary's voice is near her ear. "How touching. Your knight in shining armor came to your rescue."

"This is neither the time nor the place for your sarcasm." When Birdie looks up at Cary, he's peering at her over the top of his sunglass frames. "What happened to your eye?"

He pushes his sunglasses up the bridge of his nose. "Your lover boy slugged me."

"I'm sure you deserved it." Birdie turns her back on Patty, who is hovering nearby. Is she attempting to eavesdrop on their conversation? "Seriously, Cary, I have a right to know. What did you do to Stan?"

Cary lets out a sigh. "Stan saw me with Patty and accused me of cheating on you. When I confessed the truth, that I lied about you and me sleeping together, he punched me."

Birdie cocks an eyebrow. "Why didn't he fire you?"

"Because I'm the best salesperson he's ever had. He agreed to let me stay on if I promised not to lie again."

"As if your promise is worth two nickels." She notices Patty inching her way closer to them. "Why would you bring your girlfriend to a family crisis? She's out of place here, Cary. And she's making me nervous. Our daughter needs our undivided attention right now."

Cary glances over at Hannah who stands at the railing and

watches the coast guard prepare to leave the dock. "You're right. I'll ask Patty to leave."

Is this what Birdie has to look forward to as Cary's ex-wife? A string of his girlfriends hanging around whenever Hannah's in town for a visit or the holidays. *Whatever,* she thinks. *As long as I'm not the one who has to sleep with him at night.*

TWENTY-FIVE

Hannah watches the fleet of coast guard boats pull away from the dock. *Please, God, let them find Gus.*

Chief Summers comes up from the floating dock. "Woo-wee, it's a scorcher," he says, mopping sweat off his forehead with a folded blue bandana. "Looks like we're gonna be here awhile. Can we maybe go inside where it's cool?"

"Of course," Birdie says. "I'll get some coffee on."

When the others enter the cafe, Hannah makes no move to leave the railing. Birdie calls to her, "Hannah, honey, are you coming?"

Hannah shakes her head, her eyes searching the inlet. The tide is low and the water muddy. "Y'all go ahead. I'm gonna wait out here for Ethan."

Hannah feels closer to Gus outside. She's certain her son is still alive. Her mother's intuition would sense if something bad had happened to him. If he . . . She tears her eyes away from the water. She can't stand to think of her son lying at the bottom of the creek.

Hannah observes the Sunday afternoon activity on the inlet. Fishing boats return from a day of deep-sea fishing. A group of teenagers pass, their boat loaded with inner tubes, wakeboards, and water skis. A pair of kayakers glide by, and down the creek a way, a kid squeals as he jumps off a dock. Stan zooms past on his wave runner, and Hannah waves at him. She wants to yell at him, tell him not to waste his time, that Gus isn't in the water. But what if he is in the water? What if her son drowned? What if she never sees her son's beautiful blue eyes again, never feels his sticky peanut butter lips against her cheek?

Hannah doesn't want to know if Gus is dead. She'd rather live with the hope that he's still alive than face the finality of death.

She hears Max's voice behind her, thanking her guests for helping with the search and asking them to keep an eye out for the little boy with white blonde curls as they go about their day.

One of those guests, an attractive woman about thirty, gives Hannah a pat on the back. "Keep the faith, hon. They're gonna find your son."

"I hope so," Hannah says, even though her faith is waning by the moment.

Max comes to stand beside her at the railing. "She's right, you know. We have to keep the faith. I believe in my heart he's still alive. There's a logical explanation for Gus's whereabouts."

Hannah swallows past the lump in her throat. "I pray you're right, Max."

Max gives her a half hug. "Do you wanna come inside?"

Hannah shakes her head, unable to speak.

"All right. Let me go see what I can do to help your mama."

Time drags on. Minutes turn into an hour, yet Hannah

remains at the railing. When she hears a voice calling her name, she turns and runs into Ethan's outstretched arms.

"We're gonna find him, Hannah," he says, hugging her tight.

Hannah buries her face in his chest. She belongs in these arms. She feels safe and secure here. She trusts Ethan. She's always trusted him. Even when his father had a heart attack and she didn't hear from him for over a week, she knew deep down that he had a legitimate reason for going dark.

Birdie calls Hannah from the doorway. "Come inside, Hannah. Chief Summers is on the phone with Ryan's father." She holds the door open for them as they enter the cafe. Ethan greets her with a warm smile, and Birdie thanks him for coming.

The room is abuzz with ringing phones and the hushed conversations of police officers in uniforms and plain clothes. Chief Summers sits at the largest table in the center of the cafe with her father and two other officers. Ending his call with the attorney general, Summers sets his phone down and stands to face them. "Stevenson hasn't seen his son since this morning. Ryan left Pawley's Island around eleven. He was driving his own car, headed back to Columbia. Stevenson tried to call Ryan, but he didn't pick up. He's headed over to Ryan's apartment now. He's going to call back as soon as he knows more."

"We can't wait any longer, Chief," Hannah says, her voice raised and panicked. "What if Ryan is on his way to Texas with my son? We have to issue the Amber Alert now."

"I know the waiting is torture, Hannah, but give Stevenson a few more minutes." He squeezes her arm before sitting back down.

Hannah ignores the empty seats at the table. She doesn't want to be near her father. She saw him with that Patty woman earlier. Only a week ago, he was begging her mother to give him another chance and now he's moved on to someone new?

Hannah leads Ethan to a table for two by the window. "The chief is wasting precious time. He's stressing because Ryan's father is the attorney general."

Ethan gawks. "Seriously? Patrick Stevenson?"

"Don't be too impressed. He's not a very nice man. And his wife's even worse."

Ethan falls back in his chair. "This is definitely a game changer. Which could work in your favor. The last thing Stevenson wants is a scandal. If he thinks Ryan may have kidnapped Gus, he'll bring out the big guns to find them."

"I hadn't thought of that."

Sadie and Max bring over trays of warm ham biscuits and cheese straws, which Ethan and Hannah both decline.

"Would you like coffee?" Sadie asks, staring down at the table as though afraid to look Hannah in the eyes.

"Coffee would be great," Ethan says.

"May I have some water, please?" Hannah offers Sadie an apologetic smile. She was rude to the woman earlier, when Sadie admitted to having left the back door unlocked. They'd had a busy day, and Sadie was preoccupied. Could've happened to anyone.

"What am I missing here?" Hannah says more to herself than to Ethan. "I don't understand why Ryan would do something like this. He's not a bad guy. He's spoiled and immature, but he'd never intentionally hurt Gus." She's thumbing through the stream of texts from Ryan, looking for a clue she might have missed, when an email from Heidi Butler pops up on her screen. She reads the email and drops the phone on the table with a clatter.

"What is it?" Ethan asks.

"I just got an email from Heidi Butler regarding the apartment I told you about. Her prospective tenants decided not to take it. She says the apartment is all mine if I want it, but I need to let her know as soon as possible." Tears fill Hannah's eyes. "How can I even think about moving to Charleston with my son missing? I can't think about the next minute, let alone the next hour. What if we don't find him? How am I supposed to go on with my life without Gus?"

Ethan reaches for her hand. "Don't even go there, Hannah. You'll drive yourself crazy, worrying about something that might never happen." His gaze shifts to something over Hannah's right shoulder. "Summers is heading this way. He doesn't look happy."

Hannah jumps to her feet. "What is it? Did you hear from Ryan's father?"

"Ryan is not at his apartment, but Stevenson has a spare key, and let himself in. He found the suitcase Ryan used for his trip to Pawley's in the bedroom and Gus's stuffed alligator on the kitchen counter. This is very important, Hannah. Did Gus bring the alligator home with him from Pawley's?"

Hannah's mind races as she tries to remember. "Atticus is Gus's security blanket. He never goes anywhere without the alligator." She looks at Ethan for confirmation.

Ethan nods. "I'm positive that Gus was holding tight to Atticus when we were in the elevator on the way up to my apartment last night."

Hannah's green eyes get big. "Right! I remember now. When we ran out of gas on the bridge, Atticus had fallen on the floor, and I reached over the seat to hand him to Gus."

"All right, then." Summers runs his hand across the top of his balding head. "I will authorize my team to issue an Amber Alert."

"Let's hope they're not already on a plane headed to California." Hannah drops back down to her chair. "I can't believe this is happening. I may never see my child again."

Summers kneels down beside Hannah's chair. "Calm down, Hannah. I view this as good news. Stevenson offered his full support. He's as anxious to find his son as you are to find yours."

Elbows on the table, Hannah plants her face in her hands to hide her tears. She hears Birdie suggesting they give Hannah some space, followed by the sound of retreating footsteps. She can't see Ethan, but she senses his presence. She cries softly into her hands, tears of relief that Gus is still alive and fear that Ryan will somehow hurt him.

An alert notification, a loud and long beep, sounds on her phone, startling her. She snatches up the phone as Gus's face appears on the screen, alongside descriptions of his physical appearance, what he was last wearing, and the make and model of Ryan's car.

Texts from concerned friends blow up her phone. Liza. Miss Daisy. Robbie's mother. She doesn't respond. What can she say to them when she knows so little?

Day morphs into evening. When the cafe dims, Birdie turns on the overhead pendants, and the light casts the room in a soft glow. More coffee is distributed. More ham biscuits consumed. When Hannah grows restless, she pushes back from the table and begins pacing the floors. She's been at it about ten minutes when the door swings open and Ryan enters the cafe with Gus in his arms.

Gus shouts, "Mommy," and reaches out for her.

"Gus! My baby! Thank, God." She runs to him, and he leaps from Ryan's arms to hers. His little body is on fire. "What the heck, Ryan? He's burning up with fever."

Ryan hangs his head. "I figured something was wrong. He wouldn't stop crying. I didn't know what to do."

Ethan is on his feet and at her side. "Let's get him to the emergency room."

"Mom, will you grab my bag from upstairs?" Hannah says to Birdie, who is hovering nearby with Chief Summers and the others.

"I'm on it." Birdie goes around behind the sales counter and disappears through the swinging door.

Hannah glares at Ryan. "What were you thinking? Why did you kidnap Gus?"

The color drains from Ryan's face. "Kidnap? What do you mean? How could I kidnap my own son?"

Summers steps forward. "Parental abduction is kidnapping, son. And you're in a lot of trouble."

Ryan glances over at the police chief before setting his gaze on Hannah. "*You* left the door unlocked, for crying out loud. Anyone could've *kidnapped* him. You're damn lucky it was me."

Sadie raises her hand. "That was my fault. Not Hannah's. I forgot to lock it back when I took out the trash."

"Whatever," Ryan says. "Bottom line is, my child should not be living in an apartment over a bakery."

"We were doing just fine until you came along," Hannah snaps.

Birdie returns with her bag. "Do you want me to go to the hospital with you?"

"No. But thanks." Hannah leans into Ethan. "We'll be fine. You'd better stay here and hold down the fort."

Hannah and Ethan exit the building with Ryan on their heels. She hears Summers call out to Ryan, "Where do you think you're going?"

"To the hospital with my son," Ryan answers.

"No, you're not," Summer says. "You're gonna stay here and answer my questions."

When they reach the parking lot, Hannah aims her key at the Wrangler, unlocking the doors. At the sight of Gus's car seat in the back, she turns to Ryan. "Did you buy a car seat? Or have you been driving my child around without one?"

Ryan shrugs. "I didn't know it was such a big deal."

Hannah shakes her head. "You're pathetic." She buckles

Gus into the car seat and gets in beside him. Ethan climbs behind the wheel and reverses out of the parking space. As they're driving off, Hannah sees Summers folding Ryan's arms behind his back and handcuffing his wrists.

"If he hadn't put me through hell the past six hours, I might feel sorry for him. He didn't mean any harm. He's just clueless."

"He's a self-absorbed jackass," Ethan says to Hannah through the rearview mirror. "His cluelessness cost a lot of people a lot of trouble and heartache this afternoon."

Hannah brings her son's hot little hand to her lips, kissing his tiny fingers. "I can't worry about Ryan right now. All that matters is getting my son well."

TWENTY-SIX

Birdie is still standing near the door with Max and Sadie when the chief returns with Ryan in handcuffs. He shoves Ryan into a chair. "Ow! Dude! Take off these handcuffs. Do you know who my father is?"

"Indeed, I do. I spoke with the attorney general earlier. He went to your apartment looking for you and found Gus's alligator. He's not very pleased with you at the moment."

Ryan wiggles in his chair. "I'm allowed one phone call. Take off these handcuffs, so I can call my dad."

Jerking Ryan to his feet, Summers takes off the handcuffs. "You see my officers over there?" He aims his thumb at his officers huddled around Cary, who is entertaining them with a funny story. "Count them. One. Two. Three. There are three armed police officers in this room. If you make one wrong move, they will shoot you."

"Dude, I'm not gonna try anything," Ryan says, rubbing his wrists.

Summers jabs his finger at Ryan. "If you call me dude again, I'll shoot you myself." He sets Ryan's phone on the table in front of him. "One call."

Ryan speaks to his father for less than a minute. When he hangs up, he says, "Dad's on the way. He told me not to talk to you until he gets here."

"That's your prerogative. How far is Columbia from here? Two, two-and-a-half hours? I have a good mind to take you to the police station. But since your daddy is the attorney general, we'll wait." Summers looks over at the three women. "Can I bother you nice ladies for more coffee?"

"I'll get it," Sadie says and goes behind the counter.

Max nudges Birdie. "I'm so relieved for y'all. I hate to go, but I need to get back to my guests. Will you let me know as soon as you hear from Hannah?"

"Of course. Thanks for all your help today, Maxie. I wouldn't have made it through this crisis without you." Birdie opens the door for Max. "I'll walk you out. I could use some fresh air." She's surprised to see Stan standing by the window, peeking inside.

"Hey, Stan." Max waves at him before darting across the park to her hotel.

"What're you doing?" Birdie asks.

Stan's face beams red. "Trying to decide whether to come in. I wanted to check on you, but I hated to intrude." He inclines his head at the window. "That young man? Is he Gus's father?"

"Yes. Thank goodness. He brought Gus back. Although the poor little guy is sick. Hannah took him to the emergency room."

"I'm sorry to hear that. But at least he's back with his mama. I know you're relieved." Stan places his back to the window. "I owe you an apology, Birdie. I should never have doubted you. After a lot of soul-searching, I'm willing to admit I have bigger trust issues than I thought."

"I accept your apology. You have good reason to be cautious. This is uncharted territory for both of us." Birdie covers her mouth to hide her smile. "I can't believe you punched Cary."

"He deserved it. I'd fire him if he weren't such a darn good salesperson."

"So I heard. He was bragging about that fact earlier."

Stan grimaces. "We'll see. It may not work out with him after all." He takes hold of Birdie's arm. "Do you think we could start over?"

Birdie pauses before answering. After today's drama, she'd love nothing more than to step into his arms, to feel his lovely lips against hers. She doesn't want to lose him. If they can work through their issues, they might have a chance at something special. She thinks back on her trip to Charleston with Max. She must first make herself happy before she can make someone else happy.

"Eventually. A lot is happening at once, Stan. Hannah and Gus are moving to Charleston, and I'm considering making some major changes at the cafe. I think it's important for me to be on my own for a while, to ease into my new life."

"I respect that." He drops his hand from her arm. "How long is eventually?"

"A couple of months. Maybe after the summer is over."

Stan gives her a determined nod. "I can live with that. Does this mean we can't see each other at all until then?"

"We can see each other as friends." She flashes him a playful grin. "Will you teach me how to fish?"

He laughs out loud. "Yes, of course, I'll teach you how to fish. What say we make a standing date for Sunday afternoons? You, me, and the inlet. Just good times, no hanky-panky."

"That sounds perfect." She's fifty-three years old, but with good health and God's blessing, she has a lot of living left to do. If they can learn to trust each other, she'd like to do some of that living with Stan.

"This day has been hard on you. Are you okay?" Stan

doesn't ask if she's craving alcohol, but she knows that's what he means.

"I'm fine. I can't believe it. Not once during this whole crazy day have I've been tempted to drink."

He kisses her cheek. "You're a strong woman, Birdie."

Birdie straightens, holding her head high. "I am, aren't I?"

* * *

The emergency room is quiet, and a nurse shows Hannah, Gus, and Ethan immediately to an examining room. The doctor's serious expression and authoritative voice instill confidence in Hannah despite his young age. He performs a brief examination. Gus's throat is red and swollen, but his ears are clear of fluid.

"We'll run some tests and see what we're dealing with." On his way out, Dr. Collins pats Gus on the head. "Hang in there, little guy. We'll have you feeling good as new soon."

Gus screams his head off when the nurse inserts the IV. But after drawing blood for the tests, she gives him medicine to bring his fever down, and he falls asleep within minutes.

Hannah sits in a chair pulled closed to the bed, stroking Gus's leg beneath the blanket. "He looks so tiny and helpless with all those tubes coming out of his arm."

"But he's a tough guy. He'll beat this. Whatever it is."

"Do you think it's something serious?" Hannah asks, her tone alarmed.

"I hope not." Hunching his shoulders, Ethan holds his hands out in front of him. "But what do I know? I'm not a parent or a doctor."

When the doctor returns, he reports that Gus's white blood count is high and his strep test positive. "My gut tells me we're dealing with a secondary infection that resulted from the primary virus. We'll get him on some antibiotics, and he'll be better in a couple of days."

"Thank you, Doctor." Hannah waits for him to leave before pulling out her phone.

"Are you texting your mom?" Ethan asks.

"Yes, and I'm emailing Heidi Butler to tell her I'm taking the apartment. So what if the rent's too high? The location is ideal, and the neighborhood is safe. I can't wait to get Gus away from the inlet. Today was the second time in three weeks that I thought he drowned. Living on the water poses too many threats for an active boy like Gus."

"You won't be sorry. You and Chris will soon be making so much money the rent won't matter."

Hannah sits back in her chair. "I like your positive way of thinking, Ethan."

"I'm a firm believer in the power of positive thinking."

When the nurse returns with Gus's antibiotics and release papers, Ethan carries her sleeping son out to the car and insists on driving them back to the waterfront. On the way home, Hannah receives an email from Heidi confirming the apartment is hers.

"Heidi says we can move in as early as next weekend," Hannah says with a shiver of excitement. "I can't believe this is happening."

Ethan smiles at her. "I meant what I said about helping you move."

She smiles back at him. "And I'm more than happy to take you up on your offer."

Patrick Stevenson is a handsome man, who carries himself with the confidence of someone with wealth and power. The stuffed green alligator looks foreign in his hands, and Birdie has a hard time imagining him as a grandfather.

"What's going on here?" Stevenson asks, as though he doesn't know.

"Your son is facing charges for abducting and endangering a child," Summers says.

"Endangering how?" Stevenson asks, his gray eyes the color of steel.

"By failing to use an approved car seat."

"That's a passenger safety violation. We'll pay the fine."

"There's still the matter of the kidnapping," Summer says. "I don't care who you are. This case is going to court."

"This is an outrage." He points the alligator at Summers. "I demand you release my son."

"I'll release him after he spends the night in jail and appears in front of the magistrate tomorrow morning."

"Dad, seriously," Ryan says. "Let me tell my side of the story."

"Not until I hear it first." Patrick drags Ryan over to the corner near the coffee bar. A few minutes later, they return to the table and sit down.

Birdie's eyes are on Summers as he watches Ryan tell his story. "I freaked out when Hannah wouldn't answer my calls and texts. I was sure something terrible had happened to them, that they'd gotten in a car accident on the way home from Pawley's. I came here to make sure they were okay. And I wanted to talk to Hannah, to apologize for playing golf and for the things my mom said. The back door was unlocked. I saw Hannah behind the counter, waiting on customers. I went upstairs and found Gus asleep, all alone in the apartment. I got furious, thinking about how vulnerable he was with the back door open and no one watching him. Something inside of me snapped. I didn't think. I just reacted."

Birdie can't help but feel sorry for Ryan. Based on his sympathetic expression, Summers does as well.

"So, there you have it." Stevenson places his clasped hands on the table. "Ryan was simply removing his child from a situation he deemed unsafe. This wasn't a crime but a misunderstanding."

Across the table from him, Cary's jaw drops. "A misunderstanding? Are you kidding me? It didn't feel like a misunderstanding when we were watching the coast guard search the waters for Gus's drowned body."

"I'm sorry for the pain I caused you both today," Ryan says, looking first at Cary and then Birdie. "But I never intended Gus any harm. I haven't known my son very long, but I already love him very much."

Stevenson snorts. "You haven't known Gus long because Hannah kept him from you all these years."

Birdie jumps to her feet. "Because Ryan cheated on her. She didn't trust him with her child. And he proved how untrustworthy he is today."

The front door opens. Hannah and Ethan, with Gus in his arms, spill into the cafe. When they approach the table, Hannah says, "Gus has strep throat and some kind of secondary infection caused by the virus he had earlier in the weekend. The doctor has given him an antibiotic. He should be better in a couple of days."

Ryan jumps to his feet. "Can I hold him?"

"He's sleeping, Ryan," Hannah says.

Ryan grabs the alligator off the table and tickles Gus's nose. "Gus, look who's here."

Gus opens his eyes, sees the alligator, and snatches it away from Ryan. Hugging it tight, he nestles deeper into Ethan's arms.

Ryan's facial muscles tighten, and he drops back down to his seat.

Birdie places a hand on the small of her daughter's back. "Hannah, honey, I know you're tired, but you should be a part of this conversation."

"Why don't I take Gus upstairs to bed?" Ethan suggests.

"Thanks, Ethan." Hannah kisses her son's head. "I'll be up in a minute to give him his medicine."

Birdie's heart swells as she watches Ethan go. Ethan and Hannah make a fine couple, and if things work out for them, he'll be a wonderful father to Gus. Birdie isn't losing a daughter. She's gaining a son-in-law. *Hold on, Birdie. You're getting way ahead of yourself.* While that may be true, Hannah will one day get married and their family will grow. Birdie has lots of living left to do.

Hannah feels guilty when she hears Ryan's side of the story. Of course, he was worried about them. She shouldn't have ignored his calls. Then again, he should have told her he was taking Gus.

Seated next to her at the table, Summers asks, "What do you think, Hannah? Is this a misunderstanding or a kidnapping?"

"A misunderstanding," Hannah says to Summers and turns to Ryan. "You and I are both at fault. I made a mistake in keeping your son from you for all these years. Gus needs his father in his life. But I'll insist on supervised visitation until you learn more about childcare."

Ryan nods. "That's fair."

"You scared the heck out of me today, Ryan. Don't ever do that again. From now on, we have to communicate."

"That works both ways," Ryan says.

Hannah nods. "Understood."

Patrick Stevenson stands. "Sounds like we're done here."

Ryan's gaze shifts to the police chief. "Sir?"

Summers gives him the nod. "You're free to go." He wags his finger at Ryan. "If I ever see you in my town again, you'd better have that kid in a car seat."

"Don't worry, sir. I will."

"Well, then. It's been a long day." Birdie gets up, signaling the meeting adjourned. She shows the others to the door, leaving Hannah and her father alone at the table.

"Where's your girlfriend?" Hannah asks, cringing at the sarcasm in her voice.

"Patty went home. She didn't belong here. This is family business." He pauses. "We *are* still a family, Hannah, even though your mother and I are getting a divorce."

Hannah glares at him. "Really, Dad? Because I'm pretty sure you broke that family up when you flew off to Hawaii with another woman." She stares down at the table. "I understood why you left Mom. But the problems in your marriage had nothing to do with me. You and I were tight, Dad. We shared a special bond. I kept waiting for you to call me, to reassure me you were alive. When I didn't hear from you, I thought you were dead. Why did you let me think that? Why didn't you call?"

"Because I didn't want to be found. I'm sure that's not the answer you're looking for, but it's the truth." He lets out a deep breath. "Something happened to me when I turned fifty. Suddenly, my comfortable life as a small-town lawyer and the family I adored wasn't enough. When Melinda offered to make me a wealthy man, I let greed cloud my judgment."

"Did you ever regret leaving?"

"Every single day. But I knew if I came back, I risked going to jail for embezzlement."

Hannah shakes her head, confused. "Then why did you come back?"

"Melinda left me no choice. She did the same thing to me

that I did to your mom. She ran off with all my money and left me stranded in Hawaii with sixty dollars and a one-way airplane ticket back to South Carolina." Cary reaches for Hannah's hand, and she allows him to hold it. "I'm working toward righting my wrongs. I'm good at selling boats, and one day I'll pay Jonathan the money I stole from him. Your mother and I have made our peace. She deserves someone much better than me. An honest and good man like Stan. As do you. Don't make the same mistake your mom made. Find someone worthy of you. A man with strong values who treats you the way you deserve to be treated."

A man like Ethan, she thinks.

"I'd like to be a part of your life one day, Hannah. I miss our time together."

And she misses him, she realizes with a jolt. It dawns on her that her father and Ryan are alike in some ways, well-meaning but getting things wrong a lot of the time. She thinks about how much she once worshipped her father, and how heartbroken she'd been when he left. But he's still alive, sitting right in front of her. Maybe it's possible for them to rekindle their relationship. Before she starts this new chapter in her life, she would like to relinquish the burden of hurt and anger. But, before she forgives him, she needs reassurance that he won't take off again.

"Are you here to stay, Dad?"

He nods. "I'm not going anywhere. Palmetto Island is my home. You and Gus are my home."

"Gus needs a strong male figure he can look up to. Do you think you can be that figure?"

"He has that in Patrick Stevenson," Cary says.

"Patrick Stevenson is a douche. He may have money and power, but I wouldn't want to spend the day on the water with him."

Cary's face lights up. "Does this mean you'll give me

another chance? I promise to be a better person, for you and for Gus."

"I'm counting on it, Dad. Don't let me down."

"I promise, sweetheart. I won't let you down."

Birdie returns to the table. "Do you need a ride home, Cary?"

"If you don't mind. That'd be great."

Hannah walks with them through the kitchen to the coatroom. Cary hugs her in parting. "I'm proud of you, sweetheart. You've turned into a fine young woman."

"Thanks, Dad."

Hannah locks the door behind them and climbs the stairs to the apartment where she finds Ethan looking out of her bedroom window at the moon reflecting off the high tide.

Standing beside him, she places her head on his shoulder. "It's late. You should spend the night. But you'll have to sleep on the sofa. I don't trust myself in bed with you."

Ethan groans. "Just the thought of it makes me hot and bothered." Wrapping his arms around her from behind, he plants a trail of kisses on her neck. "How did everything work out downstairs?"

"Fine. Ryan and I were both at fault. We agreed it was all a misunderstanding, and everyone has gone home."

"Ryan should feel lucky. He got off easy."

"He seemed genuinely remorseful. He's Gus's father. Whether or not I like it, he's going to be a part of our lives."

"And it would be awkward to have to explain to Gus that his father is in jail for kidnapping him."

"Right." Letting out a contented sigh, Hannah leans back against Ethan. "I'm going to miss this view."

"Are you having doubts about moving?"

"No way. It's time for me to go. I'm beyond excited about my new life. My dream apartment. A business partner who inspires me." She hooks an arm around Ethan's neck. "And a sexy new guy in my life who makes me feel things I haven't felt in a very long time."

Closing her eyes, she relishes the warmth of his body against hers. Her life is good. Her tide is high. At least for now.

A note from the author . . .

Thank you for reading the *Change of Tides*! I hope you love the characters as much as I do. The next book in the Palmetto Island series introduces new characters and adventures. Order Lowcountry on My Mind now! Watch the trailer and learn more about other books in the series on my website.

And . . . to find out about my new and upcoming books, be sure to sign up for my newsletter:

If you're loving the Palmetto Island series, you might enjoy my Hope Springs and Virginia Vineyard series as well. Join the unforgettable cast of characters at the historic inn for romance, family drama, and adventure.

Be sure to visit my website where you'll find a host of information regarding my inspiration for writing as well as book trailers, reviews, and Pinterest boards from my 20+ other books.

ALSO BY ASHLEY FARLEY

Virginia Vineyards

Love Child

Blind Love

Forbidden Love

Palmetto Island

Muddy Bottom

Lowcountry on My Mind

Sail Away

Hope Springs Series

Dream Big, Stella!

Show Me the Way

Mistletoe and Wedding Bells

Matters of the Heart

Road to New Beginnings

Stand Alone

On My Terms

Tangled in Ivy

Lies that Bind

Life on Loan

Only One Life

Home for Wounded Hearts

Nell and Lady

Sweet Tea Tuesdays

Saving Ben

Sweeney Sisters Series

Saturdays at Sweeney's

Tangle of Strings

Boots and Bedlam

Lowcountry Stranger

Her Sister's Shoes

Magnolia Series

Beyond the Garden

Magnolia Nights

Scottie's Adventures

Breaking the Story

Merry Mary

ACKNOWLEDGMENTS

I'm grateful to many people for helping make this novel possible. Foremost, to my editor, Patricia Peters, for her patience and advice and for making my work stronger without changing my voice. A great big heartfelt thank-you to my trusted beta readers—Alison Fauls, Kathy Sinclair, Anne Wolters, Laura Glenn, Kate Rock, Jan Klein, Lisa Hudson, Lori Walton, Jenelle Rodenbaugh, and Nicole Lau. And to my behind-the-scenes, go-to girl, Kate Rock, for all the many things you do to manage my social media so effectively.

I am blessed to have many supportive people in my life who offer the encouragement I need to continue the pursuit of my writing career. I owe an enormous debt of gratitude to my advanced review team, the lovely ladies of Georgia's Porch, for their enthusiasm for and commitment to my work. To Leslie Rising at Levy's for being my local bookshop. Love and thanks to my family—my mother, Joanne; my husband, Ted; and the best children in the world, Cameron and Ned.

Most of all, I'm grateful to my wonderful readers for their love of women's fiction. I love hearing from you. Feel free to shoot me an email at ashleyhfarley@gmail.com or stop by my website at ashleyfarley.com for more information about my characters and upcoming releases. Don't forget to sign up for my newsletter. Your subscription will grant you exclusive content, sneak previews, and special giveaways.

ABOUT THE AUTHOR

Ashley Farley writes books about women for women. Her characters are mothers, daughters, sisters, and wives facing real-life issues. Her bestselling Sweeney Sisters series has touched the lives of many.

Ashley is a wife and mother of two young adult children. While she's lived in Richmond, Virginia for the past 21 years, a piece of her heart remains in the salty marshes of the South Carolina Lowcountry, where she still calls home. Through the eyes of her characters, she captures the moss-draped trees, delectable cuisine, and kindhearted folk with lazy drawls that make the area so unique.

Ashley loves to hear from her readers. Visit Ashley's Website @ashleyfarley.com

Get free exclusive content by signing up for her newsletter @ ashleyfarley.com/newsletter-signup/

Made in the USA
Columbia, SC
28 June 2022

62420637R00148